NOW IS OUR TIME

JO KESSEL

ISBN-10: 1500424080

ISBN-13: 978-1500424084

To my father
For teaching me that life is for living

ACKNOWLEDGMENTS

I couldn't have written this book without my husband Marc, who occupied the children so that I could follow my dream. Shirley Leuw, my gratitude for your editing is never-ending. David Sherborne, you are my legal guru but so much more besides – don't worry, David Sherwood QC is in no way based on you! Sam Josephs, I have never learned so much about gluten, egg substitutes and lactose intolerance – I thank and bow to your nutritional knowledge. Mark Fielden, nobody writes better blurb…I hope that 'thirteen' is always lucky for you! They say that you shouldn't judge a book by its cover, but a good cover nonetheless helps. For helping me choose this one I would like to thank Anna Maxted, Barbara Want, Carolyn Simons, Saunders, Philippa Handyside, Lisa Filipe, Gen Jacobs, Lisa Munley, Topcat, Pushy, Christine Parks, Donna Cooksley Sanderson, Act, Mireille Brett, Kathleen (a.k.a. Kat29), Paula Conway, Rhian Jones, Lucy Levison, Jemima Coleman, Jan, Annetha O, Megan Lesourd, Anne-Marie Murphy, FreeBee, Liz Martin, Nikki D, Mrs B (a.k.a. Emma b), Emily, Sam Roberts, Lisa Drury and all the other wonderful ladies (and readers) on Amazon's 'Romance Devotion – Looking for books/Can't get into another' romance forum, who voted in my poll, but forgot to leave their names! Last but not least, thank you to Nathalie, Gabriel and Hannah for making me so proud and for helping to 'spot' potential 'Jonah's on our recent trip to LA and San Diego.

CHAPTER ONE

CLAIRE

This isn't how I expected my life to be. That's what Claire de Klerk was thinking as she plucked yet another moth wing out of her threadbare beige bedroom carpet. Nobody had ever warned her that the fairytale ending might not in fact exist. Nope, she'd grown up believing in love and marriage and that Prince Charming would provide her with at least 2.5 children. It hadn't always been this way. At one point she nearly was living the dream. She had the man, the ring and a couple of years later they were blessed by the pitter-patter of tiny feet. But alas the foundations of this perfect world had proved even patchier than the carpet she was now fingering. So she now found herself not only a divorced single mother and seemingly on the scrap heap at the ripe old age of thirty-seven, but dealing with something far crueller: a moth infestation. She hated insects at the best of times, to the point that if a hairy fat bluebottle dared fly within half a meter's radius of her, she'd vacate the room in an embarrassing fluster. Single motherhood, however, had forced her to address such demons so that her precious eight-year-old daughter Miriam would feel safe and protected. She'd even honed a technique for evacuating creepy crawlies from the house without killing them. Trap the beast in question under an empty cup, slide a piece of paper underneath and carefully carry to the front door where the contents are released back into the wild. Because, whilst her daughter Miriam might not appreciate finding spiders in her bath, if getting rid of them meant murder, that was not an option. "No killing, please Mummy," she'd insist. "Put them back in the garden with their friends."

If only it had been as easy to shift the moths. Sadly their infestation had been so extreme that they'd had to vacate the house so it could be fumigated and baked to such a high temperature that no small living organism could possibly survive. Claire's fingers picked out tiny frail wings which the vacuum cleaner had failed to dislodge from the shag pile, before loading them onto a piece of newspaper. The phone rang, snapping her from her reverie.

8.30 a.m. *Shit.* Her ex-husband Anthony was going to be here to fetch Miriam any second and she hadn't yet packed her daughter's overnight bag. She considered ignoring the phone for fear it might delay her yet further, but then she realized that it might indeed *be* Anthony calling and therefore she better pick it up.

"Hello?"

Her tone was a downtrodden mix of weary and wary.

"Claire," a female voice purred in her ear.

Claire's shoulders visibly relaxed. It wasn't Anthony. It was her best friend Georgia. Whilst others had deserted her post divorce, Georgia had been a saintly rock, mopping up tears and trying to help her move on.

"George, I'm running late. Can I call you back?"

"No, I'm about to go get on the tube and just wanted to check that you're all set for later."

Claire smiled. Georgia knew Claire well enough to know that what was happening *later* could easily have slipped her mind. But actually, what was happening *later* was the most exciting thing Claire had planned in years, and whilst part of her was dreading it, an impish voice in her head was telling her she had to give it a go. We all only have one life after all.

"I've not forgotten."

"So have you decided what you're going to wear?"

Ah, no, that little matter had slipped her mind and most of her wardrobe was still sealed in protective anti-moth-munching boxes.

"Yes, I think so," she lied. "But remind me the rules?"

"Keep it simple and stylish and perhaps one statement piece of jewellery. No stripes or squiggles and nothing which could give you damp patches under the armpits. It will be hot in there, so be warned."

One more lie wouldn't hurt. Georgia getting angry that she hadn't yet selected an outfit wouldn't help expedite things.

"Ok, yep, I'm all set," she replied.

Claire waited for a response or for her friend to wish her good luck but Georgia suddenly gave her the silent treatment, sitting wordlessly on the other end of the receiver. Claire scrambled to her feet, trying to fashion the piece of newspaper she was holding into a funnel.

"Are you ok?" Claire probed further. "Or is there something on your mind?"

"I'll tell you later," Georgia replied. "I don't want to distract you from this afternoon."

"No, tell me now. Otherwise I won't be able to *concentrate* later."

Claire could hear her friend draw a deep breath.

"Ok," Georgia whispered. "I saw Jonah yesterday."

"Jonah?"

As Claire uttered his name like a question, like she was querying the very existence of somebody, anybody by that name, she knew it was ridiculous. There was only one Jonah that Georgia could possibly be referring to, but her friend answered anyway.

"Jonah Kennedy."

Claire gasped. The moisture from her mouth seemed to find its way to the palms of her hands at the mere sound of his name. The pulse thumping in her ears became louder by the second. She tried to say "oh", but instead her lips quivered feebly. That, after all this time, was all she could muster. That, after all this time, was the effect the mere mention of his name still had on her, which is why she'd spent so long trying to do anything but think or speak about Jonah Kennedy.

"He said he'd like to contact you. He wanted your phone number, but I hope you don't mind, I gave him your e-mail address instead."

The piece of newspaper fell from Claire's fingers, taking its load floating with it to the floor. She wanted to get off the phone, to guzzle a glass of icy water to clear her head and to grab a paper bag, because any second now she might just start hyperventilating. She quickly pulled herself together and coughed, to clear the atmosphere, hoping that the cough alone could erase the information she'd just been given. She didn't have time for this right now. She didn't have time for this ever.

"Claire?"

"Yes, that's fine," she reassured Georgia. "But I've got to go. Anthony's at the door. Let's speak about this later. Let's speak about everything later."

Anthony really had rung the doorbell but, even if he hadn't, Claire would definitely have used that as an excuse to hang up.

She took a moment to further digest this recent discovery and then shook her head, willing herself to just ignore it and get on with the job in hand. Downstairs Miriam must have opened the front door to her father because she could hear her squealing not *his* name but the name of her new half-brother, Jasper. A pang shot through Claire's core. She and Anthony might no longer be together, but it was still hard emotionally to deal with him having another child. He'd clearly managed to move on from their separation more quickly than she had.

Claire hadn't yet met Jasper and had been dreading this moment. Since his birth six months ago Anthony had left him at home with his mother every time he'd come to fetch Miriam and there'd certainly been no forewarning that today would be any different. Claire sighed so deeply that her diaphragm ached from the stretch and she seemed to gain a couple of extra inches in height. Exhaling slowly she headed into Miriam's room and started to mechanically fill her overnight bag. Slippers, a new pair of pyjamas which had 'Good Night Mummy' scrawled across its top, just in case Miriam needed reminding of her whilst she was away playing with her new step-brother. A hairbrush, toothbrush, clean underwear, spare T-shirt and school reading book were squeezed on top.

Job done, she attempted to fix a bright smile on her lips. As a senior defence lawyer, Anthony had once explained to her how important it was on a professional level not to allow people to be able read your expression because, if they could sense fear or uncertainty, they'd be over you like a rash and the case would be lost. Indeed, Anthony could switch his expression from impassive to cool with the click of a finger. And he wasn't alone. Many of his colleagues were similarly gifted in this department and Claire had always wondered how they managed it with such ease. It wasn't as if they were actors.

As someone who was supremely talented at wearing emotions on her sleeve, Claire wasn't sure how convincing her breezy demeanour now looked but she stuck with it, not so much as a muscle twitch affecting the broad grin she tightly pulled as she descended the creaking Edwardian staircase. Safely at the bottom she looked more closely at Jasper who was sleeping beatifically in Miriam's arms.

"He's absolutely gorgeous," she cooed, trying to draw her lips even wider as she ran a finger lightly across the soft skin on his cheek.

He *was* gorgeous. And yet it was one of the hardest things she'd ever vocalised. Just looking at him made her feel a confusing mix of envy, anger and longing. But she had to be nice, for the sake of her daughter and for the sake of 'moving on'. He was almost exactly how Miriam had looked as a baby, although perhaps his colouring was slightly darker and the curls on his head slightly tighter.

When Claire finally tore her gaze away from her daughter's arms Anthony made a point of looking her in the eye and nodding gratefully. Nothing about their break-up had felt particularly acrimonious. Their spark had just died and failed to reignite despite their best efforts.

"Congratulations," Claire tried to keep her voice steady.

"Thank you," said Anthony, shifting slightly on his feet and probably feeling just as awkward as his ex-wife. He ruffled the top of Miriam's dark head of hair which had been coiffed into two long plaits, each with a delicate pink bow tied at the bottom.

"Come on Missy, I'm sure your mother's got lots to be doing."

Claire handed him the overnight bag.

"See you tomorrow at eight?"

"Yes," Anthony replied, hooking the bag over his shoulder and taking back possession of Jasper from his daughter's embrace.

Claire took a step towards her daughter and hugged her tightly. They'd gone through this rigmarole umpteen times but it never made the parting any easier.

"I love you," she whispered into Miriam's ear.

"Love you too," replied Miriam.

Claire was about to let her go, but then had an afterthought, and pressed her mouth even closer to her daughter's ear.

"Maybe its best not to mention the moths to Daddy," she said.

Normally Claire would watch from behind the curtains as Anthony put Miriam into his white BMW Jeep and drove away but not today. She knew that in terms of timing she'd be better off looking for an outfit for this afternoon but she knew she wouldn't settle until she'd checked her e-mails. She didn't have time to think about Jonah now; she didn't want to think about Jonah ever and yet suddenly she could think of little else. She didn't want to know what he had to say, she didn't want her walls to be broken down, and yet the allure of seeing whether he'd written to her after all this time was pulling her like a drug. She ran back upstairs to her study and turned on the computer. She'd been so busy sorting out the moths that she

14

hadn't checked her e-mails for a couple of days. When did Georgia say she'd spoken with him? Where did they meet? Had Jonah recognised Georgia after all this time or had it been the other way round? Because there was no way Georgia wouldn't have recognised *him*. Half the bloody world might still recognise him – he'd certainly had a pretty keen female following back then. How come he was in London when, as far as she knew, he still lived in the U.S? What had Georgia said to him about her? What had *he* asked Georgia about her? How had he *looked*?

She did the mental arithmetic. It had been thirteen years. For thirteen years she had done her best to put Jonah Kennedy out of her mind. To not think of him, to not let anyone talk to her about him and definitely not let any news of him filter through to her via the internet or social media. If she'd wanted news of him she was sure she could have found out everything she wanted to know and more with an easy click of the finger. But for thirteen years she'd resisted this temptation. So why, now, as the thirty, no fifty, no ninety, no *one hundred and fifteen* new messages started loading into her inbox, was she so desperate to see if one was from him? What if he'd had no intention of writing to her at all and if he'd just been making polite conversation?

The house normally felt deathly quiet after Miriam left with Anthony but, now, the pounding of her heart was filling the silence. She shouldn't be doing this now. She should wait until later because if he *hadn't* sent her a mail, she would be disappointed, even though it was strictly speaking *she* who had told him to never contact her ever again.

Time heals, doesn't it? Claire wasn't convinced that time *did* heal as she clicked the down arrow and started scrolling through the new messages to see if one might be from him. No, time didn't heal, it just numbed. It didn't stop the fact that on each occasion her resistance had failed her over the past thirteen years and she had thought of him, the ache of what she'd *done*, no, what *they'd* done, was as acute as if it had been yesterday.

And then she saw it, his name in her inbox and she froze, the arrow hovering over it, daring to be clicked. Her hand paused. She could just delete it, she reflected, and let it go. She'd let it go for so long, perhaps it was preferable to leave it instead of exposing herself to the pain and hurt revisiting the past would entail. And yet, as she closed her eyes and allowed her imagination to roam free, she could smell his musky scent as if he were standing right beside her; she could remember how he'd squeeze her into his tall, broad frame, wrapping his arms tightly around her, making her feel as if she and she alone was a perfect fit, the one person on earth he was destined to be with.

Her eyes filled to the point that by the time she clicked on his name and the message came up, tears blurred the words. Wiping them hastily away with the back of her sleeve, clarity was restored.

Dearest Claire

I bumped into your friend Georgia earlier today and ever since she gave me your address it's been burning a hole in my pocket. So here I am…………after all this time. She told me all your news. Congratulations on your daughter. Like you, I've got a little girl and like you, I'm sadly divorced. So there you go. It looks like we've got plenty to catch up on. I'm working in London most of this month. It would mean a lot to me if I could see you. Just give me the green light and I'll come whenever you want, wherever you want, to meet you.

J

X

The tears that Claire had wiped away were replaced with fresh ones which started trickling in streaky lines down her cheeks. *Give me the green light.* After all these years he was still using that phrase on her. Just hearing from him took her back to a different place and erased the past thirteen years of her life. She closed her eyes – not just to stem their flow, but to try to halt the images which had started to flash in her mind one after the other, like a psychedelic slide show. Jonah running on a tennis court, racket outstretched as he tried to make contact with a fast-spinning ball; Jonah curling his finger provocatively at her, wearing a 'come hither' look; Jonah's thick, delicious lips, whose taste she could still remember as well as the deep urgent longing she felt whenever her mouth pressed into his. *Stop. Enough!* She opened her eyes and blinked hard to stop the pictures and memories from coming. She mustn't think about this now. She needed to focus on this afternoon and on selecting the perfect outfit to wear. Whether she did or didn't give the green light would have to wait.

CHAPTER TWO

Why on earth had she agreed to this screen test? That's what Claire was thinking as Dave the Floor Manager showed her round the studio. Calm though she'd been on arrival, setting foot on the set of *Morning Cuppa* - the nation's most beloved daytime programme - was hugely intimidating. The lights beaming overhead blinked furiously and were so hot that perspiration started pricking her skin. *Damp patches under the armpits*. Big cameras with even bigger lenses stared at her ominously and the flashing red lights on top of them caused her to swallow saliva nervously. If she had had an Adam's apple, it would have been bobbing up and down maniacally, a giveaway to the tension she was feeling inside.

This wasn't her world, this was Georgia's. Claire was a Nutritionist, not a TV Personality. But Georgia, who was a bigwig TV Producer, had seen an opportunity. She'd heard that *Morning Cuppa* was looking for a new, on-screen Nutritionist for a regular 'healthy eating' slot and Georgia had thought Claire would be perfect, especially because she had so many celebrities for clients. "I only got those clients because of your connections. And I've absolutely no relevant experience whatsoever, it's a ridiculous idea," Claire insisted. But somehow Georgia convinced her that she had pedigree and credentials and that there was nothing to lose by going for a screen test. "You're pretty, you're articulate, and I can't imagine anyone else in the world knowing more about food than you do. Who else would be anal enough to know the calorie count, salt content and nutritional benefit of every single thing you put into your mouth? That's *exactly* what they want. And better still, you can *cook*."

Claire didn't consider herself to be much of a cook. It was just that Georgia was such an *un*domesticated goddess that she presumed anyone who regularly used a chopping board must be on a par with Jamie Oliver. And it was true. Claire *did* like to experiment with ingredients. If she was going to recommend egg-free or gluten-free recipes to clients, she felt duty-bound to check that the end product actually tasted nice.

So that's how Claire had found herself rummaging through the anti-moth-munching boxes, finally settling on a body-hugging short-sleeve black Lycra dress. Even though her friend hadn't mentioned it, she knew television tended to add a few pounds to the way you looked, and this particular dress was like a giant spandex, holding all her wobbly bits well and truly in. She'd left her thick, shoulder- length ringlets loose and had heeded her friend's advice about wearing a statement piece of jewellery. The green velvet choker with its large copper coin pendant complemented the colour of her hair, which Georgia always laughingly referred to as 'Bordeaux', after the French red wine.

Dave dropped her off in a dressing room where a make-up artist came to apply eye shadow and foundation so expertly that Claire was incredulous at her reflection. Her complexion was so perfect it almost looked like porcelain. As she sat back, relaxing with her eyes closed whilst mascara was coated on her lashes, it was as if she were playing at being a Princess for the day. This experience was far removed from her day-to-day reality of moths, motherhood and meal plans!

Makeover completed, Claire was taken into the green room adjacent to the studio where Natasha Bridges, the voluptuous blonde bombshell Presenter of *Morning Cuppa,* introduced herself and explained the format of the show. She was very touchy-feely, tapping Claire's forearm on just about every third syllable she uttered. "I'll ask questions, so just take my cue and chat like we're the best of friends. And remember to look at *me* when you're speaking and not at the cameras. Try to relax and enjoy it. You're going to be just fine."

Natasha kept her hand on Claire's forearm for a good five seconds after she had said the word 'fine'. Luckily, Dave interrupted at this moment, popping his head around the green room door to announce that the crew were ready and that she and Natasha should make their way towards the set. Once they were in the studio, it all started feeling a little surreal. The three-piece red sofa suite which Natasha used for all the show's topical guest interviews suddenly felt so much smaller than when she was watching *Morning Cuppa* from the safety of her living room at home.

The Series Producer had telephoned during the week to decide what nutritional aspect she'd like to talk about for the test. She'd suggested they discuss how to eat on a budget and forage seasonally. As part of her slot, she also planned to do a quick cooking demo of a simple, seasonal dish: gooseberry yoghurt fool. It was June and this fruit was currently abundant in back gardens as well as in the wild. About a meter to the right of the sofas a separate faux kitchen set had been created. Bowls overflowing with fruit and vegetables had been placed on a table attached to a wheelie cooking unit, complete with a work surface, hob and sink. Behind it was a fake wall decorated with a backlit mock window. Dave demonstrated how everything worked and when she was happy that all the right ingredients and pans were ready, he positioned her on her spot, a cross on the floor marked in yellow tape.

As Dave held up his hand, commanding silence, the knots in her throat became harder to swallow and she was inwardly cursing Georgia. She could feel herself pulling the same fake smile she'd given Anthony that morning, showing her teeth between her taut open lips. By contrast, Natasha, who had plonked herself and her huge double Ds on one of the red sofas, couldn't have looked more relaxed if she'd been lazing in a bath of bubbles. Cameramen were ready behind the three studio cameras. Two of them swivelled to point their lenses at Natasha. The third one was trained on Claire.

"Stand by," said Dave as the studio hushed. Stretching his palm towards the rows of ceiling lights above them, he counted down, both verbally and with his fingers. "Three, two, one, cue........

Despite a Researcher asking if they could wine and dine her afterwards, Claire couldn't get away quickly enough. The screen test had gone disastrously and she'd been desperate for fresh air and solitude. It was a gloriously bright summer's day and the studio for *Morning Cuppa* had an enviable riverside location along the Embankment south of the Thames. And so now she found herself in a rare moment of calm, with no particular time constraints. She'd cancelled her clients for today and Miriam was with Anthony for the next twenty-four hours. She was free.

Her nude heels clicked noisily along the pavement as she walked towards the London Eye, with the Houses of Parliament and Big Ben looming far in the distance along the capital's skyline. Buskers and street artists lined the boardwalk. A golden statue of Winston Churchill caught her eye. As she stopped to admire it, she realised Winston wasn't a statue at all, but a man spray-painted all over and standing impossibly still on an empty plastic beer crate. A hat with a few coins in it lay on the pavement in front of him. Miriam would have loved this human piece of art and would no doubt have done her best to make him laugh by pulling an array of funny faces. Claire fished in her bag for her purse and took out a couple of fifty pence pieces which she tossed into the hat. As she replaced the purse she could feel her mobile phone buzzing. She pulled it out. Georgia was calling.

"Hello," she answered.

"Hey superstar," Georgia squealed in her ear. "How did it go?"

Hearing Georgia's voice made Claire smile, but it also made her remember. About Jonah's e-mail and about how she'd decided to shove all that information into a box which wouldn't be opened until after the screen test. She was still far from convinced it should *ever* be opened.

"Awful," laughed Claire. "I was awful, it was awful, and Lord knows what they made of me. Everything that could have gone wrong did go wrong. I've probably tarnished your reputation for ever, seeing as you put me forward for it in the first place."

"I'm sure it wasn't as bad as you think."

"Trust me. It was probably even *worse* than I'm saying."

They both giggled.

"Sorry," Georgia apologized. "I shouldn't have pushed you into it."

"No, no," Claire was quick to rebuff. "I had a great time. Just because I was awful doesn't mean I didn't enjoy myself. It was actually quite fun and nice to do something different for a change."

Claire meant it. There was a humdrum repetitiveness to her life which was beginning to feel tedious. Her world revolved around getting Miriam to and from school and squeezing as many clients as she could in-between the hours of 9am – 3pm. And then, after Miriam went to bed, she'd be on the computer devising client meal plans and deciphering lab test results. She'd go to bed, wake up, make breakfast and then it would all start over again, like *Groundhog Day*. It was sad to admit, but the moths had been about the only recent buck to her routine. So yes, Claire meant it when she said she'd enjoyed the screen test. People had been fussing over her and treating her as if she mattered, which made a pleasant change. Because most of the time these days she felt as if her own needs, desires and hopes had all been shoved under the front doormat and kicked into shreds. The real Claire was starting to get lost.

She walked towards the riverbank and peered over the railings, watching pleasure-boats gliding past.

"So," Claire whispered, finally allowing herself to think and talk about it, "Jonah wrote to me."

Admitting it out loud brought a well of suppressed emotions rushing to the surface. A lone tear snaked a path down her cheek, making a beeline for the river below and then from nowhere, quite unexpectedly, a monstrous sob heaved out of her tiny frame.

"Oh, Claire," soothed Georgia. "I wish I was there with you."

"I'm fine," Claire reassured, pausing to take some measured, calm breaths. She waited a couple of seconds before trying to start again. "Right, really, I'm fine now. Tell me everything."

And so Georgia explained how she'd been filming at some TV studios on the outskirts of London when she'd passed him in the corridor. She'd recognised him instantly and had wondered whether it might just be best to let him pass unnoticed, but Jonah had done a double take, and had recognised *her* and stopped. He couldn't remember her name though. He just remembered her as Claire's friend and then they'd exchanged awkward small talk for a few minutes. He said he'd just started working as a Commentator on a satellite TV sports show and was going to be in London for the next few weeks. And then he'd asked about Claire.

"And............. what did you tell him?" Claire interrupted.

"I told him the truth. That you'd recently separated from your husband and had a beautiful daughter and then I asked how he was doing, because I knew you'd kill me if I didn't. It sounds like he's in a similar position to you. So our crossing paths was fate, serendipity, call it what you will."

"How did he look?"

Claire's voice was a thin rasp. She could hardly bring herself to speak. Just hearing about Jonah stirred too many memories.

27

"He hasn't changed."

"Really?"

"No, actually, I'm lying. He *has* changed. Age has made him even better looking."

"You're joking."

"Actually, I'm not. There was some salt and pepper going on in his hair and a few more creases round his eyes that were pretty endearing. They made him look wiser and sexier somehow than however many years it's been since we've seen him."

Georgia and Claire had been nineteen-year old students and had got a last minute bargain for a week's multi-activity holiday on the Greek island of Kos. Water sports and land sports were all included in the price and so Claire, who enjoyed playing tennis, had on a whim booked up a lesson. This tall bronzed Adonis with floppy sandy hair had been waiting for her on court. He was scarcely older than she was, and when he'd sauntered over to casually introduce himself, she initially thought that maybe she was having a joint lesson with him. But it turned out he was the hotel's resident tennis coach. "A working vacation," he'd pulled a winning smile. His sexy, lazy, Californian drawl had rendered Claire coy, and she couldn't

28

take her eyes off the cute dimple which appeared on his right cheek whenever he curled his lips upwards. "I haven't played tennis for ages," she said, worried she was about to make a fool of herself in front of this impossibly beauteous male specimen. But he'd just cocked his head and grinned. "No excuses, English lady. Just give me the green light and we'll see what you're made of." Georgia had walked past the court half-way through the lesson, and when she spotted the coach she'd tried to give Claire a subtle thumbs-up from behind her back. Claire, who'd been a huffing, panting mess from being run ragged round the court, had flicked the back of her hand at her friend and told her to 'buzz off'. At the end of the lesson Jonah had admitted to being captivated by her accent and had tried replicating the phrase 'buzz off' in all its anglicised glory, over and over, until Claire had done another hand-flick, this time onto Jonah's forearm, telling him politely and yes, with a hint of flirtation, to shut up. He asked if she wanted to hook up for a drink later just so he could hear her speak. And that's how the story of Jonah and Claire had begun, a journey which had crossed continents several times over and lasted nearly five years.

She was over it, she'd moved on. Their time together had been both wondrous and painful in equal measure, and sometimes it was hard to separate the two in her mind. Yes, her life was now a tad dull, but at least she had control. With Jonah she'd always felt a little *out* of control. Could any good possibly come out of meeting up with him?

"What should I do, George?"

"What did he say?"

"He said he'd like to meet up."

"And would you like to?"

Yes, no, she didn't know. It wasn't black and white. Nothing about them had ever been straightforward.

"I'm scared," she admitted.

"I know, honey, but are you having such a fabulous time at the moment that you'd be happy to turn down this chance? Who knows where it could take you to?"

"What if it makes me even unhappier?"

"You can't go through your life running scared, Claire. Life is about taking chances. And you've been given a fucking exciting chance here. How many other women would relish the opportunity of a night with Jonah Kennedy?" Georgia paused and then chuckled. "And if you play your cards right you might even get *more* then one night. Honey, the ball is in your court."

The ball is in your court. Claire laughed at the irony of that phrase, considering how Jonah's life, when they'd been together, had been all about tennis. She said goodbye to Georgia and made her way home, stopping briefly at the dry cleaners round the corner from her modest West Hampstead terrace house to buy some moth balls.

No sooner than she'd closed her front door, she kicked off her heels and ran upstairs to her study to turn on her computer. Whilst she was waiting for it to fire up, she decided to keep herself busy to mask the jitters. It felt as if the plague of fluttering moths which had chewed through her carpet had decamped to her stomach. She took the two plastic moth balls and turned each a little anticlockwise, just how the dry cleaner had demonstrated. The scent inside wasn't the nasty naphthalene which she remembered her mother using when she was growing up, but cedar wood, which was actually quite pleasant. She hung one up in her own cupboard before shutting its door firmly and planted the other in Miriam's.

Back in her study, her inbox finally filled the screen. She ignored the two hundred unread emails and scrolled down to the only one that now seemed to matter: Jonah Kennedy. She clicked on his name, re-read the mail and pressed to reply. She kept starting, writing a sentence or two and then deleting. Nothing she wrote seemed to sound right. Had Jonah spent hours trying to perfect his tone? Not too needy or too cocky or too indifferent. After thirteen years and all they'd shared, getting the tone right seemed to matter.

Dearest Jonah
I am so genuinely pleased you contacted me. It's been too long.
Consider this your green light. I would love to see you again.
Claire
X

She quickly pressed 'send' before she could regret it and then started reanalyzing what she'd written. Perhaps *dearest* was too much. Maybe saying she would *love* to see him again was a little over the top. *Stop.* She reminded herself that she was thirty-seven years old, a grown-up, and this wasn't about playing hard to get or being cool. It was about putting a simple goddamn date in the diary.

She began checking through her other mails and within five minutes a reply pinged into her inbox.

Jonah: *What about tonight? X*

32

What *about* tonight? She was free, she didn't need a babysitter and her screen test make-up still looked fabulous. But wasn't tonight too soon? It wouldn't give her a chance to mentally prepare, or to back out.

Claire: *Tonight works for me.*
     X

Jonah: *I'm staying at the Dorchester. Can you get here for 7pm?*
     X

Claire: *I'll do my best. Hope you still recognise me. I'm not sure if I still look like Kate Winslet.*
     X

Jonah: *You'll always be my Kate. See you in the lobby at 7.*
     X

Claire spent a long time staring at her reflection in the gilt-framed rectangular mirror that filled her entrance hall. What Georgia had said about Jonah made her nervous. She'd struggled to resist the Jonah of old but, if age really *had* made him better looking, there was no hope. And the last thing she wanted was him looking at her and being disappointed that time had ravaged her beauty.

She wasn't sure what he'd think. He'd always told her she resembled a red-headed Kate Winslet and, to a degree, this was an astute observation. There was definitely a likeness in their faces and Claire even more definitely shared the same curves and body-shape issues as the English actress. She'd once had a bust to be proud of, a bust that Jonah had adored. After she'd finished breastfeeding Miriam, however, her breasts had shrunk in size and she now thought of them woefully, as two, ugly, withered prunes. She remembered joking with Anthony. "You do realise," she'd told him, "that I'll never be able to have an affair or be with another man because I'd be way too embarrassed for anyone else to see me naked." This was still the truth and she hadn't made love with another man since Anthony.

She decided to keep on the dress she had worn for the screen test but swapped her shoes for emerald wedge sandals which matched the velvet choker. Lipstick was touched up with her stick of deep-red Mac which she then popped into her fake leopard print clutch. She'd long had a penchant for leopard print, which hadn't really been to Jonah's taste, but he'd always said it looked good 'on her'. Would he even remember? She took one final glance at her reflection and wished herself a silent 'Good Luck' before locking the front door behind her.

The Dorchester, on London's Park Lane, opposite Hyde Park, held a special place in Claire's heart, although she didn't think Jonah would have known it. Her grandparents used to take her there for the occasional posh afternoon tea when she was a little girl. Little cakes had been served on multi-tiered display platters. Chocolate éclairs, scones, warm sausage rolls, tiny cucumber sandwiches with their crusts cut off. White-gloved waiters wore long black tail coats; the beverage itself was served in delicate floral china cups, the purest Ceylon blend that existed. It had always felt like such a treat. Royalty couldn't have been served better!

As she approached the hotel from the tube station Claire slowed down her pace. She felt as anxious as a pubescent teenager about to go on their first date. Thoughts raced through her mind. What should she say? How should she be? They mustn't, at all costs, talk about what she'd done. No, she reminded herself. What *they'd* done. Not today. She glanced at her watch. Five minutes late. Would he already be waiting in the lobby? She hoped so, because she didn't want to be there first. And then she heard him.

"Claire."

She could have recognised that sexy, lazy drawl blindfold from a line-up of hundreds. It stopped her in her tracks. It was a voice that had a direct passage to her heart. It was a voice that melted away her anxiety. It was a voice that ignited her desire. But she still couldn't see the man it belonged to.

"Claire."

And then, as if he instinctively knew that something was needed to put a stop to the frenzied activity going on in her brain, he suddenly appeared before her, like an apparition on the pavement, scooping her into his arms, wrapping them around her so tightly it was as if he didn't want to ever let her go. As they stood there, rocking back and forth, thirteen years of space and time peeled away like the layers of an onion.

"You feel good," he whispered into her hair.

"So do you."

"I don't want to let you go."

"Then don't."

Eventually he pulled away and held her at arms length.

"I need to take a good look at you."

It gave Claire the opportunity to drink him in too. Georgia was right. He *had* aged well. The dimple was still there, only somehow it appeared endearingly magnified as it creased his cheek. The subtle grey streaks in his hair and the more weathered skin on his face gave him an air of sexy maturity. His large grey eyes were still hot and smouldering, and they were dancing too. And as for his body, she didn't need to see it to know that it hadn't changed either. She'd felt it when they'd embraced. He still had the taut, beautifully sculpted chest and arms of an athlete and he hadn't shrunk a millimetre. His six-foot three frame towered over her, despite her being raised on four- inch wedges. As she checked out his jeans, sneakers and tight white T-shirt, she wondered how she'd ever let him go in the first place. What on earth would this Adonis make of her?

"You haven't changed," he smiled, "although maybe you've got thinner."

"It's an optical illusion," Claire grinned back. This time it was a natural smile, not the forced ones she seemed to have been pulling most of the day.

"It is so good to see you."

"You too," Claire said shyly.

"Claire Jackson, thank goodness I didn't let another day pass before seeing you again."

 It was funny hearing him use her maiden name. Although she *was* now, strictly speaking, Claire Jackson again because her divorce was finalised, she still answered to her old married name, de Klerk.

"I'm so pleased you suggested tonight," she said, "because if we'd waited any longer I fear I might have backed out."

"Why?"

She shook her head.

"I'm not sure," she whispered, "but I'd possibly have tried to convince myself that it was a bad idea."

He took one of her hands in each of his and she felt a bolt of electricity shudder up both her arms.

"How could *this* ever be a bad idea?"

Their eyes locked and despite any resolve she might have had, in that split second, she could feel herself falling for him all over again, just like she had when she was nineteen. She didn't trust herself to speak.

"Come on," he said, putting his arm around her and lightening the mood by playfully pinching the side of her waist, "I've booked us a table at Nobu."

It wasn't a surprise that Jonah had chosen a Japanese restaurant. Sushi is a sportsman's staple. Athletes need a high protein diet and you can't get much more high protein than a platter of sashimi. She'd been to plenty of sushi bars with him in his home town of San Diego, but they'd never eaten at Nobu, Old Park Lane. The sommelier poured them each a flute of champagne. When he'd finished, they clinked their glasses and Claire leaned in conspiratorially.

"Are you aware that it was in the broom cupboard of this restaurant that Boris Becker got a woman pregnant?" she asked.

Jonah raised an eyebrow at her, eyes twinkling, ignoring her piece of tittle-tattle.

"To us," he said.

"To us," she echoed.

"I don't care about Boris Becker and broom cupboards. I want to know about you," he started. "I want to know how life has been treating you."

And so, as they ordered and tucked into scallop, salmon and sweet shrimp sashimi, they gave each other a précis of their lives. Jonah had known Claire as an aspiring artist, but Claire told him how she'd decided to retrain as a Nutritionist after they'd broken up, to give her a new focus. And about six months into her course she'd met Anthony at a party thrown by one of her fellow students. A couple of years later he'd proposed to her and, for better or worse, she'd said yes. Then Miriam had come along. Jonah asked to see a photo. Claire bent down to retrieve her leopard skin clutch from between her feet and placed it on the table. "Still loving the leopard skin," Jonah joked. *He remembered.* She took her mobile phone out of the bag to give him a quick slideshow of her daughter: Miriam with a daisy chain around her neck; Miriam as a bridesmaid at Georgia's recent wedding; Miriam making a sandcastle on a beach. "She's absolutely stunning," Jonah complemented. And then he took one of her hands in his and added: "but of course she would be. She's yours."

Claire asked him to show her a photo of *his* daughter, who was called Martha. She, too, was gorgeous and a complete opposite to dark, exotic-looking Miriam. Martha had white-blonde hair which skimmed her waist and Jonah's broody grey eyes. "She's a mini you," Claire whispered, thankful that the sommelier had returned to fill her glass with more champagne. She needed it. It was hard thinking of Jonah having a child. It felt wrong. *They* should have had a child together. Things should have been different.

Stop. This was a dangerous path to tread, even if it was only in her head, so Claire quickly changed the subject. "Right, your turn," she said. "Now I don't think you won Wimbledon, but did any of your dreams come true?"

Jonah's dreams had been part of the problem. It had always been about him. When they'd met he'd already been ranked number ten in America, but he'd been plagued by knee injuries and an operation had forced him to take time out from competing. He'd taken a job as a tennis coach on the Greek island of Kos to recuperate. What he'd ended up with - a long distance girlfriend – had *not* been part of the plan. If anything, she'd been a *hindrance,* and Jonah's coach had a gift for making her feel unwanted. But Jonah was smitten. "You're my lucky charm," he'd told her. "The coach knows nothing. I need you by my side." It was a testament to how they felt about each other that their relationship had lasted as long as it did. Claire, who was studying Fine Art at St Andrews University just a few years before Prince William and Kate Middleton put the place on the map, had pulled pints overtime in pubs to pay for transatlantic flights so that she could accompany Jonah on the road at every possible opportunity. She'd been a dutiful tennis girlfriend, turning up to support him at some of the remotest and pithiest satellite tournaments. And, of course, once he'd started winning more and earning better money, he'd paid for her to join him. Bit by bit he'd clawed his way up the rankings. He'd been number three in the U.S by the time they'd split up. Not quite Andre Agassi standard but still bloody impressive! His pretty face had made him popular among female tennis fans, which was something else that Claire had found hard to deal with.

"My dreams," he paused, reflecting. "Maybe as we get older we recalibrate our dreams."

He reminded her that anybody who's crazy enough to want to compete in the world of tennis does it because they want to be No.1. He was no different. He'd wanted to be a champion. It was all or nothing. But his body had let him down. He'd had three more knee operations since they'd last met and his right elbow had also started packing up. He showed her the new scar on the back of his arm and it took all the strength she could muster to not reach out and run her fingertips over it. There once had been a time when she'd known every faded stitch and wound on his body and they'd jokingly graded each surgeon for their sewing capabilities. Some of the wounds were botch jobs and Miriam could, quite frankly, have done a better running stitch. "Did you see me play Federer in the quarter finals at Melbourne?" he asked her. She shook her head without elaborating. She didn't want to admit that she'd refused to watch or follow his career at all, because it was just too damn painful. Wimbledon had been the hardest to avoid, and she'd hated doing so because she'd been passionate about watching tennis and there was no other tournament in the world quite like it. Their relationship had, to a degree, ruined Claire's love of the game.

He told her that this match against Federer in the Australian Open had caused a huge upset at the time and had been a nail-biting one to both watch and play. As the underdog and seeded more than thirty places behind the Swiss player, Jonah hadn't been expected to win. "It was some of the best tennis I've ever produced," he said, "and whenever it rains it's still one of the classic games they broadcast until play is resumed."

"But," he said, as he sipped the remainder of his champagne and paid the bill, "I got into the world's top ten, which wasn't too shabby." He tried saying the word 'shabby' in his best British accent and they both giggled at his poor effort. "And things are good now. I've been taken on as a Commentator by Sky Sports and apparently I'm not too bad at it. That's why I'm in the UK. I'm commentating on all the tournaments building up to and including Wimbledon."

"That sounds great," Claire replied.

It really did, but all Claire could calculate as silence fell between them was that he would only be here for another month and then he'd be gone. It reminded her of how peripatetic their life had been together. She'd hated it, and yet something about sitting opposite him here and now felt so horribly right. He took her hands in his once again and suggested they go for a walk.

44

Back on Park Lane, Jonah clasped her fingers tightly into his to keep her safe as they dodged traffic to cross the busy road. Once they reached the other side, he didn't let go. If anything, he held on even tighter as they strolled towards Kensington Palace. Claire didn't resist. She liked being attached to him and welcomed the warmth and naturalness of their connection. With him, she'd always felt like she belonged.

It was 9 p.m. and the soft light was slowly starting to fade. Her shoulders shivered as the temperature dropped and Claire slipped on the crop black cardigan she'd brought with. There was an empty bench outside the wrought-iron gates which guarded the Palace, the same gates which mourners had flocked to, to decorate with flowers and wreaths and messages of condolence after Princess Diana had died. As they sat down Jonah still didn't free her hand. They stared straight ahead at the gates for a few seconds and then Jonah broke the silence, turning to her.

"I tried contacting you after you left you know," he said quietly. "I never *wanted* you to go."

Tears began welling in Claire's eyes and one dared to tumble over the edge and dribble towards her nose. Jonah wiped it away with the pad of his thumb. She nodded, but didn't dare to speak. After she'd left, she'd changed her phone number, her e-mail address and even her home address. She'd not wanted to be found. She'd thought she was doing the right thing for everybody.

"What was your wife like?" Claire whispered.

She hadn't asked in Nobu and she cursed herself for letting that question pop out her mouth now. She didn't want to know that he'd shacked up with some tall, leggy supermodel. Lord knows, there'd been enough of them around, clamouring to take him off her.

"She was a mistake," he said, tracing his finger down from Claire's wet eye and along her cheek towards the back of her neck. It was a gesture so sensitive and tender that she felt her head tilt towards his hand and her eyes close. She'd never in her wildest dreams imagined being with Jonah, ever again. This was almost too much, too soon, too hard to take in. Her life had felt dull for years and, to an extent, she'd been responsible for letting that happen. She hadn't believed she'd deserved better. *Not after what she did.* And now, from nowhere it had sped into fast forward.

"But she gave you Martha," Claire reminded him.

46

"Yes, and for that I am truly grateful."

Jonah leaned forward and cupped his other hand around Claire's face. It was safer to close her eyes and not to try to read his expression, or guess his thoughts.

"Open your eyes," he commanded.

With difficulty she obeyed and found herself staring into his deep, grey pools. What she thought she could read in them unsettled her. It felt like nothing had changed in the intervening years, even though she knew so much had. A lump caught at the back of her throat and she could feel her lower lip trembling. Part of her wanted to run away, scared of being exposed to what was sure to be emotional turmoil. But another part of her was frozen to the spot. He had her face clasped in both his hands and once again she found her eyelids closing as he caressed her cheeks.

"I have to admit something," he said.

She nodded, eyes still tightly sealed. Here it comes, she thought. He'd given her the good stuff and was now about to deliver bad news, to tell her he was in a new relationship or something. She didn't want to see him as he said it.

47

"You know I think you're beautiful," he continued. "But, I have to admit, I prefer you without make-up."

Her eyes snapped open as she giggled.

"I don't normally wear make-up. This was put on me this morning for some silly screen test Georgia put me up to."

He raised a questioning eyebrow.

"It was nothing," she brushed it off.

She wanted to close her eyes again, but his gaze held her magnetically. She wasn't sure if her thirty-seven year old heart could keep up the cracking pace it was now thumping at and she knew she must look ridiculous. Her lower lip was quivering uncontrollably and her porcelain make-up was no doubt now a streaky mess. *Idiot*, why hadn't she removed it before coming? She couldn't stop herself from looking down at his mouth, his luscious, thick, sensual lips. No-one's lips had ever matched up to his, either before or after. It was as if he could read her mind.

"I'm going to kiss you," he said.

She clamped her eyes back shut and nodded.

"I can't watch," she whispered.

She waited for so long that she considered telling him to hurry up, but then she felt his teeth gently take her lower lip in its grip, as if trying to stop the tremor. When she'd calmed down, he released it, pulled away for a second and she could feel the smile on his lips as he crushed his mouth deliciously into hers.

CHAPTER FOUR

Twelve hours later the phone rang, stirring Claire rudely from slumber. She'd been looking forward to a lie-in. 09.00. *Ugh.* She'd got back late and slept only fitfully. The evening's dramas had been playing on a loop in her mind - Jonah's voice, his touch and the dreamy moment their lips had reconnected after thirteen long years. She brusquely pulled the handset off its charger.

"Hello," she mumbled.

"You dark horse." Her mother screeched so loudly into her ear that any chance of Claire dozing off again was instantly undone. "How could you not tell me?"

Oh, no! Her mother must somehow have found out about Jonah. She'd always told her when she was growing up that she had 'eyes on the back of her head' and now Claire was actually starting to believe her. Had she been outside the Dorchester, or in Hyde Park, or driving along Park Lane? Or perhaps that wasn't it at all. Claire clapped a hand over her mouth. Paparazzi *had* been hanging around outside the entrance to Nobu but they hadn't appeared even remotely interested as she and Jonah had left. It's not as if Jonah's star was in the ascendant any more. Who could possibly be interested in him? Or was she being naive?

"Oh no," Claire groaned. "Don't tell me I'm in the papers."

"Papers?" her mother sounded confused. "I don't know about any papers. But you've been on the TV all morning. Every fifteen minutes."

Every fifteen minutes? Claire sat bolt upright and scanned her room for the remote control.

"What are you talking about?"

"You're making gooseberry fool on *Morning Cuppa*. And oh, darling, what a mess with the fruit and the milk and the whisk........shame, you poor thing. But I thought you looked lovely if that's any consolation? And so did your father."

Ah, there was the remote, on her dressing table. Miriam must have moved it. Claire jumped out of bed to grab it, aiming it at the TV set as she pressed the 'On' button. She clicked to Channel 3. Damn. The end credits were rolling. She'd missed it!

"Why didn't you call me earlier?"

51

Her tone reeked with irritation.

"Well, I imagined you must have known about it. And why on earth you didn't think to tell *me* is anybody's guess. I'm always the last person to know about everything. Your sister's just the same."

Her sister Jacqui had been living in Hong Kong for the last five years, so it was no surprise her mother knew little going on in her life.

"It was a last minute thing which only happened yesterday. It was a screen *test*. There was a clue in the title. Why are they even broadcasting it?"

"Oh, well," said her mother, "I can answer that, actually. It wasn't just you who they showed doing a nutrition slot, there were two other women and one rather dashing man. It's the viewers who get to decide who *they* want to be the new TV Nutritionist. Apparently they can vote on You Tube."

"Mum," said Claire, running downstairs to turn on her computer. "I'll speak to you later. I've got to go."

Fifteen minutes later, Claire clicked 'Play' for the tenth time on the video of her which was posted on You Tube. It was painful to watch. No, it was tortuous. The actual segment they'd filmed had lasted about eight minutes, but what they'd put online was a quick-cut, edited version of all her worst bits. 'Out-takes' she thought they called it in the business. Tomatoes tumbling and splattering to the floor when she'd tried to remove some from the bowl. The milk she'd heated for the gooseberry fool over-boiling. The food processor exploding when she'd tried to puree the cooked gooseberries. She hadn't realised how many times she'd said *oops* but she must have said it at least a hundred and, each time that she had, she'd done some idiotic jazz-hand gesticulation to accompany it. It had been a car crash, just like she'd known, but oh, the public humiliation! It hadn't been for hundreds to *see*. So much for gooseberry fool! The only thing looking foolish was *her*.

She picked up the phone and called Georgia.

"Oh my God, did you know about this?"

Claire hadn't realised that she was capable of screeching louder than even her mother but it suddenly appeared she'd inherited that gene.

"About what?" Georgia asked.

"Are you at a computer?"

"Yes. Why?"

"Go to You Tube and type in my name together with *Morning Cuppa*."

The phone went quiet on the other end as Georgia did what she was told, and then Claire could hear the video playing over the phone line.

"Hideous, isn't it?" Claire screeched when she could hear it had finished.

It went quiet on the other end again.

"Are you still there George?"

"Yes," her friend replied. "But hang on a sec, just let me check something out."

Georgia went quiet again. And then, after a couple of minutes, she gasped loudly.

"This is great," said Georgia, her voice full of excitement.

"Great?"

Claire had always considered her friend to be intelligent but now she was seriously having doubts. How her looking a fool making gooseberry fool was 'great' she had no idea.

"What on earth are you talking about?" Claire said.

"Well," replied Georgia, "I've just seen it's a competition and you've had one and a half million votes so far. The next best contender only has five hundred votes. You're way ahead. In fact, I'd say that you're pretty much going *viral*."

"Going *viral*? I don't want to go viral. I want that video taken off You Tube. I look like an idiot."

"The public clearly loves you."

Claire was getting frustrated.

"No they don't. I'm getting the pity vote. They feel *sorry* for me. Get them to take it off. Please," she pleaded.

"Calm down," Georgia laughed. "This is good news, not bad news. You're going to get the job."

"I don't want the job, I want my pride."

"Ok, I'll see what I can do," her friend reassured. "But let's put that aside just for a couple of minutes and discuss what's really important. Tell me about Jonah."

If a psychologist were to analyse Claire's habit for mentally 'putting things in a box' to deal with later, they would probably give this trait some psychobabble label like *denial*. Being brutally honest with herself, she'd put most of the baggage of her divorce into a box to never open again. Yesterday she'd refused to think about Jonah until after the screen test. And right now she refused to worry about foolish videos going viral. Not properly dealing with things had become her coping mechanism ever since the horror of what *they'd done* nearly fourteen years ago.

In keeping with her philosophy of denial, now was most definitely *not* the time for thinking about any of these matters because now the most important job in hand was to get the house ready. She'd invited Jonah round for dinner and not only did she need to decide what to cook, she needed to make the place more presentable. Not because she believed that Jonah would actually care about the mess, but for her own self-esteem. She wanted to feel proud of whom she was and where she lived and the sealed cardboard boxes scattered around her home like carelessly discarded pieces of Lego, were eyesores. Everything from every single cupboard, from clothes to crockery to toiletries, had been packed away whilst the property had been fumigated and she'd scarcely unpacked a tenth of it yet. Still wearing her pyjamas, she started in the kitchen, attacking the gaffer tape seal to one container with a penknife before slowly, bit by bit, putting plates back on shelves and returning tumblers to the glass display cabinet where they belonged.

Recipes wafted through her head as she robotically sorted through each room replacing objects to their rightful spot. One of her passions used to be experimenting with food but, since Miriam's arrival, she'd prioritised spending quality time with her daughter over making complicated dishes. It turned out that Miriam didn't have the most sophisticated of palettes anyway and it had been a case of the simpler the better.

She knew she would have fun creating something a bit fancier for tonight, and yet she didn't want it to appear as if she was trying too hard either, or to slave over a stove in front of her guest. Whatever she served would ideally be prepared ahead of time. Creamy fish pie......pasta......roast chicken.........slow-cooked lamb in the oven..........barbecue?

For the second year in a row, Britain was in the grip of a rare and uplifting heat-wave. Indeed, according to the pest exterminator, moths had become endemic in the South East as a direct result of last summers' high temperatures. Forecasts had regularly boasted that it was hotter in London than in Rome, Barcelona and even Mumbai. The weather had been so reliably good that, last year, Claire had invested in a proper gas barbecue, rendering the ridiculous little disposable aluminium ones that she'd previously used redundant. It wasn't cheap, but it was worth every penny. It was the first summer that she and Miriam had been without Anthony. The pleasure of eating freshly barbecued food in the garden had taken some of the sting out of the pain and given mother and daughter fresh new memories.

With the boxes all unpacked, Claire took a shower before dressing in a pair of high-cut fraying denim shorts with a black vest t-shirt and heading out to the shops. She smiled as she allowed herself to remember the night before. "When can I see you again," Jonah had asked as they'd walked hand in hand back to the tube station. She'd been anticipating an invite back to his room at the Dorchester but it hadn't come. And because everything was already happening so fast, part of her was relieved. Instead he'd hugged her so tightly that she sensed he really didn't want to let her go. When he did finally release her he'd murmured in her hair. "It's taken me so long to find you again, please don't make me wait too long." Without hesitation she'd whispered back, "Tomorrow. Come to mine tomorrow."

They'd exchanged telephone numbers and as Claire entered the supermarket a text message buzzed through.

I'm meant to be commentating on tennis and all I can think about is you. What time shall I come later? X

Whilst Claire had been on a couple of blind dates since the divorce, nobody had been special enough to be invited to the house. She longed more than anything for Jonah to meet Miriam, but was concerned that it was a bit soon. For some reason she also instinctively felt that Anthony and Jonah's paths shouldn't yet cross either. Anthony was returning Miriam at 8 p.m. and half an hour later she would be in bed, fast asleep.

Is 8.45pm too late?
77 Gladstone Road
NW3 1AS
X

She'd only just sent the reply and picked up a shopping basket when Georgia called. Claire answered.

"I'm in the supermarket," she warned, "and sometimes the phone cuts out when I move deeper inside. If it does I'll call you back later."

"No problem," said Georgia. "What are you making?"

"I thought I'd do a barbecue - marinated meats with salads. What do you reckon?"

"That sounds perfect."

"So," she said, eyeing up the burgers. "Has Mary Poppins sorted out the video yet?"

"Um, about that-

Georgia's apologetic starter made Claire sense trouble.

"No bad news," she interrupted, moving towards the chicken counter. "Please. I mean, crikey, what if Jonah saw it? I'd be mortified."

"Well," Georgia started, "I've got good news and bad news. Which do you want first?"

"Bad."

Claire always believed in getting the worst over and done with.

"Ok, you signed a release form, and that release form gives them permission to broadcast anything they filmed with you. So there's really nothing you or I or the hottest lawyer in town can do. Did you not *read* the form before you signed?"

Georgia was sounding ominously like Anthony. That was exactly the sort of question he would have asked Claire in this situation. One of his mantras was 'don't sign anything without reading it through properly first.' Claire had known this, but the release form was three A4 pieces of paper long and packed with small print. The researcher who'd handed her the pen had reassured that it was no big deal, just a formality. And so Claire put her signature on the dotted line.

"Tell me this isn't happening," said Claire. "Tell me there's something we can do?"

Georgia bypassed her question.

"Do you want the *good* news now?" she asked instead.

"It better be *very* good," Claire sighed.

"Have you not been on the computer since we last spoke?"

"No, because unlike the majority of the population, it would appear that my world does not revolve around a screen. I had other, more pressing things to tend to."

"Well, you should be happy with what I'm about to tell you. Or at least see the funny side. Trust me. Most people would be green with envy at the situation you're now in. You're clearly hitting the spot with the public. I was exaggerating when I told you that the video had gone viral this morning, but now it really has. They're even watching in America. Do you know how many votes you've now had? You could be gastronomy's answer to Susan Boyle. Hell, you might give *Charlie Bit My Finger* a run for its money. You've had t-

The phone cut off.

Happy: it's such a simple word, and yet its very state can be so elusive. Georgia thought her new viral status should be making her 'happy'. And Jonah had asked her an innocuous enough question last night which had hinged on just that. "Were you happy with Anthony?" Back at home, as Claire cut three lemons in half and squeezed the juice into a bowl, she thought about how she'd answered his question. She'd paused for longer than she ought to have done, her brain whirring overtime, trying to work out the 'right', or at least the 'honest' answer. In the end her reply had been feebly noncommittal. "I guess," is what she'd said.

But now, as she added olive oil, rosemary and finely chopped garlic to the lemon juice and stirred the mixture, she forced her mind to linger on the question of happiness. Had she and Anthony ever been truly happy? She thought they had, certainly at the beginning. She'd been intrigued by him and his exotic mixed race genes. His dark, chocolate skin had been as far removed aesthetically from Jonah as she could possibly get, which had helped prevent comparisons from being made. Although it hadn't escaped her notice that both Jonah and Anthony shared one pivotal personality trait. Their competitive streaks were both off the radar and she'd wondered whether her attraction to men who were driven by winning said more about her than about them. She didn't feel as if she had a competitive bone in her body – she was very British in that respect. *It's not the winning that matters, it's the taking part.* Jonah had laughed in her face at that phrase. "That's utter bullshit," he'd retorted. Perhaps on some subconscious level, however, she needed to be with someone who was more driven than her, a yin to her yang. That didn't seem to make sense though, when what she thought she wanted was an easy, non-confrontational life.

She'd thrown herself into a relationship with Anthony, trying desperately to move on from the past, but after the initial honeymoon period and birth of Miriam, the cracks had started to show. Something had been missing, something which possibly had never even been there in the first place, but she'd not wanted to admit to this. And her dissatisfaction with their marriage had turned her into someone she hadn't recognised. Someone snappy, impatient and intolerant – whatever Anthony did, he didn't do right in her eyes. He wasn't impulsive enough, he wasn't romantic enough, he wasn't thankful enough. He worked too hard and it felt as if he was never there for them, both emotionally and physically. In the end she didn't have the energy or desire to wallpaper over the cracks. It had felt easier and preferable to let it go, for everybody's sakes. They were definitely not each others' soul mates and it had been clear that Anthony felt the same way. He'd allegedly found his 'real' soul mate just a few measly months after they had separated and they'd had a baby straight away. Even though she hadn't wanted to be with him any more, receiving the news had felt like a ball being thwacked into her stomach at 150 mph.

Claire carefully spooned her freshly prepared marinade onto the chicken thighs and burgers she'd bought earlier. She believed in soul mates, and she also knew, hand on heart, that Anthony had never been the one. And the reason she knew was because she'd already found hers. Now that he'd come back into her life, she couldn't quite fathom why she had let him go in the first place. Somehow it had all made more sense at the time.

She smiled to herself as she popped the tray of marinating meats into the fridge, remembering the heady, tingling sensation she'd felt all over as she'd tasted Jonah's warm lips on hers last night. It had felt comfortingly familiar and yet excitingly new. Her skin still prickled as she closed her eyes, remembering his touch, his voice, his breath on her neck. The anticipation was almost too much. He'd be here in an hour and a half and the butterfly flutters in her stomach were betraying her calm exterior.

The home phone rang. *Shit*. He had better not be cancelling.

"Hello?" Claire answered, hesitantly.

"Hi."

Phew, the accent was British. It was Anthony.

"Is everything ok?" she asked.

"Everything's fine. I just wanted to warn you that we're running about half an hour late. I'm really sorry. I took Miriam to the cinema after school and something's gone wrong with the projector. They think it should be fixed within thirty minutes and I know that Miriam would really like to see the end of the movie if you agree to it."

Crap. Claire should have known that something would go wrong. The later that Anthony and Miriam returned, the more chance their presence would clash with Jonah's arrival, which is exactly what she'd hoped to avoid. Claire was within her rights to tell Anthony no. It had all been thrashed out in the divorce settlement and his contact days and times were set in stone. But if she said 'no' then she would feel badly for her daughter. It was a no win scenario, to hell with it. What would be would be. She uncorked a chilled bottle of Chardonnay. Some Dutch courage was definitely in order.

"Don't worry, just enjoy yourselves," she told Anthony. "I'll see you when I see you."

She hung up on the call, took two wine glasses down from the cupboard, filled one of them to the top and downed a long, generous gulp.

CHAPTER FIVE

Sometimes it's best to fear the worst so that, at least, one can be prepared. As Claire leaned against the frame of her open front door watching the scene unfold, she was thankful she'd drunk that glass of wine. It had relaxed her, allowing a natural smile to crease her lips at the irony of Jonah, Anthony and Miriam all pulling up outside 77 Gladstone Road at the same time: Anthony in his white BMW jeep, Jonah in a black taxi cab. *Hell, could this be any more awkward?* Somehow the sight of Jonah ducking his head as he stepped out of the taxi and unfurled to his six-foot-three inches calmed her. When she spotted his right hand clutching a large yellow Selfridges paper bag, it took all the strength she could muster to not coo "ah" out loud. Jonah was the first to saunter up the garden path whilst Anthony busied himself fetching Miriam's bag from the boot before letting his daughter out, all the while his beady eyes following Jonah's every step with suspicion. Claire wished she could read what was going on in his head. Did he recognise Jonah? Did he care? Did he have a strong urge to cross-examine Claire on how, why or when this man had wormed his way back into her life? Heck, they'd spoken about

67

him often enough at the beginning of their relationship, as they'd delved into each others' significant pasts. Anthony had known the name. He'd been impressed, but un-phased. He'd not even objected to Claire keeping photos of Jonah by her bedside. "I can't begin to compete with that," Anthony had kept his cool, "so I'm not even going to try." A few months later Claire had tucked the photos, face down, at the back of her bedside table drawer.

Jonah remained impervious to Anthony's gaze tracking his every movement but, even if he had been aware, it wouldn't have unnerved him. To compete professionally in any sport requires nerves of steel and Jonah had honed his into the finest titanium.

Miriam was the first to reach Claire, running to enter her mother's outstretched arms.

"Hey, darling," Claire hugged her daughter and kissed her head, before turning her attention to the supporting cast standing behind Miriam. She'd never in her wildest dreams imagined these two different men and worlds colliding.

"Jonah, this is Anthony. Anthony, this is Jonah," she introduced.

If Jonah hadn't known who this stranger was, now he knew. Cool as a cucumber he offered his hand. "Nice to meet you," he drawled. Anthony complied with the handshake but didn't reply. His steady expression was unreadable, his famous lawyer 'look'.

Niceties dealt with, Jonah smiled at the pretty little girl standing in front of him and squatted down to her level.

"And you must be Miriam?"

She nodded and duly thwacked the flat palm he held up for her to high five. "Ouch," he joked, shaking out his palm in mock pain. Miriam laughed.

"This is an old friend of mine," Claire told her daughter, "called Jonah."

Miriam spent a few seconds eyeing Jonah up from toe to top, her gaze finally settling on the Selfridges bag in his hand.

"Is that for me?" she asked.

"It certainly is," he smiled, passing the booty over.

Miriam's eyes boggled.

"What do you say?" Claire reminded her daughter about manners.

"Thank you," she said.

"It's my pleasure."

As Miriam peeked into the bag, Anthony took his cue, politely nodding at Claire and Jonah before ruffling his daughter's head and saying goodbye. Claire ushered the two of them into the house and as she closed the front door behind them, Miriam tapped gently on Jonah's arm. "You've got a funny accent," she said.

Half an hour later Claire padded into her conservatory. Miriam had now officially been put to bed, with instructions to go straight to sleep. It was late and Mummy and her friend didn't want to be disturbed because they hadn't seen each other for years and needed to catch-up.

"Is Jonah the tennis player?" Miriam had asked innocently as her mother kissed her goodnight. Claire had recoiled in surprise.

"How do you know about the tennis player?"

"You once told me about him after I broke that funny little statue of yours which is now in the lounge."

"Oh."

The things children remember! Claire wracked her brains to try to recall a kernel of such a conversation, but nothing came to her. She planted one final kiss on her forehead.

"Love you."

"Love you more."

"That's not possible."

Claire smiled as she closed Miriam's door softly behind her. The 'love you', 'love you more' ritual was part of their own personal, nightly routine. Claire was certain that Miriam *couldn't* love her more. She couldn't imagine anyone loving anyone more than she loved Miriam.

When she'd walked into the conservatory the sight before her had felt like an improbable dream. The floor-to-ceiling patio doors were flung wide open onto the small garden where Jonah was busy at the barbecue. Coming from California, barbecues were second nature to him. At his family home in San Diego, where he and Claire had spent a fair amount of time at the beginning of their relationship, there had been an inbuilt brick burner in the back yard next to the swimming pool. She couldn't remember the number of times they'd chucked some fresh fish onto the coals as they'd drunk some new age Sancerre.

Jonah's back was to her and she took the opportunity to observe him for a couple of minutes transfixed, watching his muscular arms at work, picking up the tongs and turning the chicken thighs and burgers over. She'd always loved every glorious inch of his body, warts, scars and all, but if she had to choose her favourite part, it would be his strong, sportsman's arms. She could feel her breath quicken. She wanted to touch them. She needed to touch them. She tiptoed barefoot towards him and caught him unawares, pinning her stomach against his back as she ran her hands up and down his triceps. Half a minute later he spun round to face her and they stilled, their foreheads touching as the tips of their noses performed a languorous Eskimo kiss.

"Do you know what?" he said, his forehead still glued to hers.

"What?"

"If it's possible, I think you're more beautiful now than you were when I last knew you."

"Rubbish."

"It's not 'rubbish'," he mocked her accent, wearing a playful smirk on his face. "It's the truth. I think thirty-seven must be the perfect age for a woman. You're coming into your sexual and physical peak."

He trailed his hands to the hem of her black vest t-shirt and wormed his way underneath, stroking her bare back before teasingly slipping his hands towards her front, tickling the sides of her waist as his fingers continued on a northbound trajectory, lightly grazing her breasts. Claire's breath hitched.

"Do you have any idea what you do to me? What you've always done to me?" Jonah asked.

Claire shook her head, but really she did have a very good idea. And if she could have taken her mind off his travelling fingers she might have found the courage to admit that he made her feel as nobody else had done and how her body ached for him. She floated her hands from his biceps to the back of his neck and pulled his mouth urgently to hers, whimpering as he parted her lips with his tongue, her whole body tingling with desire.

"If we wait a bit longer," Jonah whispered with their mouths still meshed, "it will be even more sensational."

Claire was pretty sure he wasn't talking about the chicken. She nodded in agreement, pulling away with a smile.

"I think we should eat then," she suggested.

Claire had prepared everything that they'd need and placed it on the counter in the kitchen which was adjacent to the conservatory. Two plates, two sets of cutlery (each wrapped in a serviette) a curried pasta salad, a green salad and a jug of home-made vinaigrette. It was still warm enough to eat outside so Jonah helped her carry everything to the wrought-iron table in the garden, to join the bottle of Chardonnay and wine glasses which were already laid there. Claire lit a scented candle to ward off the bugs and then went in to fetch one final platter which she loaded with the crispy chicken and burgers waiting on the barbecue. She'd way over-catered.

"Voila," she said, once they were both seated at the table. As she said the word 'voila' she caught herself doing the same

74

weird jazz-hand gesticulation which so embarrassed her in the viral video. It was obviously a mannerism she didn't even know she had, like a nervous tick. She must stop doing it!

Jonah refilled Claire's glass before topping up his own and holding it aloft to make a toast.

"To you," he said.

"To happiness," said Claire.

Happiness: that elusive state of mind which right here, right now, as she moistened her lips with wine, she felt she'd achieved. She felt lighter than she had done for years. She didn't want the moment or the feeling to end, ever. Watching Jonah pile his plate and tuck in made her feel that they belonged together. His very presence beside her felt so right and sent a wave of warmth coursing through her bones.

"You've got a lovely home," he said.

Her previous marital home, a penthouse apartment overlooking Regents Canal, had been much more impressive. Splitting their assets post-divorce, however, had led to the inevitable downsizing. This had been a compromise house. She'd compromised on the size of the garden and the size of every single box room for that matter, but what she had got was a house full of period character, with original wooden floorboards, fireplaces and Edwardian picture rails. Not to mention the conservatory, which she adored. She'd kept the décor simple, offsetting ivory walls with colourful rugs and furnishings in deep tones of red. And she loved the location - a trendy, vibrant pocket of London, which buzzed with cafes and ambience.

"Thank you," she said. "Do you still live in the same condo?"

He'd bought a lovely place by the ocean when they'd been together, as an investment, but travelling the world from one tournament to the next hadn't really been conducive to setting down roots. It had always felt more like a rental than a proper home. Much more of their time had been spent living out of suitcases in hotel rooms.

"No, I sold that and bought something further up the coast. It's much nicer and bigger than the last one. The complex even has tennis courts, just in case I get the urge."

He chuckled as he said this, removing his I-phone from his pocket to show her some pictures. It was stunning, bougainvillea creeping up the outside walls and spacious inside, with a divine, open plan kitchen and living space.

"Was it weird meeting Anthony?" she asked.

Claire still hadn't met Anthony's new girlfriend and she certainly wasn't in a hurry to do so. But she imagined meeting Jonah's ex would be on a whole new level. It would be hard to accept that a woman, other than herself, had borne him a child.

"A little," he admitted.

"Well, at least it's over and done with," she appeased.

Jonah downed the contents of his wine glass.

"He looks like Barack Obama."

Claire laughed. She'd not seen the comparison before, but Jonah was absolutely right. Anthony had recently shorn his mad, afro hair, and *did* now resemble the American President. Claire put down her knife and fork and pushed her plate away. Despite the meal being delicious and Jonah having barbecued the chicken to perfection, she just didn't have an appetite. Well, not for food anyway.

The Claire of old had always been at ease with her body. She'd had enviable long legs, womanly curves and a bust which too often had caused men to defy etiquette by talking to her cleavage instead of to her face. Whilst she'd never liked the tone of her skin, a pale cream which didn't tan no matter how long she lazed in the sun, Jonah had always found her colouring alluring. With her fiery hair and white limbs, he thought she looked as if she'd just walked out of Botticelli's *Birth of Venus*.

That was then, though, and this was now. Superficially, not much had changed. She'd not gained weight since childbirth and her hourglass figure was still pretty much the same as it ever was. And she still, according to Jonah, looked like Kate Winslet. Yet, as she led Jonah upstairs, their fingers tightly interlocked, two major issues were vexing her. What room should she take him to, just in case Miriam should wake up and how on earth would she avoid Jonah seeing her withered breasts?

In the end she decided on the spare bedroom and ordered him to close his eyes whilst she undressed. His lips curled upwards in amusement and she was grateful that he didn't probe further. Instead he gamely turned his back to her whilst she slipped out of her denim shorts and T-shirt and clambered under the duvet.

"You can turn around now," she smiled.

She knew this whole scenario was ridiculous. She was acting like a seventeen-year old rather than a woman of thirty-seven, but she just couldn't help herself. With Anthony, she hadn't cared. He'd been a witness to the changes. Jonah, however, was familiar with the twenty-something Claire and not her more mature counterpart. His comment about her approaching her physical and sexual peak hadn't helped matters either. He kicked off his sneakers and socks, grinning as he moved towards Claire's side of the bed, sitting on its edge and leaning over, tenderly melting his lips into hers as he stroked her hair back from her face. As their kissing deepened he positioned himself on top of her. The sensation of his entire body and hardness pressing into her caused Claire to moan with pleasure. She needed to feel him, to touch him. She ran her hands under his black T-shirt. His skin was still gloriously smooth and soft. She tugged at the top, motioning that she wanted it removed, and he obliged, raising his arms so she could pull it free. His sculpted triceps, shoulders and back felt divine under her hands and she moved down to his buttocks, pushing them tighter towards her.

"Nope," he said, removing her hands. "It's my turn."

He linked her fingers in his and raised her arms above her head, pinning her wrists down with one of his hands. With his other hand he traced a teasing line towards her elbow, then her collarbone, stopping when he reached the cup of her strapless black lacy bra.

"You're cheating," he murmured. "I've already got my top off."

She wanted to tell him to stop, to leave her bra alone, but her arms were still pinned above her head as he sneaked his fingers behind her back and expertly unhooked the clasp single-handed. She closed her eyes, not wanting to see his look of disappointment as he freed her breasts and tossed the garment aside.

He kissed her right breast and tugged her nipple with his teeth. She whimpered, writhing underneath him.

"My breasts are not what they used to be," she apologised.

He ignored her and moved onto the left breast, kissing it as if it was the most precious thing in the world before gently taking its nipple between his teeth. Even though he was pinning her down, Claire could barely keep still. She'd not felt this aroused for years.

80

"Did you breastfeed," he whispered, moving his lips slowly, languorously across both her breasts.

"Uh huh," she rasped, her voice barely audible.

"I think your breasts are beautiful," Jonah murmured, moving his lips up to her mouth.

"Now I know you're lying," she whispered.

He shook his head.

"No I'm not. They're beautiful because they're part of you."

Anthony hadn't done much to make her breasts feel anything more than a milk float since Miriam was born, but now her breasts felt alive again. Jonah unleashed his grip on her wrists, pulled back the duvet and moulded his hands over her breasts as his mouth journeyed south, snaking a path towards her naval and continuing downwards. He hesitated at the rim of her panties and then released his hold on her breasts so that he could slowly, tantalisingly, centimetre by aching centimetre, remove them altogether, tossing them in the direction of the discarded bra, leaving Claire feeling completely exposed. When his mouth found her clitoris she cried out loud.

81

"I want you inside me," she whispered.

"Not yet, baby, not yet."

He planted each of his palms at the top of her inner thighs, anchoring her legs apart as he licked and teased at her bud. She moaned louder and louder as the pleasure built, knowing she should try to restrain herself lest Miriam should hear, but unable to stop. And then, at its exquisite peak, she exploded in a series of glorious shudders. When her body had completely stilled Jonah released his hold on her legs, removed his jeans and boxers in one slick move and laid the weight of his frame on top of Claire, watching her eyes close in ecstasy as he entered her, thrusting deeply and sensually slowly.

"I love you," he whispered, his lips hovering a millimetre above hers.

"I love you too."

CHAPTER SIX

JONAH

Jonah lay on the bed, wide awake, knowing he'd hold onto this memory of Claire in his arms like this, forever. She'd been so exhausted after they'd made love that she'd fallen asleep almost immediately, lying on his chest with her lips pressed against his. Nobody had ever slept on him in such intimate proximity and he couldn't imagine doing it with anyone else but Claire. With all the other women in his life, what he'd craved most was space. He'd not been short of female company since they'd broken up and, with each new relationship, there'd been a hope that he'd finally be able to move on but nobody had ever matched up. They'd not even come close. Not even the mother of Martha. With her she'd accidentally gotten pregnant and he'd wanted to do the right thing and give this child a chance. So they'd married and given it their best shot which, in the event, hadn't been anywhere nearly good enough. Sometimes he marvelled at how well Martha had turned out, *despite* their ineptitude at parenting.

He'd always known that Claire was the one. He'd fallen for her the minute she'd stepped onto his tennis court on the Greek island of Kos. She'd been inappropriately dressed in a sexy black halter-neck bikini top and a tie-die navy sarong which she'd hitched up high by rolling it over a few times at the waist. Her only suitable piece of attire had been the sneakers on her feet but, he'd had to admit, she wasn't a bad tennis player for an amateur Brit. He'd had fun making her run around, watching her sarong split open, revealing her gorgeous creamy legs as she lunged for shots, determined not to be beaten. Claire always considered herself non-competitive but he would disagree. She didn't like to lose and the few points she'd legitimately won against him during the years they'd been together always made her do some hilarious victory dance which was so endearing it made him want to pick her up and twirl her around.

It was her mass of red ringlets which had always captivated him and as Claire finally rolled onto her side to settle her head under his arm, her hair fanned out like a peacock's tail over the pillow. *Firecracker.* That's what he used to call her. He wound one of her copper curls tightly around his finger. He still didn't dare believe that he was here with her again after so many years, their limbs interlocked, her sweet-smelling skin heating his. Her scent hadn't changed over time. She must still be using the same exotic lemon verbena moisturising cream that always so turned him on.

He'd dreamed of this moment. No, he'd *longed* for this moment, but had given up. She'd changed her numbers and moved house. It was clear that she had no desire to be found and eventually he reminded himself of that famous adage: if you truly love someone, set them free. So he'd respected her wishes and finally accepted that, much as he wished it were otherwise, it wasn't meant to be. He'd been sure that she would find someone else and he didn't want to destroy any new life she may have built for herself. But that hadn't stopped him from wanting it. He'd played at Wimbledon for at least the next five years after they'd broken up and, every time he'd been in London, a little part of him had hoped she might seek him out. She never had though.

By the time he'd got this job as a commentator, so many more years had passed that he no longer even dared to hope. He'd let it go. And when he'd crossed paths with Georgia in the corridor, he wondered if it was some cruel mirage. He'd done a double take and seen that she too had recognised him, but she'd lowered her eyes and was trying to ignore him, chatting to a colleague as they walked past. No way was he going to let this opportunity disappear. So he'd chased back after her, tapping his hand lightly on her shoulder. "Excuse me," he said, knowing it would sound ridiculous if he was wrong. "Are you Claire Jackson's friend?" He wanted to punch the air when she'd told him that Claire was divorced. Hope had seeped back into his veins. Maybe this time it was meant to be.

Georgia had scrabbled in her bag for something to write on and the creased, scrappy piece of serviette she'd finally etched Claire's email address onto had heated his pocket all day. Should he write? What should he write? What if she rejected him? The fact that this might really be his last shot made the normally cool, collected Jonah Kennedy angst a little. He'd sat at the keyboard for ages, working out what to say, writing a line then deleting it, worried he'd come across as either too flip or too desperate. He knew deep down why Claire had really left all those years ago and she'd be wrong if she believed he never thought about it. He often wondered, if he could do it all again, would he have done it differently? Being honest, he wasn't sure. He thought they'd done what they both believed was right at the time. Whatever, there was no point tormenting himself over it. The past was the past. That couldn't be changed. What made more sense was to concentrate on the future.

It had taken more than twenty-four hours for her to reply. Twenty-four hours of unadulterated agony. After he'd read her reply, he really *had* punched the air, in relief. They'd lost thirteen years and he'd not wanted to squander a second longer.

Their evening at Nobu already felt like aeons ago, but it was only yesterday. It was only yesterday that it felt as if his world had changed. Their kiss yesterday had, perhaps, been the most important of his life. It was a kiss full of hope, full of promise, full of possibility. It was a kiss that made him giddy. It had taken all his self-restraint to not invite Claire back to his room right there and then. He'd yearned for more, much more, and hadn't wanted to let her go. But more importantly, he'd not wanted to scare her off. Whilst in *his* head it was all perfectly clear - they belonged together and he was going to do everything in his power to make that happen - he'd sensed wariness in *her*. He feared she might not yet be ready. Better to play it safe than to rush her into something she might regret. So he'd let her decide when and where they should next meet and now here they were. She'd shown him *her* bedroom first, in which there'd been a divine imperial-sized sleigh bed, but they'd decided on the spare room instead, just in case Miriam should go looking for her mother in the middle of the night. In a way Jonah was pleased. True, the bed was small, more an oversized single than a double, but he didn't want space. No, he wanted to keep spooning Claire up close and to never let her go.

The next morning Jonah thought he must still be dreaming. He was woken by sunlight streaming under the curtains as well as the apparition of Claire standing at the foot of the bed, watching him, wearing nothing but the skimpiest pair of baby pink cotton shorts and a matching tight-fitting vest. No bra underneath. He stared appreciatively at her beautiful breasts. Yes, they might be smaller than before, but they were still gorgeously voluptuous, urging to be touched. Why she'd been embarrassed about them he had no idea. Perhaps it had had something to do with her ex-husband Anthony. Jonah hadn't liked Anthony. He was used to sizing up his opponents, trying to spot their Achilles heals. There was something about Anthony he didn't quite trust. Perhaps the simple truth was that there would never be any room in his heart for the person whom he would always consider had stolen Claire from him. Claire. Firecracker Claire stood before him like a tantalising angel. In one hand she was holding on the flat of her palm the biggest mug he'd ever seen, hot steam curling from it up towards the ceiling. In the other hand she was clutching some black material.

"Good morning," she smiled shyly.

Jonah shielded his eyes from the glare of the sun as he watched Claire close the door behind her and sashay towards the tousled empty sheet next to him. She placed the mug carefully down on the wooden bedside table before planting her bottom next to his chest and leaning over to kiss him. Her full, plump lips were deliciously warm.

"Mm," he moaned, leaning up to hook his arms around her neck and pull her towards him. She tasted of sugar. He grabbed her by the hips, repositioning her so she was lying flush on top of him, placing his hands at the base of her butt, tickling her skin underneath the frilly hem of her skimpy shorts.

"Be careful not to start something you can't finish," she smirked, planting a hand on the pillow on either side of his head for balance. "Miriam's downstairs and I don't want her getting suspicious."

"What's that?" he asked, nodding towards the contents loosely clasped in her left hand.

"That," Claire kissed him hard before pulling away, "is your freshly laundered underwear. I've been up since six o'clock. Miriam was singing in her bedroom and I decided to go to her before she came to find me here with you. I've already done two wash loads and made breakfast. We're waiting for you to join us."

Thankfully Claire's panic about what would happen if Miriam came to find her in the middle of the night clearly hadn't happened and Jonah was happy to play this however Claire deemed fit. Children complicated matters and everything needed to be handled with sensitivity. It was too soon for Miriam to think he was anything more than a friend and he didn't want to place Claire in a compromised position. He smacked her ass playfully.

"Thank you for doing my laundry, pretty washerwoman."

"Is that how you see me?" she feigned mock objection.

"Yes, but let me tell you, you are the prettiest washerwoman I have ever seen. Do washerwomen always wear such indecently hot clothes to do the washing? Go cover yourself up or I'm in danger of having an all-day-long hard-on. And that would not look good in front of your daughter."

"You need to control yourself," Claire teased, removing one of her hands from the pillow to feel the full length of his hardness through the thin cotton sheet separating them.

"What time is it?" he said, capturing and removing her hand before she could do any more damage.

Her brow furrowed anxiously.

"It's a quarter to ten," she started, worriedly. "I wasn't meant to wake you, was I? It's Saturday, and I just didn -

"Don't worry," he reassured her. "I've a day off. It's fine. And wow, that's the best lie-in I've had in ages. I think jet lag must have finally caught up with me."

Jonah could feel Claire starting to wriggle off him. He gripped her hips to momentarily still her.

"Last night was amazing, washerwoman," he said, punctuating this thought by kissing her lightly.

"Yes," she said, tapping his nose, before covering his face with his clean Calvin Klein boxers. "It really was."

Jonah could count on one hand the number of times he'd ever allowed nerves to truly worm into his bones and psyche. Once had been when Claire had delivered her 'I think we should take a break' speech. Another time had been when his wife had given birth to Martha, who had been born blue. Thankfully the doctors successfully resuscitated her and she'd been fine. Two matches had professionally unnerved him more than any of the others - the quarter final against Federer in Melbourne was one and the second was a game against Agassi in the US Open. It had been his first appearance on the main show court at Flushing Meadow and the occasion had got to him as, eventually, had Andre's masterful playing. But all these moments had been life-changing and monumental. They all made much more sense than him feeling nervous right here, right now, as he sat down to eat breakfast with Miriam and Claire. He didn't want to screw anything up. He wanted, more than anything, for Miriam to like him. He wanted to get it right, whatever right meant.

A veritable feast had been laid out on the table: warm croissants, scrambled eggs, crispy bacon and a bowl full of melon balls.

"Just to let you know, we don't normally eat like this," said Claire as she filled Miriam's glass with orange juice from a striped blue and white china jug. "It's a special weekend treat."

"I made the melon," boasted Miriam.

"Then that's what I'm having," said Jonah, spooning a generous helping of melon balls onto his plate before refilling fresh coffee into the now empty, enormous mug which Claire had brought him in bed.

"What's Sports Direct?" he asked, reading the blue and red logo on the cup.

"It's Mummy's favourite shop," giggled Miriam.

"It is," Claire confirmed. "It's a massive chain of stores which sells the cheapest sports merchandise on the face of the planet. And this mug once came free with one of our many purchases."

"I bet it's the biggest mug in the whole world," said Miriam.

"I think you are quite possibly right," smiled Jonah, taking a sip from the alpha mug before tucking into his fruit. "Mm," he intoned in a sing-song melody, "and these melon balls are seriously good."

Miriam eyed him as he shovelled a second, heaped spoon of melon into his mouth. Her intense scrutiny managed to elicit the impossible, to both unnerve and relax him simultaneously. Martha would have been no different and that thought made his mouth curl upwards as he matched her gaze head on.

"Do you have any children?" asked Miriam, staring him out.

"I do, a little girl who's exactly your age."

"I'm nearly nine."

"When's your birthday?"

"July the fourth."

"Ooh, that's a very special day in the country I come from."

"Is it a bank holiday?"

"Yes, it is sort of. It's American Independence Day, and everyone celebrates with a big party."

Miriam tore a chunk off a croissant before carrying on with her inquisition.

"What's your daughter's name?"

"She's called Martha."

There were many other things Jonah wanted to add. Like 'you'd really like her' and 'I've got a spare room in my apartment just waiting for you to come visit', but he held his tongue. Claire was side onto him, but he could instinctively feel that this whole exchange between him and Miriam was being keenly scrutinised by her too.

94

"When's her birthday?"

"She's just over a month younger than you. She's nine in August."

"Cool," said Miriam, stuffing the torn piece of croissant into her mouth, bringing a temporary pause to her cross-examination. It gave Jonah a chance to turn to Claire, who was wearing a warm smile. She nodded imperceptibly, a tiny gesture which perhaps nobody else would even have spotted, but Jonah knew that it was her reassuring him that all was going well. He was desperate to reach out to take her hand, but restrained himself, opting instead to fork a couple of rashers of streaky bacon onto his plate. He'd always enjoyed Claire's cooking but one of the things she did best was the full, traditional English breakfast – sausages with baked beans, grilled mushrooms and bacon. Nobody could crisp their bacon quite like hers. He'd just popped some into his mouth, enjoying the way it crackled on his tongue and oozed with smoky flavour, when Miriam recommenced her questioning.

"Did you used to be Mummy's boyfriend?"

Jonah nearly choked on the bacon. How should he answer *that*?

"Miriam," Claire interrupted.

"It's ok," Miriam continued unabashed, "I already know you were, because Mummy's already told me."

Jonah found himself stumped for words. He wished he'd read a manual on the right or wrong thing to say to someone who wasn't your child but was the child of someone you were in love with. And if such a manual didn't exist, then someone should goddamn write one!

"Are you *still* her boyfriend?" Miriam persisted.

Claire pushed her chair back, the legs squeaking against the wooden floorboards as she stood up. She moved towards the kitchen counter where Jonah had already clocked the presents he'd bought Miriam; two large white boxes still wrapped in cellophane sat next to the empty yellow Selfridges paper bag. One contained a game called Connect Four, the other was Twister.

"Why doesn't Jonah play one of these with you," she suggested to her daughter, "whilst I clear up?"

Miriam was laughing uncontrollably as Jonah found himself in a spot of bother on the plastic Twister mat, contorting his limbs into ungainly, unlikely positions as he tried to fulfil the most recent 'right hand on yellow' instruction. Claire had shooed them into the lounge and he now found himself performing some weird yogic posture, head practically brushing the floor and his legs so wide apart his groin was starting to protest. His right hand was currently his ballast. If he moved it he would surely fall. Every word Miriam uttered was like a staccato beat swiftly followed by a peel of giggles. She was precariously positioned, also upside down, with half of her frame underneath Jonah's. "You – look – like – a – wheelbarrow - that's – missing - it's - wheel," she told him. Because she kept gulping for air in-between the giggles, she now had the hiccups too.

"Watch out," warned Jonah laughing, "I'm about to try moving."

His limbs buckled and balance failed him as he lifted his right hand off the mat. Desperate not to collapse onto Miriam he did a side roll away from her, his head landing wedged between two sofas. He lay there for a while, catching his breath as the two of them recovered.

"I win," said Miriam.

She then hiccupped loudly, which began another round of the giggles from both of them. It was at this point that Claire walked in and observed them, the giggles clearly contagious and the happiness on her face clear for all to see. She was brandishing an I-pad.

"While you're both in such great spirits," she smiled, "I've got something else to show you that I think you'll find even more amusing."

It was when Jonah dug his elbows into the floor to get up that he saw it. A little ceramic statue of a cross-legged Buddha sat on a small glass coffee table. *Oh my God, she still has hers.* They'd been at some Indian fair in a hot, Arizona grass field on a day off during one of the many tournaments to which Claire had accompanied him. A stall selling Buddha statues of all shapes and sizes had caught her eye. Some of them managed to be amazingly intricate and yet smaller than a thumbnail. Others were so gigantic you'd have needed a forklift to shift them. Claire had wanted him to buy two identical statues, about the size of her hand. "They bring good luck," she'd promised. "You keep one with you at home and I'll take mine back to the UK. And whenever we're apart, our Buddha will bring us together." He'd kept his faithfully by his beside till this very day. And now he knew she'd kept hers too. He was longing to take the Buddha into his hand and to tell Claire that he also still had his, but Miriam was here and Claire had already pressed play on the I-pad. A commercial for some new razor started. Claire clicked pause to freeze the image.

"Right," she positioned herself between Jonah and Miriam, as they all shuffled together, sitting on the floor. She explained to Miriam about how she'd had a sort of audition to be the TV Nutritionist for a well known morning show and that now there was a video of her online for everyone to see. "I'd rather I showed you this than somebody else brought it to your attention. So here it is, me making an idiot of myself."

She clicked the pause icon again and the film started playing. Jonah could feel the muscles in Claire's body tense tightly and she covered her eyes in embarrassment with her hand. He couldn't see why she was so ashamed though. On the contrary, he thought she was brilliant. There was something about her that lit up the screen and her ability to laugh at herself as everything went wrong was charming. She was loveable and attractive and so engaging that had she told viewers to go and eat mud because it was good for them, half of them would probably have taken a fistful from their flowerbeds right there and then and spooned it into their mouths.

"You looked very pretty Mummy," said Miriam proudly when it had finished. "I really liked it."

Claire turned to Jonah, raising a quizzical eyebrow.

"Be honest," she warned him. "What did you *really* think? And I'll know if you're lying."

CHAPTER SEVEN

CLAIRE

"Welcome to your new home," said Dave the Floor Manager, opening the door to a sliver of space. An oval wall mirror framed by glowing light bulbs hung above a dressing table which spanned the entire length of the room. *This is insane, what's happening?* Claire wondered if she'd wake up in a few minutes and realise that she really was just humdrum Ms Jackson after all, a woman whose life largely consisted of motherhood, meal plans and moths? Or was what had just happened in the last hour her new reality? The same make-up artist who had attended to her for the screen test had painted her face so that she once again looked flawless, although Jonah would no doubt long to attack her cheekbones with a cotton ball doused in cleansing cream. Then she'd been taken to what Dave had called 'wardrobe', where she'd stood between rails of designer clothes whilst a dresser had fussed about with a measuring tape, holding different colour Prada, Armani and Whistles shirts under Claire's chin before finally settling on a royal blue sleeveless Sessun dress which finished above the knee, waist cinched in with a thin gold weave belt. "Perfect," the wardrobe mistress admired as they'd both examined

Claire's image in the floor to ceiling mirror before she'd finished off the look with a chunky black leather stud bracelet.

Afterwards Dave had led her through a warren of corridors whose walls were plastered with glossy celebrity photos. Anthony Hopkins, Paul McCartney, David Beckham, Natasha Bridges. Eventually they'd reached a door with a handle in the shape of a gold star and, next to it, Claire's name had been written in neat block capitals on a temporary plaque. It was all so improbable that Claire started laughing as Dave left her, with the instruction that she should relax because she wasn't due on air for another forty-five minutes. Flush to the mirror was a deluxe fruit basket. It was still encased in cellophane onto which an envelope had been stapled. Claire pulled it off and slipped out the little card tucked inside.

Break a leg and welcome on board.
With love from the 'Morning Cuppa' Production Team

"Ah, that's nice," Claire muttered. Then, on the end of her dressing table she spotted a vase holding a bouquet of velvety red roses. Leaning against the vase was a handwritten note.

Go get-em, Firecracker.
Jonah
X

Claire closed her eyes, holding the note to her chest as she remembered how the final stage of this new reality had come about. She'd asked Jonah what he truly thought of her hideous video but before he'd had time to answer her home phone had started to ring. Someone called Richard, the editor of *Morning Cuppa*, had apologised for calling on the weekend but said he had something urgent to discuss. The response to her video had been 'unparalleled' he'd confided and they would love her to come on board and do her first show on Monday. She'd spent the next ten minutes resisting his advances and saying that he was very kind but this really wasn't 'for her'. Richard, however, was clearly a man used to getting his own way. "Name your price," he'd shocked her. She'd politely told him that it wasn't 'about the money'. But then he'd started bandying sums around, ridiculous sums of money for just *one* show. More money than she earned in a fortnight for just *one* show. And they wanted her to be on air at least once a week but possibly more depending on whatever stories were in the news. Jonah had been watching her as she'd paced the room getting more and more agitated as the conversation continued and tugging frantically at her hair. She didn't believe one word of what Richard was saying, bar the dollar signs. Her film had been ridiculous. *She'd* been ridiculous. If she took this job, money or no money, she'd end up being a laughing stock and would lose any vestige of dignity that she had. Hell, Miriam could end up embarrassed or, worse still, *bullied* in the playground all because of *her*, and that didn't bear thinking about.

Jonah had scrambled up from the floor and gone into the kitchen, where he must have found the pad of Post-Its. He'd scribbled a message which he held under Claire's nose.

Tell them you'll think about it and call back later.

She'd blown Jonah a silent kiss in gratitude and asked Richard for his phone number as well as a couple of hours to ponder. Once she'd hung up, Jonah had acted as a sounding board. She'd explained exactly what she understood the gig would entail and they'd analysed the pros and cons. In the end Jonah had convinced her there weren't actually any 'cons' and that any negatives were a product of Claire's imagination. Yes, she'd been a bit rough around the edges and far from the slick pro she might aspire to be, but she'd also been a breath of fresh air, Jonah had insisted, with her own style and very unique charm. *She'd set the screen alight.* Those were his exact words and he refused to respond to her insistence that he must be delusional. "Do you honestly believe I'd want to set you up for failure?" he'd asked. She knew that he wouldn't and had been truly touched by his belief in her. She'd lost confidence in these last few years and Anthony had done very little to restore it. In fact, he'd been particularly uninterested by her career, never fully appreciating what a Nutritionist actually did, considering it a wishy-washy discipline which was neither a Doctor nor a Dietician, but some unsatisfactory hippy half-way house.

After she'd called Richard back and agreed to his offer, they'd all celebrated with a team bear hug. "My Mummy's going to be famous," Miriam had started singing, overexcited. "I love you so much darling," Claire told her daughter as the trio wrapped their arms around one another, squeezing tightly. She'd felt so blessed that Jonah had been there to share this moment, making sure to catch his eye so he knew that her 'I love you darling ' was addressed at him as well.

"Think of everyone in the studio being naked if you get nervous," Jonah had suggested, promising her it was a tried and tested technique which he'd employed on the tennis court. Every time he'd ever felt uptight during a match, he used to imagine his opponent running around the court in the nude. The imaginary vision of their swinging penis and bouncing testicles somehow made him relax into the game better.

The heat from the lights, the whir of the cameras and the fact that this programme was going out *live* did little to allay

Claire's fears. But instead of allowing negative 'why on earth am I doing this' thoughts to enter her psyche, she remembered Jonah's advice and put it into practice. After that it was all plain sailing. The studio was awash with tits and asses as Claire thanked the viewers for their support and neatly segued into the segment they'd prepared: How to get children to eat more fruit and vegetables.

Somehow, imagining Natasha in her birthday suit allowed Claire to relax and block out not only the immediate environment, but the petrifying knowledge that three million viewers were currently watching this from their living room. She talked to the show's presenter as if she was giving advice to a friend who was struggling to make their child eat healthily.

"I find," she said, reaching for a melon, "that making food look attractive really helps. My daughter isn't a massive fan of melon, but if I slice it up into what she calls 'melon smiles' and then cut the fruit into segments so that they look like teeth, then she can't get enough of it. Children love to use their imagination, and this encourages that, as well as helping them fuel up on Vitamin C."

As she spoke, she started cutting the melon into small curves with the knife, nothing going wrong. Even the cherries she placed on top for decoration behaved themselves, not one of them tumbling to the floor. Next she stretched for a plate of thin pancakes that had been already prepared.

"These," she began, "are not exactly a health-food and most children's idea of a tasty pancake is one smothered in sugar or honey or chocolate spread. But if you get your children involved with the actual preparation process, then it's amazing what you can get them to eat."

Little bowls loaded with different berries were lined up in a row at the front of the work station. Claire painted a large circle on the pancake with some blueberries, before helping herself to a handful of raspberries.

"Berries are plentiful at the moment. Because they're in season they're cheap in the shops or you can even grow or pick your own. I'm making a smiling face," she explained, designing a crescent with the red fruit, before adding a large strawberry for a nose and a couple of grapes for eyes. "But your child might want to design a car, or a cat or a tower. Take their lead, let them decide. And the best bit is when they get to eat it, berries and all. They'll probably ask for seconds."

Face finished, she pushed the plate toward the camera. And then she couldn't help herself. "Voila" slipped out of her mouth and her arms involuntarily performed her trademark

107

jazz-hand gesticulation. *Idiot, why did you do that?* Inwardly she cringed, but on the outside her smile remained fixed.

Next they moved on to vegetables and rather than cook anything on the spot, Claire had prepared some dishes at home which she'd brought in. One of the researchers had transferred her delicacies to the show's own branded crockery. Celery boats filled with cream cheese. Rice mixed with peas and corn. And a bowl of spaghetti, topped with cheese and spinach sauce.

Thank goodness I gave myself that manicure last night. That's what Claire thought to herself as she pointed towards each dish in turn. "Sometimes the best way to get children to eat vegetables is by being sneaky. Hide them, so that they don't even realise what they're eating. Pulses are so good for you that I never miss an opportunity to mix them with rice. As for spinach, it's one of the healthiest vegetables out there, packed with anti-oxidants and iron but very few children will actually eat it in its natural cooked or raw form. There's a very easy-to-make cheese and spinach pasta sauce, however, which should be going up on the show's website. I've yet to find a child or adult who doesn't like it and, if you want to gourmet it up a little, you can experiment by spicing it with a pinch of ground mustard or curry powder."

Natasha picked up a celery boat as she rounded off the item, thanking Claire for her fabulous tips and reiterating that details for all recipe ideas would be up on the website by the end of the show. A couple of seconds before they went into a commercial break she popped the celery boat into her mouth.

From nowhere, Claire was suddenly surrounded by a cluster of people, as if she were a sugar cube that had been sniffed out by an army of ants. They ushered her to the side of the set. A soundman unclipped the mike pack which had been attached to the back of her dress. Richard, the editor, hugged her. "Dahling, that was bloody marvellous," he enthused, "and just what we wanted." Then a photographer led her by the forearm, positioning her in front of a large, plain green screen. He did her "voila" jazz hand gesticulation. "Would you mind terribly posing for the camera just like that?" he asked.

Back in her dressing room, Claire felt somewhat dazed by it all. What just happened? *Did* it just happen? And if it did, then had she really been any good or was the crew just being terribly British and polite about it? She could remember nothing. It felt like an out-of-body experience. Someone knocked at the door.

"Come in."

The door opened and Georgia's face peered round. Claire shot out of her chair and screamed.

"Oh my God, I am so pleased to see you. Please tell me, what just happened?"

"What happened," said Georgia, sidling into the room and shutting the door behind her, "is that you, my friend, were brilliant. Honestly, you couldn't have been any better. You're a natural."

Habit meant that Claire was about to refute Georgia's claims and tell her she must be lying but, as she caught herself on the brink of uttering those words, she stopped.

"What are you doing here anyway?" she asked instead, noting that something about Georgia looked a bit different. Her mane of chestnut hair was glossier than normal. Had she had it cut? Her face was glowing. Had she had a facial? Or heaven forbid it, a face *lift*?

"I'm filming a pilot for a quiz show in a studio here today," she answered. "But we're still waiting for the presenter to arrive so I went to the staff café to grab a coffee and you, my love, were playing on the TV monitor they've got there. I didn't even know you'd been offered the job. I can't believe you didn't tell me. "

Claire couldn't believe she'd not mentioned it either. Georgia would normally have been the first person she'd have told. But the weekend had been so busy with Jonah around, not to mention having to prepare food for the show, that she'd not had a spare minute to breathe or think, let alone to call. Hell, she'd forgotten to tell her mum too.

"I know. I'm sorry," she apologised, switching on her phone. "Guilty as charged."

Her mobile predictably beeped with a message. Claire looked down. It was from her mother. *Darling, you were brilliant. Bravo. Can't believe you didn't tell me………again.* A couple of seconds later another text beeped through. *You smashed it, my little Firecracker. I'm so proud of you. Call you later. X*

"Who's that from?" asked Georgia.

"My mother," Claire began, "…………………..and Jonah."

Claire hadn't telephoned Georgia over the weekend but, now that Claire thought about it, it was a little odd that Georgia hadn't called *her*. The last time they'd spoken was when she'd gone shopping for the barbecue. George was usually the first to demand all the gory details.

"How are things going with sexy aging stud?" Georgia beamed.

"He's gone to Eastbourne for the week."

Claire couldn't help but smile at the 'sexy aging stud' reference, although truth be told she was a little forlorn about him having gone. He'd left late last night and she was already feeling his absence acutely. With him around she felt she could be anyone or do anything. "He's commentating on a pre-Wimbledon tournament from there."

"And, anything else?" Georgia probed, undeterred.

"And……..yes," Claire blushed under her half a centimetre layer of foundation. "It's going well."

She didn't feel like going into details here and now. She wanted to keep things close to her chest for a while longer and when the time came, they'd need a long, lazy evening with a bottle of wine to discuss it. A rushed, impromptu chat in a poky dressing room, even one that had a gold star for a door knob, wasn't the right time or place.

"Tell me about *you*," Claire changed the subject. "You're looking even more fabulous than normal."

Georgia turned coy. Georgia was a headstrong woman. She was the type of person whom Claire secretly thought would be difficult to have as your boss. Humility and timidity did not feature amongst her attributes.

"Really?" asked George, cocking her head shyly.

Claire watched keenly as Georgia's hand dropped protectively towards her lower abdomen.

"Oh my God," she gasped, "you're *pregnant*."

Claire emphasised the 'p' word, drawing it out as she watched Georgia's eyes darting wildly, like those of a cat dodging traffic on a busy road.

"No," she stuttered. "I mean.......why would you think that.........what makes you say that.....um-

Claire's pregnancy comment had been, at best, a guess, but her friend's bizarre reaction confirmed it as being the truth. Claire

113

reckoned that it must be early days and Georgia didn't want anyone to know.

"It's ok," Claire reassured. "Your secret's safe with me."

Georgia's eyes stilled, her hands settling defiantly on her hips. "You're a witch, do you know that?" she joked.

"Congratulations," Claire stood up and wrapped her arms around her best friend. "That's wonderful news. You'll make a fabulous mother."

They were mid hug when there was a sharp rat-a-tat on the door and the person knocking didn't wait for permission to enter. It was Richard, editor of *Morning Cuppa*. Claire was about to introduce them, but it was quickly evident they already knew one another as they airbrushed each others' cheeks with showbiz kisses. "Dahling Claire," he began, holding a tablet under her nose. "Check this out. Your cheese and spinach pasta sauce has already had more than a hundred thousand hits in just fifteen minutes. What do you say to that? You're breaking records here for us."

Claire straightened the screen so she could get a better view. Most of the typeface was so small that she couldn't make out the recipe, or the number of hits the page had had.

What she could see, however, and most mortifyingly clearly, was a very large image of her in outstretched jazz-hand pose. And a speech bubble coming out of her mouth had the word 'Voila' written inside.

CHAPTER EIGHT

June 13th

A malaise descended upon Claire as she drove in her little black mini towards the house of her favourite client, actor Orlando Goodman. Even Daft Punk's *Get Lucky* which was playing on the radio couldn't buoy her mood. Maybe it was the coming down from the high of the show. Maybe it was the coming down from the high of Jonah. Or perhaps it was none of these things because the truth of the matter was, today was June 13th.

She shook her head as she clicked her right indicator, trying to rid her mind of all negative thoughts and to concentrate on the positives. Her life had turned a corner and all was pretty great at the moment. No, not great, *brilliant*. There was Jonah, there was the new job. How many people would long to be in her shoes? But the harmful thoughts wouldn't go. *It* wouldn't go. The date kept spinning round in her head, and much as she tried to resist it, so did the thoughts that she associated with this date. She was a rational person and didn't believe in superstition. The number thirteen was inauspicious, holding so much weight for so many people, and yet she'd always refuted its force. She would happily buy a house bearing that number. She would happily stay on the thirteenth floor of a hotel.

She and Jonah had been apart for thirteen years and June 13th was a date that still pierced her heart. Perhaps she should start taking more notice of the number's significance. Perhaps there *was* some warped celestial link to it all. Perhaps that's why Jonah had come back after thirteen years, because of what she'd done, no what *they'd* done, to force her to reflect on it. For thirteen years Claire had done her utmost to put everything in a box and to not think about it, because thinking about it was too damn painful. But the problem with putting everything in a box is that sometimes it comes back to kick you on the butt. Sometimes that darn box unseals itself without your permission and its contents demand to be heard.

She shook her head. She needed to pull herself together. Orlando was one of the many high-profile clients on her books thanks to Georgia's showbiz connections and she was nearly at his house. Irritable bowel syndrome, bloating and high blood pressure were the most common complaints she encountered and Orlando Goodman had at some time complained of all three of these symptoms. He was an extremely handsome man, the sort that women swooned over until they learned that he was gay.

His home was a stylish maisonette converted from a four-storey late Georgian property located on a canal in a quiet backstreet of Kings Cross. He had bought it twenty years ago, when this was a rough, rundown neighbourhood but, with the recent introduction of the Eurostar terminal, the area saw a facelift and his property quadrupled in value. His home was the only one Claire knew that had a navigable waterway for a back garden. It was also the only home Claire knew that had a fabulous Victorian-style doorbell pulley which operated a cast iron bell above the inside front door. Claire tugged on the handle, its church-bell peels bringing a smile to her face.

"Entrez," beamed Orlando, opening both the door and his arms wide for Claire. They performed their ritual double cheek air kiss. As he released her from his hold Claire was disconcerted. Although he was deserving of the same 'sexy aging stud' status Georgia had bestowed on Jonah, today his complexion looked odd. Perhaps it was the light.

"I caught you on *Morning Cuppa*," said Orlando as she followed him down the hall. They always held their consultation in the kitchen, seated at a wooden bench table by French windows which overlooked the canal. "You never mentioned it."

Crikey, even her local newsagent had seen her on the telly and told her that he tried the celery boats on his two year old son who loved them. The attention unnerved her. The limelight was bad enough as Jonah Kennedy's girlfriend but now there was no shadow to hide behind.

"It all happened very quickly," she explained, unzipping her bag and removing the file which held Orlando's notes. When Orlando first started seeing her he was suffering from bloating and constipation. As an actor image meant everything to him and despite daily visits to the gym and intensive abdominal workouts, his lower stomach developed an ungainly bulge. Through a process of elimination Claire worked out that Orlando had an intolerance of dairy as well as problems digesting gluten. By removing both those food groups from his diet and encouraging him to drink more water not only did the constipation clear but so too did his bloating. He was delighted with the results and kept her on, seeing her monthly but knowing he could call her at any time if he had concerns. In many ways, Claire sometimes felt she was more a therapist than a nutritionist. Clients wanted to offload their problems on to her. In fact, frequently it was the offloading that made them feel better. She sometimes acted as an expensive placebo prescription.

"So, how have *you* been," she probed, anxious to move the spotlight away from her.

She planted her backside on the wooden bench and swung her legs round to underneath the table. Taking a pen out of her bag, she flipped open her notebook and poised the nib over the page. Orlando took a seat opposite her. As always, there was a bottle of Perrier and two glass tumblers loaded with ice and a slice of lime set on the table.

"Well actually," Orlando started, "since I last saw you I have been experiencing stomach pains." He placed a hand on his upper abdomen, indicating a large surface area where he was feeling it most. "Sometimes it's a dull ache, sometimes it's more acute. I've tried Gaviscon, but it doesn't help"

Claire made scrawling notes. As she wrote 'Gaviscon' she remembered guzzling it from the bottle when she was pregnant with Miriam. It allegedly cured indigestion.

"Have you noticed whether the pain comes after you eat or after something specific you've eaten?"

"No", replied Orlando, wiping beads of sweat off his forehead with the back of his hand before reaching for the bottle of sparkling water and unscrewing the top. "But sometimes the pain is worse when I lie down. When I'm busy and active I notice it less."

The sun was streaming through the French windows, flooding the room with beautiful, early morning summer light. It wasn't yet hot though. If anything there was a chill in the air and Claire wished she'd worn a denim jacket to cover her arms. Orlando, however, was perspiring profusely. He looked pasty and even in this good light she could tell that his skin was infused with an off-putting yellowish hue.

"And other than the pain in your stomach, how are you feeling?"

"Other than the pain, all seems fine."

"And is there anything else troubling you? Is work going well?"

Orlando was currently starring as Willy Wonka in the musical *Charlie and the Chocolate Factory* at London's finest playhouse, the Theatre Royal, Drury Lane. He had invited Claire and Miriam to the opening night. The whole show, not to mention his performance, was exceptional. He had won an Olivier award and there was talk of the show transferring to Broadway.

"No, everything's fine."

Claire always felt uncomfortable delving into clients' private lives but sometimes it was essential. It was amazing how depression and stress could physically affect someone's body, especially the gut.

"And, outside of work, is everything ok?" she probed.

Orlando was very guarded about his personal life.

"Everything's fine," he reassured, with neither his tone nor his expression giving anything away.

"And any other symptoms since we last met?"

Orlando swung his head from side to side, pondering.

"It's probably just because I'm getting older and my body's giving up on me, but I have started getting more back-ache than usual."

Orlando worked out in the gym regularly.

"Do you think you pulled something?"

"I'm not sure. I have stopped lifting weights but it doesn't seem to make any difference."

Claire put the end of her pen in her mouth and started chewing on it, contemplating. A brightly painted black and red gypsy barge glided past the window catching both her and Orlando's attention. Once it was out of view, she continued with the inquisition.

"Have you seen your Doctor?"

This line of questioning produced a raised eyebrow from Orlando.

"I don't need a Doctor, I've got you."

Claire took the pen out of her mouth and lowered it onto her pad, cupping her chin in her hands as her elbows found the table. She looked at him and noticed that even the whites of his eyes had a yellowy tinge. He didn't look right and from what he had told her it wasn't immediately evident what nutritional changes she could suggest to help. Georgia had jokingly called her a witch the day before. Claire preferred to call it a 'sixth sense'. And right now her sixth sense was telling her that something was untoward.

"I'm not a Doctor and the symptoms you're describing make me think it might be helpful to see someone who's properly medically qualified."

She didn't want to scare him, just in case her sixth sense was having an off-day. But nonetheless she wanted to make sure that he listened to her.

"I'm sure it's nothing, but please," she pleaded, "if you won't see a doctor for you, then do it for me."

Orlando held up his hands in surrender.

"Ok, I'll do it," he promised.

"Good," said Claire, "and I'll call you in a couple of days to check you've kept your word."

One of the perks of a home visit was that Claire performed a recipe demonstration at the end of each consultation. Something was definitely needed to temper the heaviness that now hung in the air. Claire reached for her bag and started unloading an array of ingredients onto the table: a tin of mackerel, a small pot of soy yoghurt and half a lemon.

"Oily fish is a great source of omega 3," Claire smiled, lifting up the mackerel tin, "and it makes a cheap and easy pate. So let's get cooking."

Meeting with Orlando had served as a good distraction but, once Claire got back in her car, it didn't take long for her malaise to return. She slowed and stopped at a red traffic light, tears spilling from her eyes onto her cheeks. She knew she ought to be thinking about Orlando - she was genuinely concerned about him - but the only thing now in her head was Jonah. Damn him! If he hadn't come back into her life she wouldn't be having any of these thoughts. That box would have remained firmly sealed. *For Ever*. This had been precisely what she'd feared from the beginning. That Jonah re-entering her life would open her up to a pool of pain which she just didn't want to dive into.

The car behind her honked its horn. She wiped her eyes. The traffic-light had turned green and she'd not noticed. Slowly accelerating, she wondered whether this date, June 13th, held any significance for Jonah whatsoever. Did he even remember? Well, sure he would remember, but would this particular *date* trigger an emotional response? Had he battled and struggled with this date every year like she had since they'd parted, trying to lock all that torturous emotion away for eternity? She seriously doubted it. Then what did that say about *him*?

Claire's brain felt as if its wiring had been temporarily tampered with and signals were firing off in wrong directions. *Think about something nice.* Claire tried. She thought about Georgia's exciting pregnancy news. No, that didn't help! Claire burst out crying as she parked her car outside her house, leaning her head on the steering wheel until she recovered her composure.

Lily Allen's spine-tingling rendition of *Somewhere Only We Know* was playing on the radio as her tears abated. The pure clarity of Lily Allen's voice as she sang *Oh simple thing, where have you gone* was haunting. Perhaps it was Lily Allen who was the witch and not her. Outside, a large black rain cloud drifted underneath the sun and settled there, like a heavy grey weight defying gravity.

A stiff, alcoholic drink, that's what Claire really felt like after she shut her front door behind her. But it was only 11.30 am. Instead, she boiled the kettle and decided to soothe herself with the strongest cup of tea she could brew. She made it in the mega-size Sports Direct mug that Jonah had used over the weekend, which made her smile and recall nice thoughts.

Keep thinking nice thoughts. That's what she reminded herself as she padded upstairs, switched on the main computer and took Orlando's file out of her bag, preparing to type up his notes. Her study overlooked the road and a FedEx van delivering a parcel next door grabbed her concentration, her focus only broken when a fat raindrop landed on her window pane, making a loud, unexpected splat. A few seconds later a second drop landed, then a third, until the heavens opened, unleashing their load with vengeance, the drops becoming denser and the wet splodges on the glass reminding Claire of large, watery snowflakes.

A gloom descended, matching Claire's mood. She got up to turn on the main light and no sooner than she'd sat back down, her mobile rang. A name flashed onscreen: Jonah.

She wanted to speak to him but she also knew she wasn't in a suitable frame of mind. Her mood was as low and flat as the Somerset Plains and their reconnection was still too fragile for any heaviness. Then again, perhaps hearing his voice would make her feel better. She hesitated whilst the phone rang twice, three times, four times. Against her better judgment she answered the phone on its fifth ring.

"Hello?"

"Hello babe," Jonah began, slightly shyly. "I know you're probably busy but I had a spare moment and just wanted to say hey."

In the same way that Claire had attempted to wear a fake smile for Anthony the other day, she now tried to inject levity into her tone.

"Ok then, 'hey'."

Her response was intended to sound like a joke, but its delivery came across as more abrupt than funny.

"How's it going?"

Claire started tapping on the keyboard nervously.

"Busy, busy," she said. Perhaps if Jonah thought that she was multi-tasking, she might appear less strained. Her mouth felt disconnected from her brain.

"Did you hear more news from the show?"

Claire stopped typing and tried to focus all her energy on the conversation.

"Err, no, not really, except they're pretty sure that Mondays will be my regular slot day."

She forced brightness into her voice, confident the result must sound so convincing that even Orlando Goodman would give her acting skills the thumbs up. Silence descended on the crackling phone line as she waited for Jonah to speak.

"Are you alright?" Jonah finally asked.

"Of course I'm alright."

"It's just you sound......"

"Sound *what*?"

"Different," said Jonah.

"I'm fine," she insisted. "I'm just tired. How are things going your end?"

She needed to shift the conversation away from herself.

This time it was he who sounded distracted.

"I'm sorry Claire, something's come up. I've got to go. I'll call you later."

Jonah hung up. As Claire listened to the dead tone on the phone she felt like a piece of pastry which had been pummelled and rolled so thinly that stretchy holes were starting to break across its surface, ruining its perfect consistency. One of those holes was over her heart, which now felt like a big black twisting vortex. Jonah had only just come back into her life and she was doing a very good job at pushing him away again already. Was that really what she wanted? Why wouldn't her thoughts just behave and get back into that damn box again? And if only they would, she swore she would seal it so tightly that it would survive a nuclear holocaust. Damn Jonah. Damn her. Damn bloody June 13th.

CHAPTER NINE

JONAH

Lifting the cup at a grand slam final is every professional tennis player's dream, but Jonah doubted that kind of euphoria could have felt much different to how he'd felt over the recent weekend. The benefit of maturity is that if you're an ass enough to not already know it, you soon learn what really matters in life. Love's what matters. It's having that special someone to share everything with. It's being with someone who makes you feel whole. It's being with someone who makes you feel omnipotent; that with them beside you, anything is possible. And for him, Claire was that person. Without her in his life, the glory of lifting the odd cup he'd won on the circuit had felt victorious, yes, but nonetheless, a shade empty. If he could have traded never losing Claire over winning a few tournaments, he would have.

After Jonah had helped Claire calm down from the TV network's shellshock phone call, persuading her that it was an excellent opportunity which she shouldn't turn down, he'd excused himself, saying he had to run an errand. "What errand?" Claire had asked, furrowing her forehead. Jonah loved how Claire's face was so expressive, and her scrunched-up, confused look was his favourite. It made him want to be her cocoon, a safe place where no harm could penetrate. Yes, idiot, he thought to himself. What errand could he possibly invent? "Men's stuff," he'd answered lamely. It was the best he could think of on the spot, without giving the game away. He'd given strict instructions to be let back in on his return and had headed in the direction of the local high street which he'd passed in the taxi on the way there. He'd been quietly pleased with his shopping. The champagne had been easy enough to find but he'd wanted to source an equivalent for Miriam. He absolutely did not want her to feel left out from the celebrations. And happily, in the picnic section of the supermarket, he'd found a dazzling mini-bottle range of wines and bubbles. One pretty little bottle, which even had the traditional golden champagne seal, was perfect, its contents a non-alcoholic fizzy punch.

An hour later, slightly tipsy on the bubbles, Claire had asked what his plans were for the rest of the weekend. He'd explained that the following afternoon a car was picking him up to take him to Eastbourne where he would stay for the next week, to commentate on a grass tournament taking place there. After that he'd be returning to London, first for the tournament at Queens, then Wimbledon. Happily, Miriam was out of earshot at this point, playing in the garden, whacking a rusty swing-ball which had been staked into the grass near the rear fence. "Where will you stay tonight?" Claire had wanted to know. He knew where he *wanted* to stay but he'd not dared to vocalise it.

Instead he'd let her decide. "Where works best for you?" There was Miriam to consider and, if she saw that he was staying at her Mom's again, it might look suspicious. In the end Claire hatched a plan. Jonah's bags were at the Dorchester and had to be retrieved. So they would all go, under the pretence that they were going there to enjoy a fancy afternoon tea to celebrate Mom's new job. Meanwhile he could check out, get his luggage and bring it back to 77 Gladstone Road, where he'd stay another night as their house guest. Claire doubted Miriam would even notice that Jonah's bags had materialised from nowhere.

So that's what they'd done. The finger sandwiches and scones with clotted cream and jam had gone down a treat and Miriam had been so tired from the days' antics that she'd gone to bed shortly after their return, her belly full on sausage rolls and chocolate éclairs. She'd even demanded that Jonah give her a goodnight kiss, which had made his heart swell with emotion.

Once they'd been certain that she was fast asleep they'd tiptoed up to Claire's bedroom to baptise her sleigh bed. Thanks to the mattress's imperial proportions, his feet hadn't hung off the end of it like they had in the spare room but, more importantly, it had been one of the most exquisite nights of his life. If he'd thought it had been amazing with Claire before, wow, well this felt even better. "Marks out of ten?" Claire had asked afterwards. It wasn't a serious question, but was one that held significance for them. Back when they'd been together, whenever they'd spent a special weekend away or done something new, she'd often asked him to rate the experience by giving marks out of ten. She could never pin him down though. His stock answer was always "it's all good and I refuse to compare." And that's exactly how he'd responded this time, his standard reply making her poke his side with a chuckle as she lay with her head on his chest after they'd made love. But actually, if she'd have persisted, he'd have given her a different answer this time. He'd have told her that he couldn't rate the evening, not because he didn't want to compare but because his score was off the scale. Giving it a ten wouldn't have done the evening justice.

Which is why as he now stood outside the commentary booth in Eastbourne, pressing the red handset icon on his mobile to end the call to Claire, he was dumbfounded. She'd sounded so strained and odd. Not like Claire at all. None of it made sense. Here he was, having had the best weekend of his life and here *she* was sounding every inch like she was getting cold feet. Her voice had been tight as elastic stretched to its limit, just waiting to ping. He remembered that tightness only too well. Claire did a terrible job at masking her true emotions. He'd always been able to read her like a book, much to her annoyance. There was only one time she'd taken him by surprise. One time, and he didn't want to remember it. There was only one time her voice had sounded like it just had, as if her voice box had been cut in half and all resonance swiped from it, her words thin and monotone to the ear. And that was *the* conversation, the conversation that had sparked the beginning of the end.

He leaned back against the wall, running his fingers through the salt and pepper on his temples, his brain working overtime as he tried to figure what to do. He was stuck. He was stuck in Eastbourne for work and the only reason he'd been able to call Claire in the first place was because rain had just interrupted play, leaving the three commentators who'd been holed inside the cramped booth happy to stretch their legs. He moved, heading away from the shelter to the outside courts to assess the situation. It hadn't rained for weeks in the UK apparently, and whilst this rain had come as a surprise, it shouldn't have. It was long overdue and par for the course when it came to tennis tournaments in Britain. He looked to the sky. Far from looking like it might brighten up, the clouds were mushrooming and blackening towards the horizon in all directions. The rain was beginning to pelt at a sixty degree angle. The weather forecast had been dicey at best. It had been a miracle that play had even started in the first place and from the report they'd been handed in the booth, the meteorologists predicted that the rain would last throughout the day without any let-up.

He checked his wristwatch. 11.40 a.m. Eastbourne was a good two hours' drive from London. If he got into a car now, he could be there by 2 p.m. A little voice in his head was persuading him that allowing Claire to stew in this mood was a very bad idea. Whatever was troubling her needed to be resolved sooner rather than later before it had a chance to fester. Yet dare he ask if he could be dismissed for the afternoon? He'd only just got this job. He liked this job. Perhaps he was being melodramatic about things and misreading Claire's voice. Dare he? Could he? Should he?

1.50 p.m. Jonah knocked on Claire's door. Each of the three loud knocks he gave it hammered home the fact that it was too late to back out of this now. If he'd misread the situation or his presence was ill-advised, too bad. He could hear footsteps coming down the stairs. One of the many concerns he'd pondered as his demon taxi driver had driven away from the coast towards the countryside, taking the bends on its narrow lanes as if he was Lewis Hamilton, was that Claire might not even be there. By the time they'd hit the motorway any doubts he had were futile. They'd gone too far to turn back. But hey, now he knew that, for better or for worse, she was at least in the house. A chain unlatched and the door opened. When Claire saw that it was him she sprung back in surprise, clasping a hand over her chest. She looked beautiful, but she also looked drawn, dark circles around her eyes a giveaway that she had been crying.

"I thought you were in Eastbourne?" she said.

"Well, surprise," he smiled, trying to make light of the situation. He'd not realised until after he'd done it that as the word 'surprise' had left his mouth, his arms had involuntarily performed Claire's jazz-hand gesticulation.

She stood aside, motioning that he should enter. She eyed him up curiously, tilting her head as she shut the door behind him. Her voice was tight and even her body looked tight, as if she believed that if she crossed her arms any closer to her diaphragm she might be able to make herself disappear altogether. Hell, she looked like she *wanted* to disappear. Perhaps this was a bad idea. No, it couldn't be a bad idea. This was Claire, and something was clearly wrong which needed to be righted.

"But….you…but….." she stuttered, "I don't understand, how come you are here?"

Jonah paused, searching for the right words.

"Claire, I know something's wrong."

A pensive look fell across her face. She was desperately trying to hold tears at bay.

"Do you want a drink?" she whispered, heading for the kitchen.

"Water would be good, thank you," he replied, following her.

She reached up to the cupboard over the sink, took out two glasses, ran her finger under the cold tap and when satisfied that the temperature was right she filled them up. She handed one to him and then hovered, uncertain where to put herself.

"I'm tired," she sighed, her shoulders slumping, "I need to sit."

She led the way into the lounge where she tucked a leg underneath her as she sat down in the far corner of the sofa, still nursing her glass. Jonah sat beside her and was grateful that at least she didn't flinch at his proximity. He sensed that, in the state she was in, she didn't want anything or anyone coming too close. But her alienation also felt like it was part of the problem, like a piece of her was closed to him.

"What is it babe, tell me," he spoke quietly, his words a caress which hung in the air.

138

A single tear slid down her cheek, just as it had before they'd kissed outside Kensington Palace. That time he'd wiped it away. He was about to do the same again, but she got there first, swiping it with the back of her hand. She cleared her throat and opened her mouth as if she were about to say something, but stopped. He knew for sure that she loved him, but was this all just too much, too soon? She looked traumatised.

"Is it me, is it something I've done?" he asked.

She closed her eyes and shook her head defiantly no, but after a few seconds her shake turned into a nod.

"Do you know what today is?" she whispered. Tears broke free from her closed eyes and this time she didn't even try to brush them away.

Where was this going? What had he done? Today was Monday, but he feared that wasn't really what she was getting at. He shook his head in response, but because her eyes were sealed she didn't even see. She planted the palms of her hands protectively over her lower abdomen. It was a tiny, imperceptible movement. Perhaps she didn't even know that she had done it, but it told him everything. It was his turn to close his eyes. He sighed, his exhalation a long, audible hiss. Now he knew.

"It's the anniversary of the most awful day of my life," she whispered, "June 13th."

They both opened their eyes simultaneously and her watery gaze showed thirteen years of hurt that she'd stored up. It pained him to see her agony. He reached for her hand and she allowed him to interlock his fingers tightly with hers. For this he was thankful.

"Do you blame me?" he whispered.

She nodded, tears now freely flowing. Perhaps if enough of them came they could wash the pain away.

"Sometimes I do blame you," she started, "but only because it's easier to. Mostly I blame myself. I wish I'd been stronger. I wish I'd not listened to you. We could have made it work. Couldn't we?"

Her eyes locked with his, questioning his, but no matter how much she might want to, she couldn't turn back the clock now. Much as *he* might want to, he didn't possess that power either. When she'd told him that she was pregnant all those years ago, he'd reacted badly. His career was on the rise and he was finally climbing up the rankings. Having a baby would have interfered with that and he hadn't felt ready. Hell, they'd both admitted they weren't ready, even Claire. They were young and certainly from his point of view, there was still so much he'd wanted to achieve before committing himself to fatherhood. He hadn't forced her to have an abortion, but he had made his position clear. If he'd have given her the green light, would she have cancelled the termination? They could never know for sure.

He'd tried to forget the hateful day that they'd visited that clinic. It wasn't one of their finest hours and there *had* been a point in the proceedings when the word 'stop' had entered his head - but frozen on his tongue. Half of him had expected Claire to blurt the word out instead and he wouldn't have fought it. Only she'd not known that. And if he'd have been able to predict that that day would mark the beginning of the end for them then who knows what he'd have done.

"We probably could have made it work," Jonah agreed, "but imagining things differently can't change the past. If it makes you feel better, I do regret it."

"Do you really?" Claire's voice was so quiet he could barely hear her.

"Yes, especially since Martha was born."

His response seemed to please Claire, allowing her to relax a little. Perhaps it was a relief to learn that at the very least he had shared the same burden and pain over the years. And it was true. He *had* always wondered about the child that could have been. It wasn't a thought that consumed his consciousness, but it did flit through his mind from time to time.

"I never speak about it," Claire admitted, "and sometimes I think I should have seen someone about it, a therapist or something. There's a lot of blame and resentment stored in here."

She took her free hand and placed it over her heart, her lower lip trembling. Jonah stilled her lip with his finger and then scooped her into his arms, hugging her tightly. She came across as so strong most of the time but this reminded him of her very sensitive, fragile side. He was pleased they were having this conversation. At least it gave them a chance to work through it

"I'm so, so sorry Claire," he whispered into her hair. "And I can't change the past, but we can take from it and move on. And concentrate on the future. That's what really matters now."

Claire sobbed loudly in his embrace. He was dressed smartly for a change, in a suit and tie and he could feel her tears dampening his shirt. He pulled away, not because he was worried about his shirt getting wet, but because he wanted her to see how serious he was.

"Do you see a future with me?"

She nodded, smiling through her tears. He saw her little Buddha statue sitting on the coffee table sandwiched between the two sofas. He reached across to pick it up and placed it on the palm of his hand.

"Do you know where I keep my Buddha?"

She shook her head and he continued.

"I keep it on my bedside table. I sleep with it looking over me every night. And do you know why?"

She shook her head again, smiling as she sniffled.

"I keep it close to me, because I've never stopped believing in us. I've never stopped hoping that somehow we'd be brought together again. I can't change what we did all those years ago, but perhaps it happened for a reason. Perhaps the timing wasn't right for us then. You wouldn't have had Miriam and I wouldn't have had Martha. Perhaps now is our time though. Do you believe that?"

Claire nodded, smiling once again through her tears.

"I need to hear you say it baby," Jonah encouraged.

"I do believe and very much hope," she whispered, "that now is our time."

They hugged tightly, rocking gently back and forth, not moving for a very long time, soundless. It was Claire who broke the silence.

"Why are you here when you should be in Eastbourne?"

"I'd do anything not to lose you again," Jonah replied honestly, "and I could feel you slipping through my fingers."

CHAPTER TEN

CLAIRE

Being in the presence of celebrities wasn't something that had ever fazed Claire. Five years spent as Jonah Kennedy's girlfriend had brought her into contact not just with some of the world's most iconic sports stars, but Hollywood actors and even Presidents and Prime Ministers. They were, she always reasoned, just normal people. And because of that she never reacted to their fame. If anything, she tended to give them a wide berth, because the last thing they wanted was a load of hanger-on's gushing around them. If she ever did find herself in conversation with someone well-known, her golden rule was never to discuss their work, because chances were that anyone in the public eye was probably sick to death of answering the same questions ad infinitum.

Claire would have been very happy sending Miriam to the local state primary school, but Anthony had insisted on her being educated privately. It quickly became apparent that a few choice celebrities had decided that Miriam's school was right for their child too. One of them was an A-list rock star. Whilst fellow Mums and Dads had desensitized to his presence in the playground over the years, they weren't quite so chill when his pals Beyonce and Cameron Diaz flew into town and joined him on the school pick-up. Claire had never seen such a scrum, parents and children alike ambushing them with their I-phone cameras at the ready. Their cameo appearance had been the talk of the playground for weeks.

Not Claire though. No, Claire was cool around fame. *Normally*. It was fast becoming clear, however, that today was anything but a normal day. Claire regretted that she'd not been there for Jonah the time he'd made the quarter finals of Wimbledon, especially because she was now benefiting from a perk of that achievement. A privilege for players making it into the last eight is that they become instant honorary members of Wimbledon's illustrious All England Lawn Tennis Club. And members of the club are entitled to seats to watch its championships.

When Jonah had invited Claire to come this Saturday, she'd jumped at the chance. The timing couldn't have been better. Miriam was with Anthony for the weekend which meant that Claire would be free to stay with Jonah at the lovely hotel where he was being accommodated: The Millennium Gloucester. This also happened to be where many of the players stayed too and, bizarre though it was to be in a hotel room in a city which she called home, she was thoroughly enjoying the pampering. She didn't have to make the divine marsh mallow bed with its indulgent Egyptian cotton sheets.

She didn't need to do the cleaning. She didn't even have to make the breakfast. No, they'd ordered room service. Creamy scrambled eggs with smoked salmon had arrived piping hot and accompanied by a basket of crumbly warm pastries. This was definitely the life! Jonah left early to attend a morning briefing and she called Georgia to brag about where she was going this afternoon. "Oh my God," Georgia gushed. "Can I come too?"

Claire sent Jonah a text to see if it was remotely possible and an hour later, like a fairy Godmother, he replied to say that it was. Tickets to Wimbledon were like gold dust and this middle Saturday of the tournament was one of the best days to be there. It was a mix of men and women playing and it was still early enough in the event that most top seeds hadn't yet been knocked out. It was a day for the people, for the tennis fans, with plenty of singles and doubles being played from midday till sunset. It was also, Claire now realised, a day for royalty.

When Jonah said he could provide tickets, Claire presumed they would be back row seats on some inferior, outside court, and quite frankly she'd have been delighted with anything. He nipped out from the commentary booth to meet her and Georgia at the entrance gate, furnishing the girls with VIP passes to hang round their necks. He also gave them two Centre Court tickets. Blissfully ignorant they followed signs for the stairwell and row marked on their tickets and it was only when they had been directed to their seats and turned round to face the court that she realised exactly where she was. She was in the Private Member's stand, also known as the Royal Stand.

If only Jonah had warned her she'd have worn something a little fancier than her figure-hugging calf-length navy jersey dress, but then again, it could have been worse. She could have worn jeans! Georgia was far more suitably attired, wearing a flouncy floral dress with a string of pearls and a lightweight beige blazer. They were in the front row of the stand, perched high over one end of the court. Claire had stuffed all essentials into her leopard print clutch and was bending over, about to place it against the front wall when she heard a lady behind them say "Excuse me, I think our seats are next to yours." Both Claire and Georgia rose to their feet, sucking in their stomachs to make space for the woman and her friend to pass. It was only when the woman turned to her and said "Thank you" that Claire, recognising the trademark magnetic smile and glossy long chestnut hairdo, realised exactly who it was. It was none other than Kate Middleton. Her 'friend' was sister Pippa.

Oh my God, do you realise who that is? Claire had to literally bite her lower lip to stop herself from blurting out that very question and prevent her jaw from dropping. It took even more resolve to not make eye contact with Georgia. Instead she surreptitiously double flicked Georgia's thigh and Georgia promptly flicked her leg back in response.

The crowd, by contrast, showed no restraint whatsoever. Spectators quickly cottoned on to the new arrivals, prompting a raucous cheer and slow hand-clapping. A Mexican wave began in the stand to the left of them. Little by little it travelled round the court, gaining in momentum as did the decibel levels of the accompanying whoop. The closer it got to their stand, Claire wondered what to do. Instinct was telling her that it would appear "bah humbug" if the wave came to a halt once it reached them but, on the other hand, did regal protocol permit Duchesses to flap their arms in public? In the end she couldn't help herself. Better to hear it from the horse's mouth. She cocked her head toward Pippa and asked "Are you going to do this?" "It would be rude not to," beamed Pippa. A few seconds later the wave crept round to them and the four ladies, royal and otherwise, got to their feet, sweeping their arms from low to high and back again. Kate's willingness to act like one of them made the crowd, clearly pleased by her performance, cheer even louder.

Sitting back down again, Kate leaned over her sister towards Claire.

"I love your leopard clutch," she said. "Where's it from?"

Claire could feel heat rushing to her cheeks, a crimson blush lighting up her face. Had Kate Middleton seriously just ask her that? Did she dare tell Kate where it was really from? Or should she lie and say it was Gucci or Armani?

"Top Shop," Claire admitted. "And it was in the sale for £5.99."

"Fabulous," Kate replied, tapping her nostril conspiratorially, as if she'd been let into a big secret and would be heading to the cheap fashion retailer to snap up an identical clutch next week.

"And *I,*" Pippa began, "have to thank you. I loved your mackerel pate and potato gratin. I tried them both. They were so easy to make and you were absolutely right. They were seriously tasty."

So much for Claire recognising *them*, Pippa had recognised *her*! The day was becoming more surreal by the second. This whole exchange was absurd and giddying. In last Monday's slot on *Morning Cuppa* they'd been talking about the rise of lactose intolerance. As part of the segment Claire had demonstrated the two dishes Pippa had mentioned. The potato

150

gratin tastes so indulgent it's hard to believe it doesn't contain dairy. Crikey, it was hard to believe that *anyone* at home was attempting her recipes, let alone Pippa Middleton.

"Thank you," Claire replied, "that's *so* nice to hear. I still can't believe I'm doing that show. And I can't believe you saw it. It makes me nervous."

Claire felt as if the air was being sucked out of her lungs. She was blabbering nervously and wished she would stop.

"You shouldn't be," Pippa touched her arm. "You're doing great."

At this point the players walked out onto the court. Andy Murray followed by an un-seeded Dutch player Claire had never heard of called Otto Van der Welder. Claire heard her mobile beep. Oops, she'd forgotten to turn it off. She bent down to pick up her clutch and without checking to see who was trying to contact her, she turned the phone off.

Two hours later, trailing one set to two, the Dutch player Otto Van der Welder skidded badly running for a wide forehand and twisted his ankle. Clearly in pain and clutching his calf he asked for injury time so that a medic could assess and

151

hopefully repair the damage. Andy Murray returned to his courtside seat near the net, a ball girl holding an open umbrella above his head as the spectators relaxed filling the stadium with chatter. Claire turned and saw Jonah entering her stand. Still, now, whenever she saw him her heart flipped but today he looked especially dreamy. He was normally a T-shirt and jeans kind of a guy but he'd spruced up his image for his job as a commentator. The beautifully cut grey summer suit he was wearing was stylish and sexy. Pale blue shirt cuffs hung longer than the jacket sleeves and the navy tie with silver diagonal stripes he'd chosen, together with large dark sunglasses added just the right amount of bad boy cool. *I can't believe he's mine.* She smiled broadly in his direction and when Georgia saw him approaching she graciously moved into the vacant seat beside her so that Jonah could sit next to Claire.

"Hello ladies," he grinned, settling himself between them. "How's it going?"

"It's a great match," said Claire.

"Thank you so much for letting me come," Georgia added. "They're amazing seats by the way!"

If only Georgia and Claire could have said more or, indeed, squealed loudly about their excitement but Kate and Pippa were still right beside them, chattering between themselves.

"Are you finished for the day?" Claire asked.

"No, I've got a forty-five minute break in-between matches and thought I'd check out how you were doing."

"It's a great match," Claire took his hand in hers, "and we're having an incredible time."

Claire bent down to retrieve a small bottle of water she'd stowed under her chair and her arm brushed against the leopard skin clutch. She could feel it vibrating. She discreetly slid it half out the clutch to see who was trying to contact her. It was her mother. Ten missed calls, two voice messages and now a text.

Oh my God, u r on the TV right now.
You're sitting next to Pippa and Kate. How did you get to be so lucky?
Oh my God and now Jonah Kennedy's there too. I can't believe it. Why am I always the last person to know? Are you two back together again? Call me. V. soon please. I can't contain myself any longer. Mum X

Claire slipped the phone quickly back into the clutch and laid the bag down, promising herself that she'd call her mother before the end of the day. She looked around the stands, trying to locate the camera which had given her away. It was ridiculous of her not to have thought of it. Of course the cameras would have found them. Kate Middleton was there. She suddenly became self-conscious as well as berating herself for not returning her mother's calls this past fortnight. She deserved better, but Claire had wanted to keep things about Jonah private for a while. Her mother had always loved Jonah and had been upset when they'd broken up. She'd not wanted to tell her Mum about him being back in her life until she was certain that their relationship was going somewhere. And now she knew that it was. She'd have had to have come clean with her mother soon enough anyway because the flights were booked and they were leaving in just over a week. Claire had agreed to take Miriam and spend the next two months in California with Jonah and his daughter. Better still, *Morning Cuppa* had been delighted with the idea. They'd decided to make a plus of her being the other side of the pond and had arranged for her to do live broadcasts from the US. They planned to give her nutrition slots an American twist and the fact that she was abroad would lend a summer holiday feel to the show.

"Play will resume in two minutes," called the umpire. Jonah placed his hands on his thighs and stood up.

"Excuse me?" Kate Middleton called politely. There was a tone about her voice that demanded to be heard. Jonah turned and found that she was looking straight at him.

"I was a big fan of yours," Kate told him. "And that match you played in Melbourne against Federer was one of the best I've ever seen. I was so excited when you won."

Back at the Millennium Gloucester Hotel, Jonah ordered strawberries and champagne to be delivered to their room. Whilst waiting for these to arrive he hopped in the shower and, making use of this brief moment of downtime, Claire kicked off her wedge sandals, lay on the bed and finally called her mother. It was a conversation that made her eyes well up but in a nice way. Her mother was a woman prone to criticising and, whether intentional or not, Claire was often made to feel that she was never good enough. Not a good enough daughter, not a good enough mother, not a good enough wife. But during this particular conversation her mother said how beautiful and radiant Claire had looked on the television earlier and how proud she was of what Claire was achieving with her career. She was also exceptionally pleased that she was back with

Jonah. "I'd always thought it a mistake that you two broke up," she said. "I loved him like a son." In many ways Jonah had been the son she'd never had. She'd lavished love and attention on him and had even battled her fear of flying to travel to America once to watch him play in the US Open. She'd not set foot in an aeroplane since. She hadn't disliked Anthony but she'd never warmed to him in the same way. Their repartee had always felt more forced, with Anthony and his mother-in-law being perfectly polite to one another, but nothing more or less. She'd certainly never treated him like a surrogate son.

Claire promised to visit her mother before going away and, after ending the conversation, she quickly sent a text to Orlando Goodman to check he'd been to see his Doctor. She'd just pressed send when Jonah walked out the bathroom. A white towel clung loosely round his torso and he was in the process of wrapping a second, smaller towel over his wet hair.

"I heard you talking to someone while I was in the shower," he said, as he knotted his head towel into a pseudo turban, "was it Anthony?"

"No, it was my mother. I'll see Anthony tomorrow when he brings Miriam back. I'll speak to him then. I promise."

Jonah was anxious that Claire should clear everything with Anthony about taking Miriam to the States. For some reason he sensed that Claire's ex-husband might not be overly thrilled with the arrangement but Claire didn't anticipate any problem. Nothing in the plans had changed. Miriam had two months off from school for the summer. Claire would have her for the first half and Anthony for the second.

Jonah approached Claire with sexy, mischievous intent in his eye, snatching her mobile phone from her hand and turning it off. As a quid pro quo, she was about to snatch his towel from his body but was interrupted by a knock at the door. "Room service," a man called. Jonah let the man enter and the waiter wheeled in a trolley loaded with an ice-filled champagne bucket, two crystal flutes and two glass bowls filled with strawberries. "Just leave the trolley outside when you've finished with it," the waiter said before closing their door behind him.

Jonah wasted no time in picking up the champagne and tearing the gold seal off the top of the bottle. Claire quietly watched every movement of his arms at work as he untwisted the wire and pulled at the cork. The honey colour of him, the chiselled contours of him, the height of him, the breadth of him, always made her long for him, to touch him, to feel him. She waited for the cork to pop and for the two glasses to be filled and then

157

she padded towards him, wrapping her arms around him from behind and pulling gently at the towel until it unravelled and fell to the floor. She kissed his back as her hands explored his chest, travelling lower until she found the huge size of him and held its pulsing hardness in her clasp.

"I love this bit of you," she said, still kissing his back and then sliding her hands slowly round to his tight buttocks, "and this bit of you."

Jonah whipped around, the sharpness of his movement causing his temporary turban to join his other towel in a heap on the floor. He placed his hands on Claire's long dress, lifting it in one swift movement until she compliantly raised her arms so he could remove it entirely.

"As usual," he kissed her neck as he unclasped and took off her bra, "you're overdressed."

He pushed her playfully backwards until she fell on the bed.

"Take your panties off," he commanded as he picked up the champagne bottle. She did as she was told and as she lay naked she watched him pour champagne over the strawberries in the bowl. She couldn't believe how far she'd come. A fortnight ago she'd been utterly embarrassed by her body and now she felt so free and easy within her skin. He'd done a wonderful job of making every single tiny inch of her feel beautiful. Jonah poured so much champagne onto the strawberries that it was almost sloshing out of the bowl as he climbed onto the bed lying on his side like a Roman and balancing the bowl of strawberries and champagne on her stomach.

"That's going to spill everywhere," Claire objected.

"Only if you don't stay still," Jonah laughed.

"If you could choose between Kate Middleton and me, who would you pick?" she asked, trying to ignore the strawberry Jonah was teasing her with and most definitely trying to ignore his hand moving across to her breast and the urge she had to pull him on top of her and feel his hardness between her legs. He dipped the strawberry back in the bowl again, leaving a trail of champagne dropping onto her stomach as he brought it back to her lips and finally allowed her to eat it. He carelessly served himself a strawberry, spilling yet more champagne onto Claire's stomach.

"You ask a lot of stupid questions," he replied, feeding Claire another strawberry. "I've only got room for one Duchess in my life and that, my love, is you. And by the way, this is your punishment for your stupid question."

Jonah started tickling Claire's stomach gently with two hands. At first she was able to stay still, but then it became too much and her giggles made the bowl topple a generous helping of champagne onto her, trickling in all directions. She squealed for him to stop and he finally removed the bowl and set it on the bedside table. He then set to licking Claire's skin clean, his hands never losing contact with her breasts as his mouth lapped at the champagne trailing down towards her belly button and beyond. As his mouth found her mound which was moist from desire and champagne, he slipped a finger inside of her. Claire moaned loudly.

"Duchess," Jonah whispered, "By the time I've finished with you, our neighbours are going to be bashing on the walls to get you to turn down the volume."

CHAPTER ELEVEN

ANTHONY

"Bye, sweetie," Anthony kissed the top of Miriam's head as he pulled her close for a hug. Her hair smelled so good, like a piece of sugary candy sprayed with cologne. This was the part he hated, the farewell. He never wanted to let her go and time always dragged horribly between his access days. This new reality was somewhat ironic. Back when he'd been together with Miriam's mother, he'd worked so hard that an entire week could pass and he'd barely see his daughter. He left the house before she woke and, by the time he returned, she was fast asleep. Claire criticised him for being an absentee father but since their divorce – or perhaps *because* of their divorce - things had changed. The holidays, weekends and occasional weekday nights spent with Miriam meant everything to him and he always ensured he spent proper, quality time with her. Family now meant everything to him. More than work, that was for sure, and he'd managed to engineer a better balance between the two. Since his son Jasper had been born he'd been thinking about returning to court to see if there was any way the current arrangement between himself and Claire could be altered, allowing him access to spend *more* time with Miriam. But now Claire had dropped this bloody bombshell. He didn't let Miriam or Claire see it as he left, but on the inside he was positively fuming as he got back into his white BMW four-wheel drive and slammed the door shut.

Claire had shooed Miriam into the garden so that she and Daddy could have 'a quiet word.' That's how she'd put it. And only when she could see that Miriam was actively engaged whacking the swing ball with a plastic racket did she start speaking. "I just wanted to let you know that I'm going to spend the next two months in California," she said. "And of course Miriam will be with me for the first half of that time." She was holding a red leather key fob case in her hand and kept nervously opening and shutting its popper clasp. She probably didn't realise she was doing it, but this very action irritated Anthony, an irritation which was exacerbated by the conversation she'd started. "With *him*?" he asked, not even able to say the name out loud. "Yes, with Jonah," she confirmed.

Claire had always refused to watch Jonah Kennedy when he was shown on T.V playing tennis, but Anthony had done just that, on the sly, out of curiosity. He'd wanted to observe more closely the man his wife had been with before him. He'd been her significant past, her significant ex, and Anthony had always wondered whether, for Claire, Jonah had been 'the one that got away'. Perhaps the reason she found it hard to watch him on the television, or even to *talk* about him for that matter, was

162

because she was in denial. Whenever he asked Claire why they'd broken up she changed the subject. He knew there must have been a reason but her rambling, non sequitur explanations never really amounted to much. What he *did* know was that, much as Claire denied it, he wasn't convinced she'd ever truly moved on. He'd felt it. Not so much in her actions or in things she'd said and done but by reading between the lines. When Anthony and Claire first got together she had photos of her with Jonah mounted in artisan silver frames arranged on her bedside table. If they were truly 'over' then why keep the pictures up? And whilst the pictures had finally been stowed away, a little Buddha statue she used to keep by her bed was never removed. Anthony hadn't appreciated the full significance of that Buddha until one day when Miriam was about four years old. She grabbed that Buddha in her tiny fist and raised her arm. "Look Mummy," she cried, but then she'd become distracted and the chubby fingers gripping the statue slackened open. The Buddha landed with an ungodly thud on the wooden floor, the drop decapitating its delicate ceramic head. The two pieces had lain motionless on the ground. Claire kept silent, staring at the broken fragments, and Anthony noticed her eyes filling with tears. She wiped them away, and were it not for Anthony overhearing a conversation Claire had with Miriam later as she diligently stuck the head back onto its torso with superglue, he'd have been none the wiser. He heard Miriam apologising and Claire promising it didn't matter. But then Miriam asked why was she crying then and her mother said it was because the Buddha was a present from someone special. "Was it a boyfriend?" Miriam asked. "Yes," Claire replied. "What was his name?" "He was a tennis player called Jonah, but that's all a long time ago now. It really doesn't matter darling."

Well, it mattered to Anthony. It all suddenly made sense. He'd never been able to make Claire really happy. He hadn't tried hard enough perhaps, but then again he'd always felt her pulling away and at some point in time he stopped trying to bridge the gap. He never attempted to compete with Jonah Kennedy because he knew that he couldn't. For Christ's sake, Jonah Kennedy wasn't only a successful tennis player but he was glossy magazine front cover hot male eye candy.

Two weeks ago, when he saw Jonah walking up the garden path towards Claire's home, it was as if time had stood still and someone had pressed freeze-frame on the image. In that moment, Anthony had a sense of foreboding that nothing in the nice new life he'd recently carved for himself would ever be quite the same again. Jonah Kennedy was a major threat. For starters, although it shouldn't because they weren't together any more, it felt odd to think that Jonah and his ex-wife might be an item again. It made Anthony feel that he had never been anything more than a stepping stone. But, far more importantly,

164

if this was the case then there would be an impact on Miriam. Anthony wasn't stupid. He knew that Claire was an attractive woman and that eventually she would find herself another partner. But this wasn't any man, this was Jonah Kennedy. And worse than that, Jonah lived a whopping six thousand miles away. How could that ever spell good news?

Anthony drove himself stir crazy for a week, stewing over a whole host of hypothetical scenarios. His wandering thoughts even brought about the rarest of occurrences. He lost a trial! He was defending a client on a robbery charge and whilst in his heart he believed the defendant wasn't guilty, the jury disagreed. Anthony just wasn't sufficiently on the ball. Instead he'd been pondering a whole host of "what ifs". What if Miriam liked Jonah more than Anthony? What if he tried to take Miriam away from him? What if he hurt her? What if he tried to turn her against him? He knew it was wrong, but the next time he had Miriam to stay he cross-examined her as if she was a witness in the dock.

"Oh, so you met Jonah at Mummy's," he tried to keep his tone light and casual. "Was he nice?"

"Oh yes, he was really nice. He played Twister with me and Connect 4 and he let me win."

This hurt. Anthony never let Miriam win, at least not on purpose. As a top criminal Barrister he had a hungry desire for victory, but he liked to achieve this legitimately. He also liked to teach Miriam that conquests tasted sweeter when they were earned, not when they were handed to you.

"Did he stay the night?"

"Yes."

Ouch.

Anthony's annoyance at this was irrational. Not only was he already engaged to somebody else, they even had a son together, and he'd only been divorced for a year. Claire was entitled to a boyfriend and for all Anthony knew she'd had several since their separation. Moreover, they could all have stayed the night in Claire's bed and it would be none of Anthony's business. Except that it felt like it was because Miriam was there too. Anthony had been desperate to ask which room Jonah stayed in but didn't dare steep that low. Luckily he didn't have to. Miriam offered the information.

"He stayed two nights actually," she continued. And then, with a maturity that belied her years and made Anthony think she understood the situation better than he expected, she added, "in the spare room."

"What did you do all weekend then?"

"We celebrated Mummy's new job."

"Mummy's got a new job?"

"Yes, she's going to be a TV superstar."

Anthony guffawed. Really, Claire was going to be a television superstar? Miriam's last word was spoken with great relish, and even though it wasn't intended, to Anthony it felt like a snub. It was as if Miriam believed her mother's fictional TV superstar status was far superior to any legal coups her father might achieve. Jealousy was building in Anthony's gut like venom but then he recognised he was being ridiculous. Miriam had a vivid imagination. She couldn't be right. Claire didn't even have a proper career.

"And Jonah's got a daughter my age called Martha. She's American too. Daddy, can I ask you something?"

"Yes, darling, anything."

"If Mummy marries Jonah like you're going to marry Ali, would that make Martha my sister like Jasper is my brother?"

Anthony tried to keep his face composed, an act he'd perfected for his job, but on this occasion he wasn't sure he completely succeeded. The next question he asked felt like thick molasses on his tongue as he struggled to articulate.

"Why, do you think Mummy might marry Jonah?"

Miriam beamed and then puckered up her lips, as if mimicking some teenage kiss she'd seen on *Hannah Montana*.

"I think I saw them smooching," she said.

Anthony lived fairly close to Claire, in a grand avenue of huge, whitewashed terraced Georgian houses in Maida Vale, a bohemian pocket of Central London. Both Claire and Anthony had downsized, choosing properties that were within easy reach of Miriam's school so as not to upset her any more than their break-up already had. His two-bedroom apartment had been bought with his role as a single parent foremost in mind and not really looking at the future. But, much as he loved his pad - a stylish, minimalist affair packed with African carvings and tribal painted canvasses - unexpected changes in his

168

circumstances meant that he and Ali were already growing out of it. The second bedroom was a frilly pink paradise designed by Miriam and slept in by Miriam when she was there. Jasper still shared his parents' room, but Anthony didn't really want that set-up to continue indefinitely. No, another move was definitely on the cards, a tedious prospect which made him sigh as he opened the front door.

It felt good to be back and he could smell something nice cooking. His fiancé Ali wasn't just a stunning beauty but she was also a gifted barrister, a fabulous mother and a keen amateur chef. And, unlike Claire, she wasn't constantly thinking of the health benefits of food. Ali used copious amounts of double cream and sugar in her cuisine. Sure, their cholesterol levels might be a touch suspect but, if they died from a heart attack then at least they'd die enjoying themselves. Ali didn't need to watch her weight. Perhaps it was genes or metabolic rate or stress but she somehow appeared to be one of those lucky women who, no matter how much garbage they eat, remain resolutely skinny. Even having a baby hadn't altered her shape. Her green eyes and straight black hair lent her a feline quality and Anthony was particularly partial to her long, graceful legs.

"Ali?" he called.

"Hi," she called back, "we're in the bathroom."

He made his way to the bathroom where the vision of mother bent over the baby tub washing his son calmed his rising levels of anxiety. This right here was precious. This right here was what made his heart sing, what made getting up in the morning worthwhile. He already had so much, why was he letting this America business unsettle him so? He was normally so calm and calculating that this rush of emotions felt alien and unnerving. He leaned over Ali, planting a hand on her back for balance as he held the little finger of his other hand out to Jasper hoping he'd grasp it. He did, straight away, with an iron grip.

"Hello tiger," he beamed at Jasper. "You're so strong."

Jasper gurgled merrily and performed his new party trick.

"Da......dee," he chirped. "Da.....dee."

Jasper had only recently started saying the word 'daddy' and every time he did, it was like melodious music filling the air with pure innocence and love.

"Aren't you a clever boy, saying my name so beautifully?"

Jasper opened his arms wide and Anthony took his cue, lifting his son out of the bath and wrapping him in a fluffy blue towel. With Jasper secured in the crook of his elbow, Anthony drew Ali into a communal hug with his other arm. He wanted to keep them both close forever. Indeed, he wanted to keep *all* his family close forever. If only Miriam could be part of this hug too.

"You're back later than I expected," she said, kissing him on the lips.

"I know. Sorry, but Claire had something she wanted to discuss."

Ali had always been remarkably understanding about the baggage he brought into their relationship. It can't be easy having an ex-wife in your life, let alone a stepchild. It made everything so much more complicated.

"Is everything ok?" she asked.

"It's fine or if it's not, I'm sure it will be."

This was Anthony's problem, nobody else's, so he tried to brush it off. Clearly he didn't do a good enough job of it because Ali could sense something was wrong.

171

"Your problem is my problem. If there's something wrong, please tell me."

Anthony nodded. He'd already told Ali about Jonah's reappearance in Claire's life.

"Ok, then. Claire is taking Miriam with her when she goes with Jonah to the States this summer. And because she's planning to stay on in America afterwards, she's arranged for Jonah's mother to chaperone Miriam back here in August when it's my turn to have her."

"Right," Ali raised an eyebrow. "And you don't like that?"

No, Anthony did *not* like the concept of a stranger bringing his precious daughter back on a transatlantic flight. He didn't know anything about Jonah's mother. She might be a psychopath for all he knew.

"No, I don't."

Ali raised her other eyebrow.

"But there's nothing you can do about it?"

Anthony stepped away from the group embrace, gently bouncing Jasper up and down.

"No, I don't have a legal leg to stand on. Claire could arrange for the airline to chaperone her and that would be even worse, but I still wouldn't be able to change it."

The bottom line was, when Miriam wasn't with him, Claire was in charge and vice versa.

"You know," Ali cocked her head sympathetically, "Claire has already had to come to terms with having me in Miriam's life. I'm a total stranger to her and yet she has to trust me. It must be incredibly hard, I'm not saying it isn't, but you've been lucky that she's not been with anyone sooner."

"It's not just that," admitted Anthony. "It's the whole America thing. I've got a bad feeling."

"Have you met Jonah?"

"Yes."

"Did you like him?"

He hated him. He hated everything he represented.

"I don't know him."

"What are you worried about?"

"What if Claire decides to move to America and take Miriam with her?"

"There's no way she'd be able to do that. Miriam's life's here. Her father's here. Her school's here. Her family's here."

They were both criminal lawyers, but nonetheless Ali had a basic understanding of family law.

"I know," Ali continued, chewing her lower lip the way she did whenever she was hatching a plan. "Why don't we go to America for our holidays too and that way you can pick up Miriam yourself and check out the situation? There's no law against that."

Eureka. Anthony crashed his lips into Ali's.

"I love you," he said appreciatively. "That's a brilliant idea. And you don't mind all that long haul travel with Jasper? He's ever so little."

"I'm sure we can make it work," Ali insisted.

In less than a second Anthony went from being as tense as a tightly wound coil to feeling euphoric. He liked a plan. A plan made him feel in control. To win, that's what was needed, and if there was one thing Anthony didn't like, it was losing. If there was one thing he was never going to lose, it was his daughter. The very concept was unthinkable.

CHAPTER TWELVE

CLAIRE

"Babe," said Jonah, struggling to squeeze Claire's toiletry bag into the suitcase. "The zip's going to break. You've got to take something out."

Claire was anxiously peering through the stained-glass window adjacent to her front door, willing her mother to hurry up. Her mother had insisted on driving them to the airport. "I'm not going to see you for at least the next two months," she'd argued, "so the least I can do is to wave you off. Besides, I've not seen Jonah for fourteen years and I want to see him again. Is that a crime?"

It wasn't a crime, but Claire still had misgivings. Not only did her mother have a bad track-record when it came to timekeeping, she also had a car that Claire was fearing by the second would be too small to accommodate their needs. Crumbs! Even the cases appeared to be unfit for purpose. "Get Miriam to sit on it," she suggested but Jonah wasn't listening. He flung the case open and peered at the contents: body lotion, bubble bath, foot cream, hand cream, sun block, three different factor sun creams, shampoo, hair conditioner and a large box of organic tea bags. One by one he deposited them with a clunk onto the wood floor. "I've got all this stuff at my place and, if there is anything you've forgotten you can always buy it from the shop round the corner. We're not going to some remote wilderness." "Ok," Claire conceded, "but not the teabags. Yours aren't the same." Jonah grinned and tossed the box of tea bags back in, closing the suitcase with ease on the next attempt.

"She's here," cried Claire, watching the silver Ford Focus pull up outside.

The last week had been manic. There had been so much to organise, from visas to packing to touching base with all her clients, arranging to hold video consultations with them from the States. She'd done her last *Morning Cuppa* broadcast the day before. This had been followed by meetings to bandy ideas around for the weekly segments they would be airing from California. Much to her relief Claire learned that she would have her own dedicated American producer.

Miriam had celebrated her ninth birthday a couple of days previously with a cook-your-own pizza party at their local Italian restaurant. Because Miriam now knew that her birthday was on American Independence Day she insisted that her girlie guests should each receive a US-themed goodie bag containing a packet of Oreos, a chocolate Hershey bar and, the pièce-de-resistance, a red, white and blue Alice band.

More importantly had been the 'chat'. Miriam already knew that she was spending the summer in America with Jonah and his daughter Martha. She was very excited about it but Claire didn't want any confusion about Jonah's status in her life.

"You know Jonah and I are good friends," she began, wishing there was a divorced mums' 'how to' manual.

"Isn't he your *boy*friend?"

Thwack. Claire hadn't been expecting that.

"Well, err, yes, err, he used to be, b-

"Mum, it's ok. I know he's your boyfriend again and I'm happy for you. I really like him. I think it's great."

Miriam had then reached up to her mother, wrapping her arms around her neck and pulling her down so that she could kiss her cheek.

"I'm happy for you, Mummy," she said. "Daddy's got someone and I want you to have someone too. Does Jonah make you happy?"

Tears pricked Claire's eyes.

"Yes, darling, he does. But your happiness is more important to me than anything. You've had to make a lot of adjustments in the last year and I'm sure it can't be easy. So promise you'll talk to me if anything's ever troubling you?"

Miriam promised faithfully and now here they were, a merry trio, standing next to three large suitcases and three smaller carry-on bags, waiting by the open front door as Claire's mother walked up the garden path. Jonah stepped forward, arms outstretched as he greeted her. Their soft spot for each other had been mutual.

"Mrs J," his voice oozed warmth, "it's so nice to see you again."

They hugged each other and it was almost comical how Jonah's height swamped her. The top of her head reached barely higher than Jonah's armpits and Claire made a mental note to ask him later if he thought her mother had aged significantly in the intervening years. Certainly her hair had turned from 'Bordeaux' to white.

"Please, call me Dolores," Mrs Jackson insisted.

She'd always preferred Jonah to address her by her first name and he'd always struggled. He'd been raised to call men senior to himself 'Sir' and women 'Ma'am.' For him, the 'Mrs J' tag was already a serious nod towards intimacy.

"You're looking very well," he flattered.

Claire swore she saw her mother blush.

"Now, what's all this I hear about you taking my daughter and granddaughter to the other side of the world? I've already got one child in Hong Kong and really don't want to lose another. You remember I don't like aeroplanes?"

Dolores wore a smile on her face and her tone was definitely playful but still there was a level of warning in her words. America was not round the corner and her fear of flying was very real. Jonah couldn't forget. None of them could. Claire's father had hilariously recounted the story of how, dosed up on Diazepam to calm her nerves for the one flight Dolores *had* taken to America, she'd been high as a kite. So high that she'd

180

flirted outrageously with the man at US customs. When he'd refused to stamp her passport she'd started slowly undoing the buttons on her shirt, staging an erotic protest. Her behaviour had apparently been so suspicious that they'd taken her into a side room for further questioning, grilling her like a criminal. She'd giggled uncontrollably. If she'd been sixteen she might have got away with this behaviour but she'd been fifty-six! Eventually the effects of the medication wore off and they let her through but nobody in the family had forgotten this incident. It still made great dinner table conversation.

"Mrs J," grinned Jonah, picking up a suitcase in each hand and heading out to the car, "I hear they've made a supersonic boat that can do the trip from Southampton to New York faster than Concord."

Claire giggled as she followed him down the path with the third case.

"Really?" asked Dolores, incredulous.

"Really," joked Claire, even though she knew she shouldn't because her mother always took everything literally and would probably be on the phone to the travel agent that afternoon asking for more details. "And it's cheaper too."

"But how would I get from New York to California?"

"Train," said Claire.

"Greyhound bus," said Jonah.

"Another supersonic boat?" suggested Miriam.

"You're awfully quiet in the back dear," said Dolores, as they passed the 'Welcome to Heathrow' sign. Claire *was* quiet. For starters she was uncomfortable. She and Miriam were jammed so tightly into the back of the car that she could barely breathe. The only way Jonah had been able to squeeze everything in was by making the car's cargo, human and inanimate, into some warped, living collage. Claire had a bag under her feet, a case jammed between her and Miriam, and another nudging at her cranium. The back of the driver's seat was rammed into her knees, holding her like a vice.

She also suddenly recognised the enormity of what they were doing. Was this a reckless decision made in haste? What if Miriam didn't like it in the US? What if Miriam hated Martha?

182

These were all legitimate concerns but the real reason Claire was quiet was the conversation she'd just had with Orlando Goodman. She'd failed to reach him in the last few days and, in one final attempt, she'd telephoned from the car and he answered. Whilst he sounded upbeat, what he told her was making her introspective. His doctor had organised multiple investigations: an abdominal ultrasound, organ function tests and blood tests but, to one of them, he'd attributed a number. "The 999," he joked. "Sounds ominously like an emergency." Claire wasn't medically trained, but her work as a nutritionist had taught her not only how to analyse results but also the names of different tests. There wasn't, as far as she knew, a '999'. There was, however, a CA 19-9. This test filled her with fear.

She was thinking of this as she mechanically helped Jonah load their luggage onto a trolley at Heathrow. She was thinking of this as the lady at the check-in desk lowered her voice to inform: "I'm pleased to tell you, you've been upgraded, which means you can also use the VIP lounge." It wasn't until her mother pulled her into her arms and told her to be safe that Claire finally snapped out of it.

"We'll be fine Mum, I promise. And we'll video speak on the computer every few days. You remember how to do it, don't you?"

Claire had visited her parents home a few days earlier to download Skype onto her father's laptop and teach them how to use it.

"Yes, I remember."

Jonah held out his hand.

"Thank you so much for bringing us to the airport, Mrs. J."

"Don't Mrs J me," ticked off Dolores as she kissed two fingers and placed them onto Jonah's cheek. "And make sure you look after my girls."

"I promise," Jonah reassured.

Dolores crouched down, pulling a $10 bill out of her burgundy cardigan pocket and handing it to Miriam.

"Buy yourself a couple of ice-creams my love," she told her, "and be good for your Mummy."

It's easy to pass each day going through the motions, with every hour accounted for by either a mental note or a scribbled reminder in the diary about what needs to be done. Make packed lunch, take Miriam to school, drop off the dry cleaning, client consultation, devise meal plans, catch up on *Downtown Abbey*, conk out exhausted, most likely with *Downtown Abbey* still playing on the TV in the background. A very, very long time ago, or so it felt, Claire had been a free-spirited soul, following her heart and going with the flow. She'd lived in the moment and it had felt good. No fixed plans, no fixed abode, she'd inhabited a space where anything and everything was possible. Something had somehow gone wrong, however, and she wasn't convinced it could entirely be blamed on the responsibility or constraints of parenthood. Jonah was right, there was no point dwelling on the past; what mattered now was the future. Fourteen hours after their plane left British soil and their taxi pulled up outside Jonah's home, Claire experienced the strangest of sensations. It was as if she'd been holding her breath for the last decade and now, suddenly, she could breathe freely again. For thirteen years, despite being a vehicle that ran on unleaded petrol, she'd been fed on a diet of diesel. Now, finally, she was being filled up with the right gas again and it wasn't the economy version, it was the premium brand.

She'd always loved California. Everything here was bigger and brighter; the sky, the ocean, the sun, and yes, dangerously, the restaurant portions. Even Jonah's house fitted that bill. He referred to it as an apartment but it was actually a luxury two-floor pale terracotta villa set in a gated cliff-top community in Del Mar, a beachside resort north of downtown San Diego. Beautifully manicured gardens flush with palms and cacti shaded the glorious private patio out back. This was clearly where Jonah enjoyed escaping from the hubbub. A Mexican hammock swung between two tall palms whose trunks were so spindly they looked as if a wisp of wind could blow them over. There was a gas barbecue which was at least twice the size of Claire's and the terrace boasted not only a table with chairs but a large, plush, wicker sofa suite assembled around a glass coffee table.

The interior was even more beguiling - pale carpets complementing oyster painted walls and a great sense of space and light flowing through the open plan ground floor. The kitchen spilled seamlessly into the lounge and everything was oversized, from the tropical indoor plants to the beige sofas dotted with bright scatter cushions, to the majestic old-fashioned ceiling fans. A white painted staircase swept from the entrance hall up to the first floor with its stunning bedrooms. First along the hallway was Martha's room. Claire noted it was decorated in the same neutral tones as the rest of the house which meant she clearly didn't share Miriam's passion for pink. Martha was due to arrive the next morning and the briefest of prayers flitted through Claire's head: 'please let the girls get along'. There were two pretty guest rooms, both sharing the same grey and fawn décor. The only difference was that one had bright pink starry cushions plumped up on the bed, whereas the furnishings in the other room were blue. Claire knew exactly which one Miriam would select, way before she squealed the inevitable "this one's mine."

Whilst Miriam unpacked, Jonah showed Claire his room.

"Actually," he corrected himself, "*our* room."

"Who designed this place?" she gasped. "It's amazing."

"A friend who's an interior designer," he answered. "I gave her carte blanche for the whole place."

This friend had given the place an inspired Louis 1Vth meets California chic vibe. Whilst his bedroom with its en suite bathroom was way superior to hers at 77 Gladstone Road, their personal boudoirs shared two key similarities. For starters, they both had a sleigh bed although Jonah's had a more decadent, Marie Antoinette feel, with padded velvet ends and distressed white paintwork. But it was the object perched on a bedside table which caught Claire's eye.

"Oh," she gulped when she saw it, reaching it in three quick steps and placing it on her palm. It was Jonah's Buddha, still unblemished and free from superglue. She spoke to it as if it were a baby. "Hello. It's nice to see you again. Next time I'll be sure to bring your friend. I think he's missed you."

Jonah came to her side, rubbing his hand up and down her back.

"I love you so much," she said, tilting her head until it rested on his shoulder.

"Welcome home," he said, resting his head on top of hers.

"How is it possible that we take off at 10 am and land at 1 pm, when we've been flying for eleven hours?" Miriam asked.

Now, there was a conundrum. Claire tried to explain about time differences and that due to its position on the other side of the world California was eight hours behind London, but it was a hard concept for a nine year old to grasp. Jonah encouraged her to keep busy for as long as possible, knowing that the later she went to bed the more in tune she would become with her new time zone. After unpacking, they all lounged by the communal outdoor pool for a while whilst Miriam perfected her diving technique. When they'd returned to the villa, Claire noted that there was a good view of the pool through their kitchen window.

The beds were made and the fridge was full, thanks to an arrangement Jonah had with the Mexican wife of the complex's caretaker, who kept an eye on the villa whenever Jonah was away. After the swim, Jonah made his version of a 'California Smoothie', a blend of strawberries, lemon yoghurt and orange juice mixed with crushed ice. Miriam must have drunk at least a gallon of it, declaring it to be her new favourite drink. Soon afterwards she lay on her bed and mere seconds after her head touched the pillow she fell asleep.

Claire kissed her goodnight and headed back downstairs. She found Jonah on the patio, lazing in the hammock in his swimming shorts, nursing a glass of white wine. On the round mosaic table an open bottle sat in a cooler next to a spare glass. Claire glanced at her watch and did the arithmetic. It was now 6 pm local time, which made it 2 am in Britain. She was tired and yet the sun still hadn't fallen below the level of the trees shading the terrace. The thick vegetation surrounding them made it impossible to see the Pacific but they could hear it. Claire closed her eyes, listening to waves crashing against the shore.

"I'm tired," she yawned, making a beeline for the wine and pouring herself a glass. She was only wearing a bikini and yet the heat of the day was wrapping around her like a healing balm.

"It's my favourite Sauvignon Blanc from a local winery called Hawk Watch," Jonah told her. "And you know why I picked this one?"

"Why?" asked Claire, taking a generous mouthful and letting the flavours settle on her palate. It was sensational. Cool and dry.

"What can you taste?"

"It's a fruit, but I can't work out which one."

"Remember, it was picked with you in mind," teased Jonah.

"Tell me, what is it?"

"How can *you* of all people not know?" Jonah laughed.

"Is it a berry?"

"Yes, but which one?"

Strawberry, blueberry, loganberry, blackberry, none of them felt right.

"I'm too tired to guess," Claire gave up, "just tell me."

"Ok," Jonah conceded, holding out his spare hand as an invitation for Claire to join him in the hammock. "It's *gooseberry*."

He was messing with her.

"Very funny," said Claire.

Jonah took Claire's glass from her and leaned carefully out of the hammock to lay both of their wines on the ground. He then sat up, wrapped his long arms around Claire's back and yanked her playfully on top of him. She squealed as the hammock tipped precariously, but after they'd wriggled back into its centre, it settled and stilled.

"I've got the best cure ever for jet lag," he said, easing her into a comfortable position as they gently swayed.

"What's that then?" she murmured, her smile hitting his lips as he pulled her close. He tasted deliciously of wine. And yes, a

191

hint of gooseberry. His skin felt so good against hers under the warmth of the sun. He slipped his hands underneath her black bikini bottoms. She wriggled nervously.

"I've got to put on some more clothes," insisted Claire, "or the neighbours will see."

"Pretty English lady," Jonah inched the bikini bottoms lower, "nobody can see here, I promise you, and even if they could, the jet lag cure I've got in mind means that whatever, these are going to have to come off."

CHAPTER THIRTEEN

Claire lay in bed, her limbs paralysed. It was as if she'd been drugged. She was awake, yet she was not awake. She was aware, yet she was not aware. In a fug of semi-consciousness she heard voices. Was she dreaming? At first she heard a woman's voice. Perhaps it was the caretaker's wife, Maria, checking in. She strained her ears. No, the voice was too young. Was it Jonah's ex-wife? She willed her body to wake up. She didn't want to be seen but, perhaps if she could manage to roll out of bed, she might be able to hide behind the wall at the top of the stairs and spy. But try as she might to force her legs to swing over the mattress and take her body with them, she couldn't. She drifted back off into blissful slumber. Minutes, hours, who knew how much longer later she heard children's voices, girls' voices accompanied by lots of laughter and running. Jonah calmly called "Careful, your feet are wet from the swimming pool, don't slip." Miriam, one of the girls must be Miriam? Claire had to wake up and check she was ok, but still she couldn't move and drifted back off. Minutes, hours, who knew how much longer later, those voices became louder, chasing up and down the stairs. Martha, one of the girls must be Martha, had a sweet accent. "I've got a twister in my room," she called. Claire had to wake up. She had to meet Martha. Jonah had told her that Martha was being delivered this morning. How rude that she hadn't been there to meet her, but still she couldn't move and drifted back into a dream about cars and parking tickets and supersonic vehicles that didn't make any sense whatsoever.

"Claire," someone shook her shoulder.

This time it was a man's voice.

"Claire, you've got to wake up, I've brought you some coffee."

She didn't want to wake up, she wanted to snooze and return to the supersonic vehicle dream where she'd now patented the car and was about to make a fortune for having been the first person clever enough to design it. She heard the sound of a cup land on a table next to her and then felt a hand on each of her shoulders. They tugged at her and pulled her to sitting. She reluctantly opened an eye, then immediately closed it. The room was too bright. She slumped, wanting to lower herself into the refuge of the bed once again and to shroud herself back into darkness.

"No you don't," said Jonah, pulling her back to sitting. "If you don't get up now, you'll be stuffed later. Trust me."

Now she was awake. She yawned and ran her forearm over her eyes.

194

"What time is it?" she croaked.

"It's ten o'clock and you've been asleep for thirteen hours."

Thirteen hours? Wow, Claire was normally lucky to get seven hours. She looked at the mug of coffee by her bedside. She usually started the day with tea.

"You need the extra caffeine to wake you," Jonah read her mind. "Drink it because we've got plans for the day already."

"Plans, what plans?"

She'd envisaged a nice, chill day by the pool, perhaps followed by a beach walk.

"It's the perfect cure for jet lag," smirked Jonah.

No, he couldn't mean *that* again?

"Honey, I haven't even woken up properly yet," she protested, remembering last night's hammock shenanigans. She had a seemingly insatiable appetite for Jonah, but really, now, again?

"No," he laughed, "I don't mean sex. We've got something completely different planned. The girls chose it. Blame them, not me."

The girls! She had to check on the girls and meet Martha. Claire quickly finished her coffee and popped in the shower. The water spray revived her, which is what she needed because now, as the moment approached, she found herself nervous. Jonah had seemed so cool when he'd met Miriam so why did she feel like such a bundle of nerves? It mattered that this went well, it mattered that Martha liked her.

Once dry, she put on a pair of green denim shorts and a grey ribbed vest top and searched in her only half-unpacked suitcase for the main present they'd bought for Martha. It wasn't there. She flung all her remaining clothes onto the beige carpet in a fluster. She couldn't have forgotten it. Or could she? She'd been juggling so many balls that perhaps it was inevitable that something would slip through the net. Oh well, at least she knew that the other smaller present hadn't been forgotten. Claire had rescued that one from the suitcase as soon as they'd arrived, before it had had a chance to melt into oblivion. Miriam had been so disappointed when she'd tried one of the Hershey bars that she'd insisted on bringing Martha some 'proper' chocolate. So they'd bought her a massive bar of

Cadbury's Dairy Milk, which was now in the fridge. She could hear the girls playing in one of the upstairs rooms. Her heart thumped a little faster than normal as she followed the noise.

"Oh," she said, smiling when she found them. They were playing in Martha's room, huddled around a plastic box whose many compartments, to the untrained eye, looked as if they contained a multicoloured array of elastic bands. "*That's* where Martha's present is. I was worried I'd forgotten it."

Martha did a half-spin on her bottom, finishing facing Claire. She was even prettier in the flesh than she'd been in the photo. Her hair was almost phosphorescent in its whiteness and her eyes were spookily similar to Jonah's, perhaps even a deeper shade of grey. Despite her fair colouring, she too had deeply bronzed skin.

"I came to take it out of your bag," explained Miriam, "because I wanted to give it to Martha."

"Great idea," said Claire.

Martha's gaze was boring a hole in her head.

"Hey, Martha," said Claire, approaching and squatting to join the girls. "It's so nice to finally meet you and sorry I was such

197

a sleepyhead this morning. Miriam chose this present. I hope you don't have it already."

"No Ma'am," said Martha

"No," laughed Claire, mortified. Now she knew how her mother felt. "Please call me Claire."

The gift was called Rainbow Loom and was the latest craze in bracelet-making. There were a thousand and more ways that these rubber bands could be fashioned into different weaves. Martha held up her wrist for inspection.

"Miriam made me this one," she said.

It was blue, black and green.

"And Martha made me this one," Miriam showed off her new pink and purple bracelet. Yep, the girls had already sussed out each other's tastes.

"Thank you Ma'am, I mean Claire," Martha giggled. "I love the Rainbow Looms."

"It's my pleasure."

"And now that you're up," Martha scrambled to her feet wearing the same impish grin as her father, "we're going out. Miriam thinks you're going to love what we've got planned."

It was a good thing that Claire had been busy in the run-up to San Diego because that had given her less time to fret. She was a worrier, perhaps not one of her better traits, and it had become worse since having a child. Series of 'what ifs' would rattle round her brain before there was even a sniff of a concern. If she'd had a proper chance to worry about this particular trip, it would have mostly pivoted around Martha. What if Martha doesn't like me? What if Martha doesn't like Miriam? What if Martha resents her father for introducing this new family into their lives? What if she resented the lot of them for invading what was hers and her father's space and time. If Claire had been in Martha's shoes, she wasn't certain how happy she'd have been about it.

Jonah, by contrast, took life in his stride. He worked on a philosophy that things only became a problem if you made them into one. And so far he was right. It was early days yet, admittedly, but far from appearing annoyed that her home and father had been usurped by foreigners with funny accents, Martha seemed delighted to have a ready-made play mate. It was indeed fortuitous that she and Miriam were so similar in age.

Martha also thought Claire's reaction to where they'd come was very amusing. They all did. It was hard for Claire to pale, given the shade of her skin, but somehow she'd managed. She was running around flapping her arms nervously, as if being chased by an imaginary swarm of bees. It was lucky that Claire hadn't had a chance to fret in advance, because not only would she have worried, she would have told them there was no way she was coming here to do this. When they'd driven through the entrance of the San Diego Zoo Safari Park, she was excited. She'd heard about this place. It was a massive reserve where wild animals roam free over vast expanses as they would in their native habitats of Africa and Asia. There were white rhinos, buffalo, gazelles, lions and elephants and a smorgasbord of different safaris on offer. Sadly, the 'safari' the rest of the posse had in mind was far from conventional. Their idea of a great way to take in the wildlife was by observing it not only from a height, but at a speed. The park had a zip-line and Jonah kept referring to the four-hundred-feet long aerial flight as 'the perfect jet lag cure'.

There were signs everywhere posting contra-indications. "Do not do if you've got a bad back". "Do not do if you've got heart problems". "Do not do if you're under 130cm". "Do not do if you weigh less than 75 pounds". "Do not do if you're under 10 years old".

"Jonah," she whispered. "They're under age."

"Come on babe," he whispered back, "they're so excited. No-one will know. They're both tall enough and weigh enough."

She knew he was right and she also knew she couldn't disappoint the girls who had started jokingly referring to her as a 'pussy'.

"All right, girls," Claire jogged on the spot, trying to gee herself up. "I'll do it."

They were given helmets and a safety briefing, before being let loose on what was referred to as a 'fledgling' training zip-line. Children under sixteen had to fly with an adult, and the fact that she wouldn't be doing it alone felt vaguely comforting. Claire wanted Jonah and Martha to go first, but the staff had different ideas, trussing her and Miriam into harnesses, clipping them onto a line, and with a "three, two, one" pushing them from the take-off platform. The fledgling line was actually quite enjoyable. It was fairly low to the ground and the speed was gentle as they flew between fragrant, shaded forest. If the line broke and they fell, there'd be the odd graze or cut, but nothing too serious. Why had she made such a fuss? Hell, this was *fun*.

They were then loaded them into a truck and were driven across the dusty savannah towards the *real* part of the course. In the distance she spotted a steel platform which resembled some weirdly shaped electricity pylon. It wasn't until they got out the vehicle and walked across a bouncing metal bridge that she fully appreciated that it was from the top of this towering pylon, one hundred and thirty feet high, that she would have to take a leap of faith. Perhaps even Miriam might want to back out. "Wow, that looks awesome," squealed Martha, watching as someone in the distance flew along the zip. "I'm so excited," Miriam jumped up and down.

Nope, clearly Miriam was unaffected.

"I need a Diazepam," Claire pulled a weak smile, vowing she would never mock her mother again for being scared of flying.

There was an eerie quiet in the atmosphere, as if this really was far, far away from civilisation. She felt Jonah's hand like a caress on her back.

"You ok babe?"

"If I die," she smiled weakly, "remember I love you."

"You're not going to die," he comforted her.

They could all do it together, apparently, on two parallel zips. And so they formed two lines, Jonah and Martha next to Claire and Miriam, all being clipped and trussed and choreographed for simultaneous take-off, like some crazy, blended *Brady Bunch* family. "Three, two, one...................

"Three cheers for Claire being brave," said Jonah, as they drove out of the Safari Park.

"That was *soooo* much fun," said Miriam, "thank you for doing it Mummy."

"Hooray for Claire," giggled Martha.

Claire wondered what Martha really thought of her. She was being ever so polite when her own mother couldn't possibly be quite such a wimp.

"I love this photo," chirped Miriam.

"Me too," echoed Martha.

The girls had both loved the photo so much that Jonah had bought two copies of it so they could have one each. An aerial camera must have captured the moment at some particular scary point during the flight, perhaps when Claire's stomach had started to lurch from the G-force. The picture said it all. Three passengers were beaming from ear to ear, eyes alive with excitement. The pussy member of the party had her eyes and lips firmly sealed.

"My dad plays tennis," Martha informed them, "and when he serves, the ball goes 130 mph which is way faster then we went on the zip-line."

"My mum plays tennis too," said Miriam.

"I do *not* play tennis," said Claire.

"Yes, you do," Miriam boasted. "You got to the final last summer."

Claire laughed. Miriam was referring to her small local club, which could hardly be compared to Wimbledon. She'd always enjoyed playing tennis and whilst she might not have watched the game for the last thirteen years, she never stopped hitting balls.

"Yes, but only recreationally. Jonah did it competitively," Claire explained. "It's not the same."

"I want to see your Mom play tennis," said Martha.

"And I want to see your *Dad* play tennis," said Miriam.

Wasn't a zip-line enough for them?

"No. You guys have just done what you wanted to do and now *I* get to plan the rest of the day."

Whilst Claire would never admit it, she was on a minor high after completing the zip-line. There's something to be said for challenging oneself from time to time and pushing limits. If she'd not done it then she would have regretted it. Now Claire had successfully completed that challenge, she felt she'd earned some chill time by the pool. But weirdly, another crazy plan was hatching in her mind.

"Tell you what," she touched Jonah's forearm. "When we get back home, I challenge you to a set of tennis. If I manage to win *one* point off you, you make dinner."

"One point?" asked Miriam. "That's ridiculous. Of course you can win one point."

Martha laughed. She clearly knew the truth of it.

"He's a man," Claire explained. "Men are much stronger than women. Even the thousandth best male tennis player in the world would probably beat Serena Williams. I'm a rubbish tennis player. I've only won about five points off Jonah in my life, and most of those were because he made a mistake."

"Are you sure you want to do this?" Jonah grinned.

He knew the odds were hugely in his favour. Claire was setting herself up for failure.

"I'm sure," Claire grinned back.

"For dinner," said Jonah.

"For dinner," Claire agreed.

They shook hands on it.

"Girls," he jibed, "this is going to be fun."

CHAPTER FOURTEEN

CLAIRE

You know you're getting older when the people working with you start to look as if they've just graduated from high school. Despite the fact that Claire's American TV Producer Chad and their cameraman Ben looked too young to legally drink champagne, she was having a blast. She felt way more relaxed out on location than in the studio. Her regime for *Morning Cuppa* had changed for the duration of her stay in the US. Instead of her usual Monday morning studio segment, she now had two weekly tasks. The first was a live outside broadcast via satellite link, which would be at some ungodly hour due to the time difference. The second was to make a short report featuring a Californian nutrition twist which she would present and Chad would produce. This week's film was putting theme park food under the microscope. Miriam and Martha would be envious to learn that her morning had been spent at Legoland, filming holidaymakers tasting the park's famous Granny's apple fries and asking what, if anything, was healthy about them despite their promising title. Now they'd come to SeaWorld, together with, it would appear, the rest of the world's press. SeaWorld was celebrating its 50th anniversary and the banks of microphones and cameras in the confined space of the restaurant where they were filming made it slightly claustrophobic.

Their focus was currently on the killer whale enclosure. Adjacent was a private outdoor patio where visitors could dine, choosing from a delicious buffet serving sustainable, responsibly fished seafood. A thin glass screen separated the restaurant from the whales, and animal trainers had just arrived poolside. The main attraction was killer whale Shamu and the unique selling point of the restaurant was that diners could eat their nutritious repast whilst watching a display of mind-boggling marine acrobatics.

"What we ideally want," said Chad, "is for you to start speaking to camera just as Shamu leaps out of the water."

"Yes," cameraman Ben agreed. "Timing is everything."

"No pressure then," joked Claire.

It can take years of experience for reporters to perfect their timing, doing a piece to camera about an aeroplane just at the moment that a Boeing 747 takes off in the background.

"I'll cue you in," said Ben, focusing the camera.

208

"Ok," said Claire, taking her position.

Despite several reporters jostling for space, Claire wormed her way into the prime position. She'd loaded up a plate with scampi, salmon, prawns, salads and vegetables and had worked out in her head what she wanted to say. A whistle blew and the whales swam up to the trainers. Claire cleared her throat and positioned herself in front of the camera. She waited patiently, following Ben's eyes as they darted left to right, until eventually he raised a finger and nodded. That was her cue. She held the plate like a prop, just above waist level and started speaking to camera.

"Behind me is the killer whale enclosure and Shamu is the star attraction which means this restaurant has one of the most original views I've ever seen. It's also got an impressive menu. Theme parks are notorious for selling unhealthy, overpriced food and usually there's not a vegetable or a piece of fruit in sight. But here you can feed your family without taking out a second mortgage. Better still, the food is all sustainable, organic and locally sourced, right down to these fresh California salad greens and vegetables. So as well as being fresh theme park food, it's carbon-footprint- friendly food too."

Chad had taught her that whenever she'd finished speaking she should stay looking directly down the lens, preferably smiling, and count to five in her head. Only then would they stop recording.

"Cut," said Ben, holding up his thumb.

"Great work," praised Chad. "Shamu leapt out the water just as you said his name and then he leaped again as you were finishing. And you didn't fluff once. Well done!"

Chad and Ben wanted to scoot round the rest of the park to get some general shots. They didn't need Claire for the next hour or so, so they left her to peruse the schedule for the following fortnight. She flicked through their upcoming programme. Next week they were filming at some local Californian vineyards and the week after they were doing a round-up on several farmers markets. Chad had given her the choice to either film each week's report on a Sunday and do the live outside broadcast on a Monday, or they could squeeze everything into one mega long day. She'd discussed it with Jonah but in the end the decision had been easy. Nightmare though the mega days sounded, starting at 7 am and finishing around midnight was preferable to having work eating into two precious days. She was having too much fun and wanted to spend as much time with Jonah and the girls as possible. The holidays were already passing way too fast. In just over three weeks Anthony would be picking up Miriam.

Each fresh day somehow felt better than the last as the four of them got to know each other. Whilst the first twenty-four hours had been crazy, they'd since calmed down, spending time chilling by the pool or by the sea, flying kites, body surfing and enjoying long beach walks. Well, she and Jonah enjoyed the walks at any rate. The girls inevitably grumbled as they traipsed in their shadows, only cheering up when they found thick strands of seaweed with bulbous heads, which they used as toy microphones.

And then there was the tennis. Martha clearly took after her father with a natural, raw talent for the game and she was trying, sometimes not so patiently, to teach Miriam. She also had her beady eye set on Claire. Martha kept challenging her to a match and so far Claire had managed to avoid the issue. She wasn't sure if she was ready for the humiliation of being severely beaten by an eight year old.

Claire chuckled as she remembered the other humiliation. When they'd got back after the zip-line adventure, Jonah had opened a cupboard that was literally so packed with rackets that several of them had crashed out of the door the second it was ajar. He'd handed one to Claire before selecting his own.

"I hope you're giving yourself a dud," Claire had said.

Claire was starting to regret opening her mouth. But then again, she only had to win one point.

"Just give me the green light, firecracker, and let the challenge commence," Jonah grinned. "There's a baseball game I want to watch at 7 pm."

He clearly had every expectation of putting his feet up whilst she prepared dinner. Out they'd gone to one of the complex's courts, armed with a basket of balls and two young spectators. The first game she'd lost to love. Then the second, then the third and by the end of the fifth game she still hadn't managed to return one of his serves. "Come on Mummy, you can do it," Miriam encouraged. "Go Dad," Martha batted for her team. Claire had imagined being drenched with sweat from the exertion, but there was no exertion. She simply couldn't get her racket to most of his shots and every time *she* served he whopped a winner back. It was the last game, and she was already thinking about what she would cook later, debating posh macaroni cheese over egg frittata. She needed to check what Martha liked to eat. *Concentrate*. Jonah was serving. But before she had a chance to prepare herself, the ball was firing right at her. She instinctively raised the racket to protect her body like a shield and, as she did so, she managed by some miracle to miss-hit the ball. It spun back over the net, deep and long and Jonah didn't even move to return it, he was so certain it was going to land out…………………………..but, hell *no*. It landed unquestionably, indisputably and miraculously on the line. Claire had jigged about on the court, twirling around with delight. She'd done it. She'd got her one point.

Claire was smiling at the thought as a man approached. She'd spotted him earlier because he'd reminded her of a shorter, squatter version of Anthony. He was another member of the press.

"Forgive me for interrupting," he said, offering his hand, "but I noticed you doing some nice presenting earlier and I just wanted to introduce myself. Will Ryan, Executive Producer at ABC."

Claire shook his hand.

"Claire Jackson," she said. "Channel Three, UK. It's nice to meet you."

"That's a cute accent you've got going there," he handed her his business card.

Claire smiled, and fished in her bag for her purse which had some freshly minted *Morning Cuppa* business cards in it. Georgia had told her that this, in the business, was called 'networking'.

"I'm sorry," she apologised as she handed him her card, "the telephone numbers are British, but my e-mail address is good."

She didn't know why she was bothering to explain. Her path and Will Ryan's were unlikely to ever cross again.

"Tell me Claire, how does American cuisine compare to food in the UK?"

"Do you mean at theme parks or in general?"

"Let's say in California."

Claire considered and then remembered that there really had been something about American food which impressed her.

"What you do well in California are organic supermarkets. They're everywhere and their produce is really good value. I can do the same shop in Whole Foods here as in a mainstream supermarket in the UK, and not only is everything organic but it's half of the price compared to back home. It makes me angry that we lag so far behind in Britain. Organic food should be the norm and not a commodity that only the super rich can afford."

Her answer seemed to please Will Ryan, who nodded sagely.

"There might be an opening at the network which I think would suit you," said Will. "I'll be in touch."

Shortly after six o'clock, cameraman Ben dropped Claire back home for a few hours rest before they'd return to SeaWorld for the outside broadcast. It was funny, she thought to herself, as she made a cup of tea. She'd only been here for a week and she already felt as if this was home. Steam wafted from the mug. She sipped gingerly. She was tired from the long day and desperately needed a pick-me-up. Natasha Richardson would be speaking to her live just after the 8 o'clock news on the next day's *Morning Cuppa,* and even though it would be midnight her time Claire needed to look fresh as a daisy. *Ugh.* The tea was nasty. She checked the box to see whether she'd used Jonah's American teabags by mistake. Nope, she'd used hers.

Perhaps she'd make a coffee instead. The extra caffeine wouldn't hurt.

She brewed some fresh coffee and took it to her room together with the tea, just in case she changed her mind. The girls were watching *School of Rock* and Jonah was in the shower. She set the cups down on her bedside table, found her laptop, kicked off her shoes and threw herself onto the mattress. Mm, that was nice. Perhaps she'd just lie here for the next few hours and not move. She turned the laptop on. She could hear Jonah humming the theme tune from *School of Rock* as he showered and it made her smile. He might be great at tennis but he was completely and utterly tone deaf.

The shower door opened and a minute later Jonah padded into the bedroom with a towel already crafted into a turban on his head.

"Hey babe, how are you doing?" he smiled and came straight to her side, kissing her lips tenderly.

"Exhausted," she sighed, "but happy to see you. How was your day? What did you do?"

"We had a great time," he said as he went round to the other side of the bed and lay down next to her. "We went to see the

216

new panda cubs at the zoo as well as the polar bears. Martha wanted to show them to Miriam."

"Oh," said Claire disappointed. "I wish I'd been there. That sounds amazing."

"What did *you* do? Did you get dehydrated or something?" Jonah asked as he caught sight of Claire's two hot drinks lined up side by side.

"No," said Claire. "I'm trying to keep myself awake, but the tea tastes horrible and the coffee smells funny."

"Do you want me to get you something else?"

"A new face?" she joked

Claire knew Jonah hated her make-up, but she'd been instructed that she had to put on 'her face' whenever going in front of the camera. Before she'd left the UK the make-up artist had given her a lesson in how to apply foundation and the best shades of eye shadow to use to complement her colouring. She thought she'd not done too bad a job this morning, but it felt like the California sun had melted the products coating her cheeks.

"No babe, you look gorgeous," said Jonah, lying down on the bed next to her. He took her hand. "The girls are watching a movie and you've got a couple of hours. What do you reckon?" he suggested, lifting her fingers to his lips before returning their clasped hands to settle on her right breast.

The sight of Jonah in a towel was arousing, but wouldn't sex ruin her make-up? She so didn't want to have to put on her face again. She was about to air these concerns when her laptop buzzed. It was Orlando Goodman calling on Skype. It was 2am in the UK, a weird time to phone.

"Shit, babe, I've got to take this, sorry."

Jonah nodded. Claire had told him all about this client.

"I'm going to go," Jonah mouthed at her as she answered the call. It took a while for Orlando's picture to come up on the screen but, when it did, her heart leapt to her mouth. He looked wan and drawn, his cheeks were sunken hollows. And it had only been three weeks since she'd last seen him. Perhaps the pixels were distorting his features.

"Hello," she said. "I've been thinking of you, wondering how things were going."

She couldn't bring herself to ask for his news. He'd obviously called for a reason. He never just telephoned for a chat about nothing. Especially not at 2 am.

"The test results came back this end. Not good I'm afraid."

Claire kept quiet. Orlando Goodman, one of the country's finest actors, was clearly struggling to compose himself and find the right words. She didn't want to interrupt his flow. There was a long silence. She was about to say something to encourage him to continue but then he started speaking again.

"You were right to be concerned, because it looks like this old boy has got cancer."

Claire felt as if she'd been thwacked over the head with a sledgehammer. If only her sixth sense had been wrong.

"Oh no, I'm so sorry, Orlando. At least we got you checked out early."

What's the prognosis? What kind of cancer? She was scared to ask.

"Not early enough it would seem," Orlando was matter-of-fact in his delivery. "It's pancreatic cancer and it's already spread to the liver and kidneys according to the oncologist."

Claire fought the urge to cry. The 19-9 test must have come back positive. She wanted to bash the computer, reach in to grab the image of Orlando and hug him. She felt so helpless. She was seven thousand miles and a glass screen too far away. Pancreatic cancer is about as bad as it gets. It's virtually a death sentence. Hardly anyone beats it. Not Patrick Swayze, nor Steve Jobs, despite showing such determination.

"Do you think the right diet can help?" whispered Orlando.

"Yes," said Claire firmly. "I can't promise you that it's a cure but we can get your body in the best possible place so you can fight the illness and cope with the chemotherapy. What's your treatment plan?

"No treatment dahling. I've said no to the treatment. If the cancer doesn't kill me then the chemo will. No, I want to fight this beast with food."

Three hours later, the girls were in bed and Jonah massaged Claire's shoulders as she re-applied her make-up. So much for worrying about sex ruining her face – as soon as she'd finished talking to Orlando the tears had done it instead, leaving chalky streaks trailing her cheeks and black smudges under her eyes. She'd given Orlando his meal plan there and then, telling him what he absolutely *must* eat (lots of oily fish and vegetables) and what he absolutely must not (sugar and red meat).

"Life's not fair," Claire whispered.

"And life's too short," replied Jonah. "Stuff like this reminds one to seize each day and live for the moment."

Claire inhaled deeply, closing her eyes as she did so, trying to calm down. Chad and Ben would be here any minute and she needed to pull herself together. The last thing she felt like doing was a live broadcast, but to coin one of Orlando's favourite phrases, *the show must go on.*

"He wants me to help him fight this with food," Claire told Jonah, "but that's impossib -

A stabbing pain shot across Claire's lower abdomen, stopping her in her tracks.

"Are you ok?" checked Jonah.

She nodded, planting a hand over her tummy to massage away the thud.

"It's nothing," she said.

It actually hurt like hell but, compared to Orlando's predicament, a touch of belly ache was insignificant. To complain felt wrong.

CHAPTER FIFTEEN

JONAH

"Right little ladies," said Jonah at the precise moment that Miriam and Martha decided to perform a synchronised jump into the pool, showering him with spray. Using the end of the white towel slung around his neck he wiped his eyes and waited for the girls to surface. "You've got half an hour to decide what you'd like to do today and my challenge will be to see if I can combine all three of our ideas. Got it?"

"Got it," said the girls.

"Be good," said Jonah, "I'm watching you."

The complex had a small but well-equipped gym which overlooked the pool. Its position enabled Jonah to keep an eye on the girls while he worked out. Most days he liked to run on the treadmill for half-an-hour followed by a few minutes lifting weights. He'd been forced to relax his regime whilst he was in the UK but, even then, when he could he'd snatch a few moments in the hotel gym. You can't go from being a professional athlete, training for eight hours a day, to doing absolutely nada. Well, you *could*, but it wouldn't feel good.

He threw his towel onto a bench, switched on the treadmill and started with a gentle jog as he watched the girls practicing their dives. Jonah couldn't have been happier with how things were panning out. Claire was under the impression that nothing ever scared him but she was wrong. Scared wasn't quite the word he would use but he'd certainly been concerned about how his daughter would react to Claire and Miriam trespassing on her turf, day in, day out. Martha was an only child used to getting her own way and her mother's style of parenting was questionable at best. Much to Jonah's dismay, she'd always pandered to their daughter's every whim and spoiled her rotten, but that was the problem with divorce. When your child is in the other parent's charge, you're impotent. He'd observed Martha playing with friends and she wasn't a great sharer, which had boded badly for the introduction of potential step-siblings. And so he'd waited with bated breath for tantrums and the green-eyed monster to rear their ugly heads but so far so good. In fact, so far it had been an unexpected breeze. True, the girls had had their fair share of squabbles and that was only to be expected. Goddamn, even siblings can fight the hell out of each other. But Martha and Miriam's tiffs were all short-lived and inconsequential. They were largely TV focused. Who should have possession of the remote control, what programme should they watch, that sort of trivial nonsense. Claire was always quick to break up the fight and referee it fairly. She was a fantastic mother. Watching her interact with the girls had deepened his love and respect for her even further.

He'd not mentioned it to Claire for fear she'd give him some health and safety lecture but, the other day he'd found the girls in one of their rooms huddled round Martha's sewing box. She'd taken a pin and they were both pricking their fingers and holding their wounds against one another's. "Now we're proper sisters," Martha said. "Blood sisters," Miriam declared. There'd also been a lot of mattress shifting. One night, about a week into the stay, Martha had invited Miriam to sleep in her room. The next night it had been vice versa. On the third night something very interesting had happened which Jonah felt, on some social, anthropological and psychological level had a greater meaning than he could ever fathom. They had both moved their mattresses into the spare room. The 'blue' room as Miriam called it, and that's where they'd slept. And now, whenever they chose to sleep together, it was in this new, neutral territory that they convened.

Splash, bomb and dive: three more children joined the girls in the pool and Miriam showed them how to do underwater handstands and somersaults. A few seconds later her head bobbed back out of the water as she held her nose. "Say bairth," one of the girls told her. "Barth," said Miriam. They all giggled. "Now say hart," said one of the other girls. "Hot," said

Miriam. Now they were all laughing and trying out the different versions of the words, the American youngsters seeing if they could sound British. Amused, Jonah chuckled to himself.

He didn't mind the days Claire worked at all. He enjoyed having the girls to himself and he was pretty sure that they had a good time too. This was the third Monday that she was out filming and time was passing way too quickly. In just over a week Miriam's father would be coming to pick up his daughter as would Martha's mom.

The girls were all having such a good time in the pool that Jonah managed to eek an extra ten minutes to work on his triceps. "Tom – ay – tow," the girls were saying to Miriam as Jonah left the gym. "Say 'tom – ay – tow'." Miriam copied their accents and sounded wonderfully Californian as she did so. Again, Jonah smiled, wondering how pleased Claire would be if her daughter lost her British accent.

"Very good Miriam," he told her.

"Really?" she asked, swimming up to the edge of the pool.

"Yep, you sound 100% American."

Miriam looked pleased.

"Right girls, have you decided what you want to do?"

Martha came to join Miriam at the pool's edge.

"I want to go cycling," she said.

"I want to eat ice-cream," said Miriam.

Jonah nodded, contemplating.

"Ok, we've got one ice-cream, one cycling and I want to go to the park."

"The *park*," said Martha, looking sceptical.

"Uh-huh," said Jonah. "We all get one choice, no complaints."

"So where are we going then, what are we doing?" said Martha as she scrambled out the pool.

"We're doing cycling, ice-cream and park," said Jonah, heading back towards the villa. "Come on now. Chop, chop."

As the girls followed him inside, he reminded himself that there was one more activity to add into the mix. Jonah had to stop at a pharmacy. Claire wasn't herself since Orlando Goodman told her he had cancer and Jonah was starting to worry.

Claire had once told him, very proudly, that London had one of the greatest urban concentrations of parks in the world, if not *the* greatest concentration. The royal parks alone covered a whopping eight miles of green land and Jonah's favourite was Hyde Park. He could get lost there for hours and its Serpentine Lake was truly a thing of great beauty. It was so quintessentially English that it reminded him of a Constable painting. You could hire boats by the hour to row on the water and he and Claire had done that, years ago. She'd been lazy, declaring her arms way too weak, and lay back basking in the sun whilst he put in the muscle power. "See, now you don't have to go to the gym later," she told him as she watched his triceps in motion. "I've done you a favour." When the sun came out in Britain the colours were extraordinary and, the day that they'd rowed, Jonah remembered thinking the park had looked like a scene from Mary Poppins, the one where the characters hop into the painting. The green foliage and the cornflower blue sky had been so impossibly bright that the colours looked as if they'd been photo-shopped.

But while Jonah loved the Serpentine, his favourite park had to be the one back home. San Diego's Balboa Park was the biggest cultural urban park in the United States and he loved its variety. As well as housing the zoo, theatres, museums and gardens, it was also home to sixty-five miles of hiking and biking trails. So the fact that Martha had wanted to cycle today was a bonus. He could kill two birds with one stone by coming here.

They'd stopped off twice en route, first at a deli where they'd bought freshly made sandwiches, iced cupcakes and drinks to take on a picnic and, next, at a bike rental hut. He and Martha already had wheels which were locked to the bike rack on the rear of his Porsche Cayenne, but Miriam needed kitting up. There was a gleaming pink model out front which was the right size and also had a front basket. That's the one Miriam had picked. Jonah loaded up its basket with their feast and they set off down a six mile trail marked 'golden hill', bumping along a dirt track shaded by oak and eucalyptus towards the canyons. There were a fair few uphill sections which required some hard-core effort which left the girls panting, but they managed it and were impressed with their efforts when they looked back at the gradient of the slope they'd just climbed. They found a large, shady tree under which Jonah unfolded a rug he'd loaded in his backpack. They took the sandwiches wrapped in

229

greaseproof paper out of Miriam's bike basket, along with the sodas, and tucked in.

Martha had pastrami as a filling, Miriam had picked turkey with coleslaw and Jonah had chosen salt beef.

"Mm, this is good," said Jonah, biting a massive chunk out of his roll.

"Mine too," said Martha appreciatively.

"Jonah," said Miriam, eyeing her sandwich but not yet eating it. "I was wondering, actually, err, we've been wondering, if you marry my mother then will Martha and I be, err, like, sort of, err sisters?"

Jonah nearly choked on his salt beef, freezing mid-chew as he digested this direct question. He loved how children could throw such curve balls. Nothing was too embarrassing and there was no filter button. Was this question actually about the sisterhood thing or was it a clever way of getting into the marrying issue?

Goddamn it, he wasn't sure what to say. If Claire were sitting next to him what would *she* say? Miriam was capable of flustering him way more than his own daughter ever could. *Be honest and just say it how it is.* That's what Claire would say, wasn't it? Or would she dodge the issue? Marriage was a big word but not one he'd even discussed with Claire. And he certainly wasn't going to let his thoughts be stolen by a nine-year old.

He swallowed his mouthful with a hefty gulp of Dr. Peppers.

"I guess that would make you sisters, yes."

"Cool," said Martha, linking her little finger with Miriam's.

"How's your sandwich?" Jonah asked Miriam, trying to change the subject, but she wasn't having any of it. She stared him directly in the eye, as if daring him with her gaze.

"So," she asked. "*Are* you going to marry my mother?"

Marriage wasn't what was on Jonah's mind as they steered towards the edge of the park. Think! Think! Think! He racked his brains. Where is there a chemist near to an ice-cream parlour? Wasn't there one near to Mariposa Ice Cream? In summer they made this special watermelon sorbet which he always left to melt in the heat a little, so he could drink it. To

231

hell whether there was a pharmacy or not next to it. Now that he had Mariposa in his head, that's where they were going. The girls would love it.

Claire's stomach aches were becoming more frequent and whilst she kept brushing it off as nothing, he wasn't convinced. The pain came and went, it wasn't constant. Some days she was completely fine but, occasionally, when she didn't think he was looking, he caught her doubling over and clutching the lower right part of her abdomen. Wasn't that where the appendix was? Couldn't a burst appendix kill you?

"You really should see a doctor" he told her.

"It's just wind." she reassured him. "I know my own body."

Well, if it really was wind, then he knew just the thing. His mother used to give him these little charcoal pills when he was a child which always did the trick.

"Let's park the bikes here," he said as he caught sight of Adams Avenue.

He chained the bikes up to a lamppost and they crossed the road. Yep, there was the pharmacy, two doors down, but first they made for the ice-cream parlour. Nobody could decide:

white chocolate macadamia, white chocolate raspberry, heath butter toffee or maple walnut. They even made ice-cream pie, although that needed to be ordered a few days in advance. Eventually they all decided they were so hot that it had to be refreshing sorbet. Martha went for orange sherbet and mango, Miriam chose peach and pumpkin and Jonah inevitably selected the watermelon sorbet. No sooner had they got outside than the ice-cream started melting!

"Girls, why don't you stay here," he suggested, handing Martha his cone. "I've got to go into the pharmacy for a minute and I don't want these dripping everywhere."

Leaving them licking the damage from their cone stems and fingers, Jonah dashed into the chemist. He ran straight up to the pharmacy counter.

"Do you still sell charcoal pills?" he asked. "I think the brand name is JJP."

The pharmacist disappeared and returned with a little grey plastic bottle in his hand.

"Here you go sir," he handed them over. "Work like magic."

CHAPTER SIXTEEN

MIRIAM

Grown-ups can be so stupid sometimes. That's what Miriam was thinking as Jonah tried to sidestep her "Are you going to marry my mother" question. If grown-ups weren't trying to prise information out of kids then they were trying to withhold it instead. Or trick them. Miriam's mother was a prime example. The lengths she'd gone to, to hide the fact that she and Jonah were way more than just friends was laughable. The first night that Jonah had stayed with them at 77 Gladstone Road, Miriam had woken with the larks and had gone to check to see if her mother was awake yet. She'd found her mother's bed empty but roughed up, as if she *had* been sleeping in it, and then she'd heard snoring from the spare room, a man's snoring, a sound she was unfamiliar with. She'd pushed the door ajar to have a peek and that's when she'd seen Jonah and her mum lying in bed together, really close, fast asleep in each other's arms. It was actually rather cute and, bizarrely, the sight of them had made Miriam feel happy.

Grown-ups think children don't notice things, but they do. Miriam's parents had never been particularly touchy-feely. Well, they were with *her* but not with each other. She couldn't remember them kissing or cuddling or holding hands the way some of her friends' parents did, so it hadn't come as a complete surprise when they'd split up. Miriam hated the 'D' word, it felt like she'd been branded, the way she noticed sheep in fields that had letters inked on their curly white fur. She hoped the 'D' tag was a label that she could some day shake off.

Her life had been turned so upside down by the 'D', that when her father had introduced Miriam to her new step-mother and step-brother, it hadn't actually felt that odd. They'd all seemed very happy together, a proper family unit just like the one Miriam had been part of before. She'd felt a pang of jealousy for her brother but had swallowed it. He was very sweet and utterly blameless. Because her father had found happiness again, she wanted her mother to be happy too. She'd seen that her mother was tired and lonely, always putting Miriam first and saying that she was "the light in her life" and assuring her that that was enough. Miriam had felt certain that she'd needed more. Jonah was nice. She really liked him. And whilst she'd been shocked to stumble upon them sleeping so intimately, it had pleased her too. She hoped he'd stick around. She'd never seen her mother smile so much or laugh so much or look quite so pretty and sparkly as she did whenever he was around.

The thing about the 'D' was that she had no control. No control over which parent she saw and when. No control over what she wanted to do because grown-ups made all the real decisions. And she had no control over her mother's happiness. But as she'd pedalled uphill in Balboa Park she'd been toying with an idea. Perhaps she *could* have control over her mother's happiness. Perhaps she was more powerful than she thought. The very concept had taken her mind off the pain in her thighs which felt as though they were circling through thick treacle as she conquered the steep slope. Whilst she'd watched Jonah shake the creases out of the green tartan picnic rug and smooth it flat under the branches of a tree, she dared herself to ask him the 'M' question. If she knew that he had every intention of sticking around then that would give her an element of control, both over her own life as well as over her mother's.

She kept willing herself to ask as they'd sat down and the other two had begun to un-wrap their sandwiches, but the words had become lodged in her throat. Then she'd counted down from three to one in her head and told herself that she must, absolutely must, ask that question after she reached number one. If she didn't, she convinced herself that something bad would happen. That fear alone was enough to make her blurt

236

out the words. She saw that the question made Jonah very uncomfortable and, much as she liked him, which she really did, making such an impact on him made her feel in control. That's why she didn't leave the matter alone. Her first attempt had been more cleverly couched, the question hidden in a ramble about whether Jonah marrying her mother would make her and Martha sisters. The second time round there was no side-stepping the issue.

"So, are you going to marry my mother?"

Jonah's eyes boggled, but he largely stayed calm, chewing his food with a thoughtful expression on his face. She wanted to ask him 'a penny for them', meaning she'd give him a penny for his thoughts if he dared to divulge them, only she didn't want to distract him or interrupt his thought processes. *Darn*, as Martha would say. She wanted him to answer that question. It was very simple. Yes or no, with no murky grey area in-between.

"Do you think I should answer that question?" he asked.

One of her pet hates was a question being answered with a question. Well, two could play at that game.

"Do you think I think you should answer that question?"

237

Martha started giggling. Thankfully Jonah was too grown-up to keep playing this game, which could have continued ad infinitum with a never-ending series of 'do you think I think you think I think you thinks'.

"I do think you think I should answer that question," Jonah started. "And so I will try by saying that asking a woman for her hand in marriage is a very special thing and really, there's only one person who should know about it first. Who do you think that is?"

Oh boy, another question.

"The person you're going to ask to marry?" Martha suggested.

"Exactly," said Jonah.

Clearly Miriam didn't have the control or power that she hoped for. Reluctantly she realised that she had to move on. She opened the packaging to her turkey and coleslaw sandwich. It looked yummy. She took a mouthful. It *was* yummy. She hummed in appreciation. Miriam loved American food. Everything was so much tastier than at home.

"Dad," asked Martha, "how did you ask Mummy to marry you?"

Jonah had just taken another mouthful of his salt beef sandwich and Miriam felt sorry for him. These pesky girls just wouldn't stop asking questions.

Not only was Martha very bossy, she was very competitive too. Back at Lily Beach - that's what Jonah's house was called - Martha challenged Miriam to a game of Connect 4. They were pretty evenly matched but one game had turned into 'best out of three', which turned into 'best of five', which turned into 'the first to twenty'. Martha was keeping a tally and somehow they were able to carry on a conversation as they played. So far, Martha was in the lead at eleven games to nine and her non-stop questions were probably some clever distraction tactic.

"You don't look much like your mom," she said. "Why is that?"

This wasn't the first time Miriam had heard this. Friends at school often asked her the same thing. Whilst *she* could see a resemblance between herself and her mother, it was clear that others found it trickier.

"My Dad's black," Miriam explained. "So I guess that makes it harder for you to see the similarity. But my mother says that I've got her nose and lips. You can check it out later."

Martha had the red discs, Miriam had the yellow. Martha made a bad move, allowing Miriam to complete a yellow row of four. Bingo!

"Ten, eleven," said Miriam.

They emptied the discs out the frame and started again.

"Would you like to be my sister?" asked Martha.

"Yes," said Miriam.

She answered very quickly. Too quickly perhaps, for this was a concept to which she'd not yet given proper consideration. This was weird considering she'd pretty much asked Jonah if he was going to be her step-Dad. But if he became her step-father then Martha would become her step-sister and, actually, that would be pretty cool. As far as step-sisters went, it could be much worse. For starters, Martha could have been a boy. Not that she had anything against boys and she loved Jasper, but it wasn't like she could *play* with him. And she actually enjoyed playing with Martha. She was pretty sure that if Martha had been at her school then they would have picked each other to be friends. So the fact that they had been forced together was pretty neat. Miriam laughed as she found herself thinking the word 'neat'. Clearly Martha's influence was rubbing off on her. In England that word had a completely different meaning.

It was also great that they were both in the same position. They were both products of the big 'D' and that meant they shared a great understanding. It was hard having two homes and being passed from pillar to post. It was hard to hear your parents fight over you, to feel you were a pawn in their game of chess. It was hard if there wasn't parity between your parents, if one was happy and the other wasn't as a result of the 'D'. It was hard when one of them had a boyfriend or girlfriend and the other one didn't. Martha said her mother had *lots* of boyfriends since the 'D' and she didn't like it. Claire was the first girlfriend her dad had introduced her to. She didn't even know if there'd been others. So it was nice that Miriam had Martha and vice versa, because they understood each others' pain in a way that others might not. They could be, and were, mutually supportive.

That didn't stop the fact that Martha could be a pain in the arse and frequently was! She always wanted to watch reruns of *icarly* whereas Miriam was hooked on The Gameshow

241

Network which showed '80s reruns in which the female contestants all had hilariously big curly hairstyles and wore enormous shoulder pads.

"Maybe we could go to the same school," said Martha. "That would be cool, wouldn't it?"

"I win," said Miriam, spotting a possible line of four on the diagonal and slotting in a yellow disc. Martha grunted. She'd lost her lead. That was the thing which most irritated Miriam about her, her competitiveness. Martha always had to win and was a bad loser. Not that Miriam liked to lose either but, if she did, at least she did it graciously.

"I don't want to play any more," said Martha.

Miriam's father was fiercely competitive, just like Martha, and he was also a prime example of a grown-up trying to extract information from a kid. He thought he was being clever and that she didn't see what he was up to, but one time, the first time she stayed with him after meeting Jonah, he fired question after question at her. What did she think of Jonah? Had Jonah stayed the night? What did you do together? Rat-a-tat-tat, rat-a-tat-tat, the questions had come at her as steady and rapid as gunfire. Miriam didn't think it was any of her father's

242

business. Her mother never interrogated her, and her mother had got used to the idea not just of Daddy with another woman but Daddy with another child. And so she decided to wind up her father, as much as an eight year old child was able. She had a fair idea of his pressure points and she played to them, aggravating him with what was entirely the truth. She knew how much her father believed in the truth. What were the words he told her, the ones that witnesses were forced to swear on the bible in court? *I promise to tell the truth, the whole truth and nothing but the truth.*

And so she had. She told him she liked Jonah a *lot.* She told him that he let her win games. "Which you never do," she added as an afterthought, to stick in the knife and turn it painfully. She told him that he stayed not one but *two* nights. And then her favourite part of the conversation had been when she told her father that her mother was going to be a TV superstar. He'd been really mean. He opened his mouth so wide in disbelief that she could have stuck a football between his teeth. And then he laughed sarcastically. That wasn't nice. Miriam loved her mother even if her father didn't. Weren't grown-ups meant to behave better than children? And see, he'd been wrong. Mummy really *was* turning into a TV superstar.

Miriam's father was coming to pick her up in just over a week's time and already she knew that she didn't want to go.

243

She loved him. He was her *father* after all and she wanted to spend time with him. The thing was, though, these last three weeks had been some of the best in her life and she didn't want them to end. She loved it here. Yes, Martha could be a pain but she was a nice pain. She enjoyed being with her. They swam, they played tennis, they *did* things, but not in a forced way, in a natural way. She loved Jonah's home, the surroundings, the sea, their lifestyle. Dinner was her favourite time of day. They'd started the way they meant to continue that first night, after her mother had won one miraculous point off Jonah in the tennis match. He'd fired up the barbecue in the garden and, even though strictly speaking it was Jonah who was meant to be the sole chef as his punishment for losing the bet, everyone had played a part. Martha had helped her dad with the sausages and chicken legs. Miriam and her mother had been in charge of salads. They'd made a potato salad with caramelised onions, a green salad and a simple corn salad. Most nights they had a barbecue and ate together on the patio but, occasionally Claire cooked something different. So far Martha had gone crazy for her beef lasagne as well as her homemade fresh fish in breadcrumbs. "You're a much better cook than my mom," she praised.

Miriam would never admit it to her mother, but she even enjoyed the long beach walks Claire insisted they do every few days or so, dodging the incoming tide as they walked round tight coves overhung by cliffs garlanded in purple flowers. Her mother loved to walk in the fresh sea air. The *ocean*, as Martha called it. Everything her father did felt contrived. Jonah was completely different. He made it up as he went along. There was a quiet casualness about him which she found incredibly appealing. She felt wicked for admitting it but part of her wished that Jonah was her real father. He was *fun*. He was cool. She saw people turn their heads, recognising him when they were out and about, and he never alluded to any fame or past history. He just *was*.

She wished her father wasn't coming to America. She feared that wherever they went, whatever they did, wherever they stayed, she'd wish that she was at Lily Beach instead. She loved Jasper. He was sweet, but after a few minutes he was boring and Ali was always focusing on him instead of her, as if Miriam was a slightly tiresome afterthought. With Jonah she never felt anything less than part of the family. She never felt less than equal.

Miriam was in a state of turmoil. She felt bad for having these mean thoughts about her Dad, who she knew loved her. But these last few days she'd been wondering if she dared ask her mother if she really had to go. Her father, Ali and Jasper could all have a great time without her. Heck, they'd probably have a *better* time without her.

245

CHAPTER SEVENTEEN

Much as Claire loved the children, her favourite moment of the day was after they'd gone to bed. She always put in maximum effort to ensure that a good time was had by all, and so the peace and quiet that came after the youngsters were asleep felt well and truly earned. It had been the same back in the UK and it was no different here in the US. Only now, with Jonah in her life, there was more of an incentive to achieve that precious child-free solitude earlier rather than later. The girls were always so active, swimming, body surfing or flying kites that most evenings they were happy to be tucked up by 8 pm. In fact, most nights they were *begging* for bed. Plus she *was* more fatigued than usual. That was the problem with her long Mondays. She was so exhausted from the pressure of performing in front of the camera for what wasn't far off a twenty-four hour shift, that for the remainder of the week she felt as if she was playing catch-up. And the whole Orlando Goodman situation was preying on her mind. Their regular skype conversations always left her feeling as heavy as if she were shrouded in a blanket of lead. Her meal plans for him weren't working. He said they were but every time she saw him when they video-spoke the sunken hollows on his cheeks were deeper, his complexion slightly greyer. His illness was being completely kept under wraps and he was still somehow managing to perform on the West End stage. *The show must go on.* She'd repeatedly asked if he might reconsider conventional treatment but he was adamant. "If I die on stage, then I die happy," he'd said. "Better than dying in a hospital bed somewhere."

Now though, she tried to block out such thoughts. The girls were sleeping and the "mm" that left her lips as she lay back on the patio sofa said it all, the sound conveying ecstasy and relief. She raised her feet on the pile of cushions scattered at one end. Today had been, quite possibly, one of the best days of her life. Jonah had taken them all to Coronado Island, one of the most desirable zip codes in the USA. It's not a real island, he explained, but just looks like one because a bridge attaches it to the mainland. A beautiful two-hour coastal cycle ride had been followed by an al fresco lunch at the Hotel Del Coronado, overlooking the ocean. The girls were delightfully entertaining and well behaved, charming the waiters and appreciating their breadcrumb coated cod with Yukon mashed potatoes. "This is the nicest food to ever cross my lips," Miriam praised. Claire felt the same way about her meal – lobster risotto followed by diver scallops covered in orange pine-nut gremolata. At one point Jonah had taken her hand and lifted it to his lips. She could tell that he felt it too. That here, at this table, as they ate, chatted and drank wine, it all felt right. They'd somehow evolved into the perfect, blended family, a special unit. She wished she could pocket the feeling of elation and for nothing to ever change.

It was a sultry evening, heavy with the type of heat that sticks to you, wrapping its moisture across your skin in an invisible sheen. Despite the mercury on the thermometer tipping 80 degrees Fahrenheit, Claire had brought out a mug of boiling water into which she'd added a slice of lemon. This was the only drink that seemed to quench her thirst at the moment. As she waited for her laptop to fire up she took her cup and blew the steam across its surface, watching it waft in curly squiggles towards the sky.

"Hey you," said Jonah, coming out with a bottle of Budweiser.

He clanked the beer onto the glass coffee table, tossed the cushions onto the floor and placed her feet on his lap as he sat down. He started gently massaging her arches.

"Mm, that's nice," she said, closing her eyes.

"Pretty toes," he admired.

The girls had given her a pedicure when they'd got back and it actually wasn't half-bad. They'd removed her blue polish, filed and scrubbed, and had repainted her nails with a chocolate-

248

colour varnish. It was a fairly professional-looking job and they'd done the same on each other. All three of them now had matching pinkies. This lovely girlie session had been tainted with a touch of sadness. In two days' time both Miriam and Martha would be handed back to their respective other parents and, whilst Martha would return for a weekend in a couple of weeks' time, Claire wouldn't be seeing her daughter again until she got back to London. She knew the girls wished it was otherwise. Martha would be celebrating her ninth birthday in a fortnight and she so wanted Miriam to come to her party.

"I know," she smiled, trying to focus on the good and not the bad. "San Diego's beauty salons better watch out. The girls will steal their trade."

The screen of Claire's laptop was facing Jonah. He scrunched up his forehead quizzically.

"Who's Will Ryan from ABC?" he asked.

"I've no idea," said Claire, turning the screen to face her and clicking on the mail. Her jaw dropped as she started to read. "Ah yes," she muttered, remembering. And then: "Oh. My. God," she gasped.

"What?"

"Will Ryan is this Executive Producer who introduced himself to me when I was filming at SeaWorld. He's asking if I would like to do a screen test for some new healthy eating programme they've been commissioned to make. Apparently accents are in vogue at the moment and they're keen to hire someone British, if they can find the right person."

Jonah pulled the laptop closer and read the mail.

"Wow, babe, that's amazing."

Claire sipped her hot water, although now she had a sudden urge to celebrate on something stronger. She was reaching for Jonah's Budweiser when her tummy was wracked by one of those irritating cramps. She was on the brink of crying out, but happily the pain disappeared almost at once. Perhaps the pills Jonah bought her were starting to work. Luckily he appeared not to have noticed, his eyes still fixed on Will Ryan's email.

"It's a screen test," she carried on. "I'm sure they've got lots of other candidates lined up. And, besides, how many viewers does ABC have?"

"I don't know, tens of millions for sure."

Claire's jaw dropped even wider.

"Exactly," she said. "I don't think I can cope with that. That's just insane. And I'm completely inexperienced, so let's not get too excited."

Nonetheless, Claire could feel a rush of adrenaline racing through her veins. This was madness. She had to tell Georgia. She drew her laptop closer and started clicking out of her mails and onto Skype.

"What are you doing?" asked Jonah.

"I'm going to call Georgia."

"It's four in the morning in London," Jonah reminded her.

Oh damn! In her excitement she had forgotten about the time difference.

"And besides," Jonah murmured, tracing a teasing line up her inner leg towards her thigh, "the thought of you being some international TV superstar plus the gorgeous dress that you're wearing is making me hot."

The dress *was* nice. It was Martha who spotted it in one of Coronado Island's chichi boutiques, her eye drawn by its pale grey fabric and funky pink floral print. The top had narrow straps and a tight-fitting bodice that enhanced Claire's breasts. Its long floating skirt was asymmetric, shorter in the front than the back. Jonah began to ruche up the material gathered around her legs as his fingers inched higher. Words formulated in Claire's head as well as the feigned angry tone she would assign to them. *You mean you weren't hot for me when I was just plain Claire Jackson, the Nutritionist?* But the second Jonah's palm found her panties and rested itself there, the words evaporated into the ether, forgotten. Moments later he wriggled his way onto her bare flesh, his fingers tickling her clitoris and then thrusting inside her, deeply. Her breath hitched as she closed her eyes. She could sense Jonah watching her and felt uncomfortably exposed.

"We haven't baptised this sofa yet," he whispered.

"We can't do it out here," she whispered insistently. "What if the girls aren't properly asleep yet?"

His finger was now nudging her G-spot, causing her to wriggle and writhe under his intense gaze. The sensation was divine. So divine she was starting not to care who did or didn't see them. So divine she didn't want it to end. Jonah placed his spare hand

252

lightly on her collar bone, slowly lowering it towards her breasts. Whenever his fingers grazed her skin she felt nothing less than beautiful. How was he capable of doing that to her with just a touch?

"Ok," he said, removing her panties and leaning forward far enough that his lips hovered a millimetre above hers. "Let's go inside."

Jonah locked their bedroom door behind them. In this heat he would always be found bare-chested around the house, but Claire wasted no time in removing his khaki shorts and Calvin Klein boxers in one deft move. As he stood there, a sculpted, perfectly-formed naked Adonis, it was clear that Jonah was more than ready. Claire pulled the hem of her dress upwards, about to take it off.

"No," barked Jonah, "leave it on."

He scooped her in his arms and carried her to the bed, landing her on top of him as he fell backwards onto the mattress. "I want to watch you," he said, manoeuvring her to his centre so she could straddle him. He placed his hands on the sides of her lower waist, controlling her as she eased herself onto him until he was filling her completely. He loved that look of unadulterated ecstasy on her face as she rode him and circled him and taunted him, moving slowly and tantalisingly up and down and around, driving him to wild places that made him feel he couldn't contain himself any longer. He scrunched her dress up so he could see her sex, caressing the skin on the divine, creamy soft flesh of her thighs. He loved her ripe breasts and how they spilled when she wasn't wearing a bra. He reached up to touch them, feeling her swollen nipples hard underneath his hands and rolling his fingers over them. The dress had four buttons down the front. He undid them, slowly, one by one as Claire pushed him even deeper inside her, moaning as he hit her core. He unhooked the lowest button and freed her breasts, fondling them in his hands as he observed her, watching her red corkscrew curls dangle in a sexy mass down her spine as she tilted back her head, a few stray strands sticking to her face in the heat of the room. The extra heat their connected bodies generated as they rocked was tempered by a gentle breeze blowing from the overhead fan. Jonah didn't mind the heat. If anything, it increased his libido. There was something inherently horny about the combined sweat of two people intertwined whilst making love. He pulled her face down so he could kiss her, their tongues matching the gyrations of their hips. It was exquisite.

"I love you," he said.

He loved her so much that four more words formulated in his head, as a question. He was about to vocalise them when he felt a much more urgent desire building within. Instead he concentrated on that, watching Claire to see if she was close too and when he saw that she was he pulled her harder down on him and found her clitoris with his finger, bringing them both slowly and deliciously to climax.

In the aftermath Claire placed her head on Jonah's chest. He gently stroked her hair, hooking curls around his fingers. Her focus was glued on the ceiling fan and the whirring rotation of its blades, its action almost hypnotic.

"What are you thinking?" asked Jonah.

She was about to tell him what an amazing day it had been and to ask if he'd care to give it marks out of ten, when the appendix side of her stomach went into sudden spasm. It felt like being speared with a hot dagger. The agony was so excruciating that the shriek which left her lips sounded wild and bestial.

"What is it?" Jonah sat bolt upright.

She wanted to tell him that she was experiencing pain on a level which was off the radar, but she was suddenly overwhelmed by nausea and summoned all the energy she could muster to make a mad dash to the toilet. She only just made it in time, kneeling over the bowl, retching violently. Jonah must have come with her and held her hair in a ponytail, placing a calming hand on her shoulder.

"Do you think its food poisoning?" he asked her in between retches.

"I - don't - know," she mumbled, barely audible, indicating with a hand on her pelvis that she was still in pain.

"Claire, I'm going to take you to the hospital. I don't like it. Something's not right."

She tried to tell him 'no', to not be ridiculous, that it was probably some gastric bug which would pass and that she didn't want to trouble the girls, but then she started retching again. Jonah went to fetch his mobile and returned to her side as he called the complex's caretaker, apologising for telephoning so late and asking if his wife Maria could come to baby sit, urgently.

"It was the way Jonah said 'urgently' which alerted Claire. He was usually so calm and cool, but she heard his voice crack and his panic unnerved her.

The next half hour passed in a blur. She was aware of Jonah manoeuvring her limbs into loose-fitting trousers and a t-shirt. She was aware of the doorbell ringing and of hushed voices as Jonah explained that he would be back as soon as he could and that he should be contacted if the girls woke up and were in any way alarmed. She was aware of being belted into a car and then carried out of it the other end. She was aware of being lain on a bed. "Ma'am we need to take a blood and urine sample," a voice instructed. She was aware of a pin pricking her forearm but the pain barely registered because it was nothing compared to the throbbing in her stomach. Someone handed her a receptacle to pee into. She was aware of Jonah trying to help her accomplish this task but, after that, she had no idea. She dropped her head back on the pillow, exhausted from the effort and fell asleep.

Scary words filtered into her sub-conscious.

*Blood… … … … … … … … …..urine… … … … … …positive… … …
…..when… …how… … …afraid… … … … …soon… … … … …sorry
… … …waiting… … … …soon… … …sorry… … … … …..possible
… … … … … … …..ectopic… … … … …..appendicitis… … …burst
… … … … … … … … … …ectopic… … ….*

Claire opened her eyes. Phew. There was nothing but silence around her. It must all have been a dream. Inches from her bed a white curtain was drawn. Where was she? She turned onto her other side. Jonah was sitting in a chair next to her, looking at her tenderly.

"Hey, Duchess," he grinned. "How are you doing?"

Now she remembered. He'd brought her to the hospital. At least he didn't look panicked any more. How *was* she doing? She sat upright. No pain, no nausea.

"I feel great," she smiled. "Can we go now?"

Jonah furrowed his brow. An extra crease seemed to have etched a path on his forehead. He shook his head.

"We've got to wait for the doctor. A specialist is coming to see you."

Claire swung her legs out of the bed.

"I don't need a specialist. I feel great. I told you there was nothing wrong."

Jonah pursed his lips and his eyes misted.

"Sweetheart," he took her hand in his. "They did a pregnancy test and it came back positive."

She clapped a hand over her chest. She wasn't sure whether to laugh or cry. Pregnant, she was pregnant. She couldn't understand quite how that had happened, but this was good news, wasn't it? So why did he look so morose? Did he really want this so little? Was this going to be a replay of what happened fourteen years ago?

"Claire," Jonah leaned in close and clasped her hand tighter. "At first they thought you had appendicitis but now, because of the positive test and all the pain you've been experiencing, they're pretty sure it's-

She finished off his sentence, the word 'ectopic' a whisper which dissolved in the air. So she hadn't been dreaming that word, someone had said it. It was true. She sat back down on the bed and bowed her head, a tear plopping out of an eye and landing on her lap.

Their day in Coronado already felt so long ago. She hadn't said it out loud, but after lunch, when they were sitting on the beach

259

watching the girls jump waves, she was so happy with how the four of them felt together as a family unit that she'd thought that having any more children would be a bad idea. It was far better to nurture what they already had than to complicate matters. She was going to ask Jonah if he felt the same way, but the day was so perfect that she hadn't wanted to start any heavy conversations.

If there really was a baby growing in her fallopian tube, however, she knew the chances of her getting pregnant in the future would be greatly reduced, or possibly non-existent. Another tear and then another fell onto her trousers. An ugly thought entered her head. *This is my punishment for what we did fourteen years ago.* She decided to spare Jonah from sharing it with him.

A white-coated doctor wheeled an ultrasound machine into her cubicle. Her demeanour was professional and caring. Her head was cocked sympathetically.

"Hello, my name's Julie," she said. "Would you mind lying back down and scooting to the end of the bed?" she asked.

Like a robot, Claire did as she was told and felt bizarrely detached as Julie squirted icy cold gel onto her tummy. On her other side Jonah sat on a chair, holding her hand, staring in fear at the blank screen. Julie placed the probe onto the gel and started moving it around, searching for an image. Claire was only thirty-seven. It wasn't young in fertility terms but it wasn't exactly ancient either. It was too soon to be told that you could never bear more children.

"When was your last period?" asked Julie.

"What does it matter?" replied Claire rudely. "It's not as if it will make any difference."

Julie temporarily stopped circling the probe.

"I know this is hard," she said, "but I just need to work out the size of the foetus I'm trying to look for."

"I don't know," Claire burst into tears. She couldn't think straight.

Julie circled the probe again, looking puzzled and frowning as she dug more deeply into the flesh of Claire's lower stomach. Claire turned to Jonah looking for reassurance but nothing on his face gave it to her. His eyes were wide and sad as they

261

stared into the far distance. Julie swivelled the screen so that it was out of view. She started taking measurements and printing images.

"Have you found it yet?" asked Claire quietly.

Julie moved the probe across her stomach and dug in again.

"Hang on a sec," she said, "I'm just trying to get a better view."

There was nothing for it but to wait.

"I'm just trying to check if there's anything I'm not seeing."

Julie printed up some more images and rose to her feet.

"I want to get someone else to look at these images, for a second opinion."

Julie left and Claire and Jonah waited in silence, each deep in their own thoughts. A couple of minutes later Julie returned with another doctor. She squeezed some fresh gel onto Claire's stomach and began circling the probe again. "Here," she pointed on the screen, showing her colleague. She moved the probe. "And here," she pointed again. The colleague nodded and raised an eyebrow before leaving.

"Right," said Julie, swivelling the screen back so that Claire and Jonah could see. "There are a couple of things I need to show you."

It sounded ominous. Perhaps it was worse than a foetus implanted in her fallopian tube. Perhaps there were growths of a more sinister nature.

"Right," she said, moving the probe to the far left. She pointed at a black mass on the screen. "This here is one lovely healthy baby, about eight weeks old I'd say, judging from its size." She adjusted the volume knob and the sound of a pulsing heartbeat came up loud and clear. Claire turned to Jonah. She didn't understand. Julie ran the probe back over Claire's stomach and dug it in sharply to the left.

"Ouch," yelped Claire.

"Sorry, it's hard to see, but I wanted to show you this here," Julie pointed to the screen again, "is another lovely healthy baby." Again, she upped the volume and the heartbeat came across loud and clear.

"I'm sorry," said Jonah, "I don't understand what you're trying to say."

"Me neither," said Claire, confused. Did she have a foetus stuck in each of her fallopian tubes?

"I've had a good look and I think the pain you've been experiencing is as a result of cysts on your ovaries, which we'll need to keep a close eye on. As for the nausea, that's most likely morning sickness associated with pregnancy. I thought there might be a third for a minute," explained Julie, "but I've had a good look and I'm fairly certain it's just two. Congratulations. You're having twins."

CHAPTER EIGHTEEN

JONAH

Getting a good night's sleep used to be high on Jonah's agenda. At one point in his career it had become a vicious circle. If he didn't sleep well then he wouldn't play his best tennis and the more he panicked about it, the less he slept. He'd tried everything in his time, from meditation to herbal remedies to heavy-duty sleeping pills. The problem with the latter was that it frequently left him feeling groggy the next day, which wasn't advisable for a competing athlete. The one thing that had always been a sure-fire cert as a slumber aid had been sex, but the rumours about athletes being advised *not* to have intercourse the night before an important event were all true. His coach had always warned him that it depleted energy reserves for the battle that lay ahead. Jonah hadn't heeded this warning, however. Instead he'd come up with an alternative theory, preferring to believe that sex increases the amounts of testosterone in the body which in turn increases aggression. Who knows which theory was more correct? It was all speculation and he wasn't going to abstain just because of some scientific mumbo jumbo, plausible or not.

Last night, after they got back from the hospital, Jonah didn't sleep at all but, this time, he hadn't cared. He didn't once think about reaching for a tablet, herbal or medicated, and he'd already had sex. No, he simply hadn't slept because he was too goddamn excited. Claire was pregnant. They were going to have a baby. And once she'd got over the initial shock of it, she too had appeared genuinely pleased. They'd twirled and hugged and kissed as the news had sunk in and, after Claire's "oh my God, oh my god, oh my God, I can't believe it," had been repeated on a never-ending loop, she'd remembered that she'd done lots of things she shouldn't have. "That must be why I've gone off tea and coffee. And crikey, think of all the alcohol I've drunk and goat's cheese I've eaten. Plus I did that stupid zip wire, not to mention all that *sex* we've been having. Crikey, do you think the babies are ok?"

Then her concerns had moved onto the girls. "What on earth do we tell them? How will they take the news? Where will we live?" She'd started to panic. "Shush," he calmed her. "Everything's going to be ok. We'll look at all the options and make it work for us. There's nothing that can't be overcome. This is our new beginning. It was meant to be."

At Coronado they'd gone to sit on the white sand after lunch whilst the girls waded in the ocean. He had watched the children, thinking how much he'd like to have more kids with Claire. He'd debated whether to mention it but the day was so perfect he had been scared of ruining it. In case she didn't feel the same way, he had kept quiet. They decided to stay quiet now and not say anything to the girls yet, seeing as the youngsters were both leaving in a couple of days. Then, when it was just the two of them together, they could work out the logistics.

As soon as they'd got back from the hospital Claire had fallen asleep and Jonah had lain awake watching her, marvelling at the new lives growing inside of her, dreaming of their future. At about seven o'clock he got up to make the girls' breakfast. Claire stirred too.

"Shush," he told her. "Go back to sleep. You can rest all day if you want to."

Jonah was on that same sort of energised "high" one experiences after falling in love. It's a kind of buzz that doesn't require sleep. It's the best natural buzz that exists. Jonah had never taken drugs but he imagined that this kind of euphoria might come from a Class 'A' narcotic, only it couldn't possibly feel *this* good.

"Hang on a sec," he called after the girls as they ran to the pool shortly after nine o'clock. "Wait for me." Where were his sneakers? He liked to take advantage of them swimming by working out in the gym. He needed his sneakers. He ran

267

upstairs to check in his closet. They weren't there so he ran back downstairs and checked the back patio. They were hiding underneath the hammock. He ran outside with them still in his hand. The girls were already in the pool, swimming underwater. He sat on a sun bed whilst he put on his shoes, eavesdropping on the girls' conversation as they resurfaced at the far end.

"I really want you to come to my birthday party," said Martha. "Do you think you'll be able to?"

"I hope so," Miriam replied. Her tone didn't sound so certain.

"Why don't you get your Mom to ask your Dad?"

"I've already tried that," said Miriam. "And she said she wasn't sure that my Dad would like it."

"What about if my Dad asked your Dad, do you think that would work? It's a fashion designing party and you *love* designing. You could design yourself some cute pink denim shorts with frayed edges."

Miriam didn't reply so, instead, Martha turned her focus on her father.

268

"What do you think, Pops? Can you do something about it?"

Jonah tied up his second lace, not wanting to make promises he couldn't keep.

"I'll speak to Claire about it again," he said as he got up. He pointed to the gym. "Right, I'm going for a run now. I'm in there if you need anything. Be good and don't make too much noise."

For the first couple of minutes Jonah jogged on the treadmill, his mind was completely blank, focusing on the movement of his legs and on his breathing. As the pace picked up, however, thoughts started slowly seeping in. He pondered his finances. He may not have been the world's number one tennis player but he had been shrewd. An athlete's career is invariably short, so the most has to be made of it. The main bulk of the small fortune he'd amassed wasn't from prize money, it was from sponsorship deals. He'd been popular among companies promoting sexier brands, who'd sought him to promote their image. Nike, Coke, Rolex, Calvin Klein, Jeep Cherokee and Wilson had all sponsored him handsomely over the years. His arrangement with Calvin Klein had gone way beyond their logo being sewn onto his tennis tops. For years he'd done a series of TV ads and glossy magazine photo shoots in the US, modelling their latest range. He felt uncomfortable under the glare of the camera, especially stripped down so bare, but the monetary rewards were worthwhile. That deal alone had bought him not just Lily Beach, but another couple of properties he rented out in California as well as a penthouse in New York - and a lifetime's supply of underwear!

If he didn't want to he needn't work another day in his life, but he liked working. It gave him a sense of purpose and he didn't want Martha to grow up thinking that her father did 'nada' for a living. Occasionally he was hired as a motivational speaker and the tennis commentating work had recently taken off. Not long ago his agent had mentioned another possibility for him in television, which Jonah said 'he'd think about'. He didn't really think it was for him but, now that he knew there were two babies on the way, perhaps he should reconsider. If he remembered correctly, that job would at least keep him in one place. Much as he liked it, following tennis tournaments around the world as a commentator wasn't conducive to family life. He would call his agent later.

Jonah was running steady and hard, watching the girls as he mulled this over. He checked his watch. He'd done ten minutes, time to pick up the pace. He adjusted the speed on the treadmill. He started to think about Claire and the twins again but then, from nowhere, the hairs on his arms pricked up. He was hot as hell, sweating profusely, and yet his skin was suddenly pocked with goose-bumps. His skill at being a great observer of people and situations, with a sixth sense for second-guessing others, now told him that he was being watched. But it didn't make sense. There was nobody else in the gym or by the pool except for the girls. He decided that the exciting news combined with not having slept all night must be playing havoc with his sixth sense and he carried on running. Nonetheless, his hairs still stood stubbornly on end. Disconcerted, he slowed his pace down and ground to a halt, stepping off the machine.

Jonah didn't like interrupting his training. Something felt wrong. He felt as if he was being watched. He left the gym and went over to the pool.

"Hi Dad," said Martha, "that was quick."

He was struggling to catch his breath, panting heavily as he slowly circled, taking in his surroundings, looking first at ground level, then higher. There was a rustling in the bushes that camouflaged the complex's outer fence.

"Hello?" called Jonah.

"Who are you speaking to?" asked Martha.

271

Jonah checked himself. He didn't want to scare the girls.

"You!" he grinned, lying down on the sun bed. Forget it. He'd do some exercise later. Slowly, as he lay there, wincing as Martha and Miriam willingly performed belly flops to see who could make the greater splashy thwack, the feeling of being watched dissipated. Either he'd been imagining things or whoever had been doing the watching had gone away.

Back inside, Miriam went upstairs to check on her mother, leaving Jonah and Martha alone in the kitchen. He liked it being just the two of them. Over the last month there hadn't been much of that and he hoped his daughter didn't resent him for it. She didn't seem to and he knew that, if she had been upset about something, she would definitely have said so.

"Hey kiddo," he wrapped his arms around her. She was growing so damn fast. Just that thought made him think about the new babies and how tiny they would be in comparison. Would Martha hate them, resent them or just accept the new status quo? He felt a stab of worry shoot through his gut. It made him understand better how Claire felt about it. Her concerns were all valid. However, Jonah knew that, when it came to the bottom line, it would all work out - it had to!

272

"Do you want me to make you a smoothie?" he asked.

"Yes, please."

The kitchen had a central island with high stools around it.
Martha scrambled up onto a seat, watching as her father cut the
stalks off the strawberries and tossed them into the blender,
smothering them with lemon yoghurt and orange juice before
replacing the lid and turning the machine on.

"*Could* you ask Miriam's father if she can come to my party?"
she shouted so that her voice could be heard above the
whirring.

"I've got a better idea," said Jonah, turning the blender off. The
strawberries had turned the yoghurt nicely pink. "Why don't
you ask her father? It's harder for grown-ups to say no to kids.
He's coming to pick Miriam up about an hour before I take you
back to Mom's tomorrow. You'll meet him then."

"Great idea," said Martha.

Jonah took two tall glasses out of the cupboard and loaded
them first with crushed ice from the freezer and then with the
smoothie mixture. He pushed one of the glasses towards
Martha and raised the second one towards his lips.

273

"Mm," Martha approved as she tasted. "You make the best smoothie."

"I'm going to miss you tomorrow," said Jonah.

Damn, he didn't mean to say that. He always *thought* it but he was never actually dumb enough to say it out loud, because it made the parting process so much harder. The lack of sleep, the sense of being watched, the baby news, it was all making him act out of character.

"Me too," said Martha. "I've had the best summer. And Dad -

"Yes, sweetie?"

"I want you to know that I really like Claire."

Jonah's heart sang.

"She really likes you too."

Martha started shifting uncomfortably on her stool, as if she'd sat on a nest of ants that had started to crawl all over her backside.

"And Dad," she continued, "you never answered Miriam's question. *Are* you going to ask Claire to marry you?"

Jonah held his daughter's gaze as he put down his glass. Perhaps this was an opportunity for a heart to heart.

"I'm not going to answer that question for the same reasons that I gave Miriam when she asked. But if, hypothetically, I *were* to ask her, how would you feel about it?"

Jonah held his breath, half regretting his question. If Martha wasn't happy about a marriage then chances were that she definitely wouldn't welcome a baby, let alone two.

"That would be good," said Martha.

Phew, Jonah could breathe again.

"She makes you happy and that makes me happy. Plus she's a much better cook than you are."

"Excuse me, young lady," Jonah pretended to be offended. "What about my smoothies? And don't forget, I am King of the barbecue."

"Sure," grinned Martha, disbelieving. "Whatever."

"I love you kiddo," said Jonah, placing an arm around her shoulder and kissing the top of her head. "And I'm very proud of you for accepting Claire and Miriam into our lives. Thank you."

Martha nestled into Jonah's chest, crushing her nose into his stomach.

"I love you too," she said, before pulling away so she could breathe properly. "And also -

"Yes?"

"Can we play tennis this afternoon?"

"Of course we can," smiled Jonah.

Martha was a *bloody* good player, as Claire would say. She was built like an athlete and her talent had been spotted at a very young age, when her agility combined with excellent hand to eye coordination already made her a force to be reckoned with whenever a racket was in her grip. She already had a wide arsenal of shots, with a mean hook forehand and a two-handed backhand with wicked topspin. She whacked the ball back and

276

forth like a mini Sharapova. In fact, she *looked* a bit like Maria Sharapova as she targeted her shots long and deep to the left, then long and deep to the right, alternating with great precision as their rally continued. Jonah had no doubt that, if she wanted it enough, she could have a chance on the professional circuit. That wasn't what *he* wanted for her though. Too many sacrifices have to be made to get to the top of your game and experience told him that came at a price. Yes, his life was getting back on track now but had the hiccups along the way really been worth it? If he could do it again, would he do it differently? It was far better to look forward not backward and to live without regret.

Jonah couldn't think of one tennis champ whose child had followed in their footsteps, and that couldn't just be coincidental. Doctors often bred doctors. Lawyers frequently bred lawyers. Children liked to emulate their parents. Not in tennis though. Perhaps those children could see that the pain just wasn't worth the gain. The chances of being the absolute best were too slim. Nonetheless, Martha had been 'spotted' and was coached in the US regional squad and regularly competed in tournaments within her age group. However, Jonah noticed that she liked to play less now than previously. Usually, when he had her with him over the summer, she wanted to play with him every day for at least an hour, sometimes more. This holiday, however, she'd only gone on court a handful of times

277

at the beginning and ever since had chosen instead to play with Miriam *off* the court. This pleased Jonah. Not just because he wanted the two girls to get along, but because this meant his daughter was actively choosing a normal childhood over training for four hours a day.

"Go get it tiger," Jonah fed her another smash volley.

Martha ran backwards, her eye on the ball, racket raised. Thwack. The sound the strings made as they met the ball told Jonah that she'd made perfect contact on the racket's sweet spot. He turned to watch where the ball landed. It grazed the baseline.

"Brilliant," he praised.

He picked a ball out of the basket, about to feed her another shot.

"No," she held up her hand, panting as she ran into the net. "Enough. I've had enough. I'm going to cool off in the pool."

At this point Miriam appeared, with sneakers on her feet and a racket in her hand.

"You said you'd help me play better before I left," she said to Jonah shyly. "Would you mind or have you had enough now?"

"I'd love to teach you," smiled Jonah, delighted she'd asked. "Martha, won't you stay and watch?" he asked as she headed off to the pool.

"Nah," she said. "I'll go hang out with Claire instead."

Again, this made Jonah sing on the inside, the fact the girls were each happy to be with the other's parent.

"Right," he said, "Let's start at the beginning. Show me how you hold your racket."

She had one of Martha's cast-off Wilson's. He checked her hand position on the grip. It was too tight and in the wrong place. He swivelled it round a touch.

"There, that's perfect. See the way your thumb lines up with that W? Right, don't move your hand from that position."

Jonah demonstrated how she should swing back her racket on the forehand and then follow through, making her practice the movement a few times, finishing with the racket in front of her

279

nose. Satisfied that she'd got it, Jonah stepped back round to his side of the net, taking the full glare of the sun in his eyes.

"Ok Miriam, we're going to play half-court only for now, so move back to the middle of that first line."

Miriam got into position and waited. Jonah gently fed her a shot, which she missed. And then another, which she hit into the net.

"Relax Miriam. And remember that you need to hit upwards with the racket and not down."

He fed her another ball. Bingo. She got it back, a good, clean shot which landed about half-way down the court. "Excellent," he encouraged. "Give me another one of those." She did, and another and another. She was getting into the rhythm of it and starting to move her feet nicely to get to the ball when it happened again. Jonah felt the hairs on his arms stand on end and the goose bumps returned. He was definitely being watched. He swivelled to face the bushes adjacent to the court. The leaves rustled and moved and yet the atmosphere was as still as could be, not even the gentlest of breezes was blowing.

"Hang on a sec, Miriam. Martha hit a ball out earlier and I think I've just seen it," he said, moving slowly to the court's

280

entrance gate. If there was someone there, he didn't want to give them a chance to escape. He gripped tightly onto his racket. It would have to double up as a weapon. Once at the bushes he moved along the hedge, hitting out at the leaves hard, this way and that. He went behind the bushes and walked up and down the narrow gap between the vegetation and the perimeter fence of the complex, thwacking at the foliage. He stopped and stilled, listening carefully. There was nothing but silence. What was the matter with him? Was he imagining things?

"Jonah, are you ok?" called Miriam.

"Sorry, honey," he reassured. "I'm coming."

Back on court, he started feeding Miriam balls again. "Nice," he praised, "good swinging action. Now maybe take a couple of steps back and we'll try hitting a little farther."

She did as he asked and assumed ready position, racket in front of her nose and knees slightly bent. Jonah picked a ball out of the basket. His arm had already started swinging forward to meet it when, a nanosecond before impact, Jonah heard what he swore was coughing coming from the bushes. What the heck. He wasn't imagining it. Something, someone, was definitely there. Instead of his arm stopping, however, as his

281

brain knew that it should, for some reason it carried on swinging like an automaton, hitting the ball robotically, firing it in Miriam's direction. Fast, too fast. She couldn't possibly get her racket to it, nor could she move out of the way in time. Jonah was still looking at the bushes and didn't even realise what he'd done until it was too late.

"Ouch," squealed Miriam as the ball whacked her arm hard, very hard. She immediately comforted the pained area with her other hand, rubbing it up and down. Jonah jumped over the net and ran to her.

"Honey, I'm so sorry," he said, taking over the rubbing and inspecting the red imprint the ball had made on her flesh. "I'm an idiot. I wasn't concentrating."

He didn't dare tell her that he thought they were being watched and that's why he'd been distracted. Again he heard rustling from the bushes and a weird sound, a bit like a muffled sneeze. Miriam was bearing up. She was being brave and, thankfully, wasn't crying. He wanted more than anything to go back to those damn bushes to investigate but the responsible adult in him knew that it would be better to tend that wound first.

"Come on," he led her away from the court, "let's get some ice and Arnica onto you before it's too late."

282

CHAPTER NINETEEN

CLAIRE

Claire wasn't an 'eye for an eye, a tooth for a tooth' kind of person. She was more an 'I can't possibly even kill a mosquito' type of woman who adhered to Zen and Buddhist principles that harming should be avoided in all but the most extreme of circumstances. And despite her fear of wasps, the couple of times she'd been stung by one, her instinct had been to set it free, as opposed to the more natural reflex action of thwacking it into a gooey mush with a rolled up magazine. She didn't believe in retribution, so it was quite bizarre that she experienced a sense of satisfaction watching Anthony's unease at being in Jonah's villa. He hadn't wanted to enter, but Jonah insisted, making it hard for him to refuse. Anthony was shifting uneasily from one foot to the other, surveying the property in a peculiar manner, eyes circling and darting from left to right, as if he were committing an inventory of the place to memory. Either that or he was on drugs.

"Can I get you a drink or something?" Jonah asked.

"No."

283

Anthony's tone was clipped and, quite frankly, rude. A 'thank you' wouldn't have gone amiss and the lack of it seemed to echo round the room, a perfect example of how, sometimes, silence speaks louder than words. The silence didn't last long though. The girls ran down the stairs, filling the space with peels of giggles. Their sudden appearance seemed to make Anthony appear even more awkward. He looked from one to the other, shaking his head, as if he was trying to erase the vision of them. Where was the composed man that Claire had once known? Nothing normally fazed Anthony and he prided himself on being able to fit into any milieu. Something was clearly unsettling him. Perhaps he didn't like getting a taste of his own medicine, Claire wondered. Or perhaps it was just jet lag making him act queerly.

As soon as the girls reached the bottom step and caught the stern look on Anthony's face, their laughter stopped. Miriam ran up to Claire, hugging her so close it was as if she was trying to wriggle back into the womb. Perhaps Anthony couldn't accept that Claire was moving on. Well, it was tough. He'd been the first to move on and now it was his turn to face up to the situation. And he didn't know the rest of it! This was no longer just about Jonah. If Miriam hadn't been squishing her mother's stomach with her nose, Claire would have placed a protective hand over it, a gesture that would have guarded the

284

lives growing inside of her from the evil glare of her ex-husband.

"This is Martha," Claire introduced. "Martha this is Anthony, Miriam's dad."

Anthony barely acknowledged the introduction. He made the weirdest of noises, as if gutturally clearing his throat.

"Hello, Sir," Martha stepped forward, offering her hand.

Claire and Jonah made eye contact, clearly both on the same wave-length and both proud of Martha for taking the initiative and for being the bigger person of the two. Anthony was now forced into dialogue.

"Hi," he said, reluctantly taking her hand and shaking it. It's hard being rude to a polite child. It could almost be deemed abusive. "It's nice to meet you."

He didn't suggest she call him Anthony. The deferential 'sir' was probably pleasing to him. In court it was always 'My Lord' this or 'My lady' that or 'Pardon Your Honour'. So 'Sir' was speaking his language.

"Sir," Martha began shyly. "It's my birthday in two weekends' time and I'm having a party. It would be so cool if Miriam could come."

Martha looked towards Miriam, seeking corroboration that her new best friend would like to come but Miriam stayed still, breathing deeply into Claire's stomach, her hot breath making her mother's skin feel sticky underneath her t-shirt. Claire hadn't seen her daughter act like this in front of her father before. She was normally so excited to see him. What was going on? She shouldn't have let Anthony come here. Anthony had insisted on it for some reason and in the end she caved in.

"It's time to go," said Anthony, completely ignoring Martha's question and instead walking towards a small silver suitcase which was waiting by the front door. "The others are in the car outside."

"I don't want to go," Miriam whispered into Claire's flesh.

Goddamn it, Claire didn't want her to go either. She'd been dreading this moment and trying not to think of it these last few days but now she was actually starting to empathise with Anthony. If the roles were reversed and Miriam hadn't wanted to return to *her*, how awful would that feel? Claire crouched down and nuzzled her lips into Miriam's right ear.

"Come on darling," she whispered, "your Daddy loves you so much. I'm sure you're going to have a wonderful time. Mummy loves you very much too and we'll be together again soon."

Anthony held out his hand. Claire nudged her daughter away from her body, a manoeuvre which defied all of her maternal instincts. Miriam reluctantly unpeeled herself from her mother but she didn't go to her father. Instead she went to Martha, offering her a hooked little finger.

"Friends for life," she said as Martha hooked her finger with hers. Both of them looked deadly serious, as if this was some sort of ceremonial sealing of the deal.

"Friends for ever," said Martha.

Then Miriam looked at Jonah. He crouched down and held up his hand for a high five, but she ignored his hand, instead wrapping her arms around his waist, making him wobble a little. He chuckled as he lost balance and then placed his hands on Miriam's upper arms. She winced as he touched the sore bit where the ball had hit her yesterday.

287

"Oh, sorry, sorry," he apologised, taking his hands away and leaning forward to give her a quick peck on the forehead. "Bye kiddo," he nodded at her reassuringly as she finally stepped towards her father. "See you real soon."

"Enjoy the rest of your summer," said Anthony, the faintest of smiles finally creasing his lips. And then, as a subdued quiet descended upon the grand entrance hall of Lily Beach, Anthony opened the front door, took the suitcase in one hand and Miriam's palm in his other and they trailed slowly down the garden path.

Half an hour later Jonah left to take Martha back to her mother. "I won't be long," he promised before going. The silence which descended in their absence was eerie. Claire hadn't been alone in Lily Beach for a second since their arrival and it felt alien. First she stood in the hallway, still as a statue, staring at the closed front door for perhaps five, ten minutes, barely moving a muscle, her mind slowly filling with thoughts. She was pregnant. With twins. *Oh My God.* Part of her was exalted by this wonderful secret. Would they be boys, girls or one of each? Would they breed tennis players or nutritionists? Would they have red hair or blond, blue eyes or brown, a dimple on their cheek? Would their accent be English or American? She smiled as she thought of this and moved to the kitchen,

288

fidgeting with appliances, moving the scales to the right, the kettle to the left, the never-used-bread-maker to the corner. She couldn't settle. She opened the fridge. The smell from inside caused her to gag and she quickly shut it. She needed fresh air. She opened the patio doors, sliding them apart just enough so that she could squeeze through the gap and planted herself in the hammock.

Perhaps it was best not to think of the babies. Perhaps instead she should prepare for her imminent screen test with ABC. They'd asked her to come up with ideas. Apparently they were recording a pilot and if the network liked what they saw, they might broadcast it. This was the biggest career break she would ever have in her life. There must be hundreds, nay thousands, of struggling actors and wannabe TV presenters who would be chomping at the bit for this break and Jonah kept insisting that they wouldn't be wasting their time on her if they weren't interested.

What would happen if she actually got the job? Would the fact that she was pregnant affect the situation? Would they still want her? This thought sobered her. Just seeing Anthony reminded her of the practicalities. Much as she knew she would love the babies, they complicated everything. Where would they live? Claire didn't want a peripatetic lifestyle and that had been part of the problem years ago when she and Jonah had been together. Jonah was always moving around whilst Claire preferred to stay in one place. How would Miriam feel about moving to America? How would Anthony feel? If Jonah came to London, when would he see Martha? *Would* Jonah agree to come to London? What about her new career on *Morning Cuppa*? They were expecting her back in the UK in a month. Was she ready to lose all that she'd just gained career-wise? There was so much to think about.

All this and more whirred uncontrollably through Claire's head so that, by the time Jonah came back and found her in the hammock, greeting her with a casual "hi babe", she'd worked herself up into such a state that she burst out crying.

"Shush," he calmed, wrapping his arms tightly around her as he knelt by her side. "Let it out," he reassured. "It's just the hormones."

"Is it?" she sniffled, uncertain.

"That depends on what you're crying about."

"I'm crying about the babies."

"That's what I thought."

290

"How did you know?"

"Because I know you better than you think. Sometimes I wonder if I know you better than I know myself."

"So why am I crying about the babies then?"

Jonah hooked a finger under Claire's chin and turned her face so that she was looking at him.

"Because you're worried about how it's all going to work out – am I right?"

Claire smiled through her tears, nodding and then wiped her eyes with the back of her hand.

"And like I've told you, there's nothing that we can't work out together, absolutely nothing. Do you trust me?"

"Yes," she nodded again.

"Right then," he said, lifting her to sitting. "All this can and will be discussed later but, right now, we need to pull ourselves together because we're going out."

291

"Out? Out where?"

"Out to celebrate."

CHAPTER TWENTY

ANTHONY

Anthony was starting to wonder if he was bipolar. Mostly he was a loving father who absolutely doted on his little princess. More recently, however, he was finding that he had this alarming alter-ego. He was filled with such anger and hatred and, more worryingly, he felt increasingly out of control. He *never* felt out of control. He considered his ability to stay cool and calm under pressure to be one of his major assets. Half the barristers in London had at one time or other tried to emulate his 'look', which they'd amusingly labelled as the 'de Klerk', after his surname. Anthony chuckled as he thought of it, although he should have been alarmed, because the 'de Klerk' was in itself bipolar. The glassy intensity in his eyes had the power to perform the impossible – it could simultaneously unnerve and entrust. It was a look whose harshness made witnesses for the opposition crumble under his questioning and yet, at the same time, there was sensitivity in his gaze which made juries believe every word he was saying, even if it was a load of bullshit.

This California trip wasn't going well. He wanted to blame Ali for dreaming up the idea in the first place but he knew that was unfair. And actually, on the one hand it *had* been a success for all the reasons she'd suggested. *To beat the opposition you've got to understand them.* That was a maxim they swore by. It helped lawyers notch up victories. And Jonah was now the opposition although he didn't act like it; in fact, he acted irritatingly affably and it was hard to find fault with him. But, damn it, Anthony would. Because Jonah was becoming dangerously attached to Miriam and Anthony would not risk losing his precious daughter to another man. So it *had* been useful to come out to San Diego a couple of days early, to case the joint, so to speak, and to create a profile of the enemy. Not to mention the enemy's daughter. She'd really caught him off guard and her wanting to invite Miriam to her birthday party had been a humdinger. He seriously didn't want his daughter to attend. By rights he didn't need to. The party was during *his* contact time and every second of every day that he was entitled to spend with Miriam was precious. He didn't want to give up that time, and yet by saying 'no' he came across as the bad guy. He *had* already said 'no', a response which went down like a ton of bricks. Miriam accused him of being mean. "You don't care about what *I* want," she accused. "It's all about you." She'd never spoken like this to him before. Was this all Martha's influence? Anthony wished he'd been able to create a better profile of the enemy's daughter, but that had been difficult. Like her father, she'd been so goddamned polite.

Catching a glimpse of Lily Beach was the only part of the trip which had so far been a success. He'd made notes of several things which could come in handy as evidence later. He even had photographs to back up some of the evidence. It had been tricky. At one point he was nearly caught in the act but he not only managed to cleverly snap photos of what he now considered to be the key incident itself, he had post-incident exhibits too. And although she didn't realise it, his daughter was helping him as the lead witness. Who knew that such simple questions could elicit such crucial information? "Oh no," he said, observing the large red patch her arm. "How did that happen?" Even more interesting was when she told him about the zip-line. He knew about the zip-line because he'd tried to book it up for himself to go with Miriam, and failed. "How old is Martha by the way?" he asked vaguely, not wanting to make it seem as if he actually cared about the answer. She was tall and looked older than his daughter, but that meant nothing. The reply had come back as 'eight'. This titbit was duly added to the series of notes in his little black book.

This was all excellent stuff but, in other respects, Anthony was kicking himself for not having second-guessed how things might turn out. Why had he chosen to stay in San Diego? Of course Miriam was going to make comparisons. He'd rented a luxury two-bed property with its own small heated pool in the trendy and historic downtown Gaslamp Quarter. It was charming, brilliantly located, next to lots of restaurants, cute shops and museums, with pretty little streets and Victorian-style architecture. And yet when he asked Miriam what she thought of it she said "It's fine, but Jonah's place is nicer. It's literally on the beach."

It was hard keeping his cool. He'd spent a lot of time after hours in London creating an itinerary specifically designed to please Miriam. The day after he collected her he arranged to go to SeaWorld. "I've already been," she said flippantly. "Mummy filmed there and was given special VIP passes to take us afterwards. We did this amazing thing where we got into the water with the dolphins and learned how to communicate with them using hand commands. I kissed one of them on the nose and he even gave me a ride."

Anthony had already bought expensive, non-refundable tickets so they still went, and Miriam happily still enjoyed it. They managed to find shows and rides that she hadn't yet done but, nonetheless, Anthony was annoyed that Claire and Jonah had stolen his thunder. That evening he suggested they visit the zoo, thinking that Jasper would enjoy seeing the animals. "I've already been there," sniped Miriam, "twice." Anthony thought he was going to scream. He *wanted* to scream. If he could have escaped to another room to open a window, stick out his face

296

and shriek his frustration into the ether for the neighbours to hear, then he would have. They'd not gone to the zoo, even though Anthony and Ali wanted to see the polar bears and pandas. Instead they went to an aqua park full of water slides which Miriam loved and Jasper disliked. He was too young to appreciate it and the noise and water made him tetchy. Jet lag was messing with his sleep patterns and turning him into one of those babies other parents used as contraception. If they *had* been thinking about procreating in the near future, then one look at Jasper in action made them question their plans. Perhaps they were too ambitious taking a long haul trip with a baby. Whereas Miriam used to fuss and fawn over her little brother she now appeared disinterested. Who could blame her? Whining isn't endearing to anybody. Sensitive to the issue, Anthony suggested to Ali that he spend the following day with just Miriam. Ali wasn't overwhelmingly in favour of the idea but she didn't say no. Anthony found Miriam sitting in front of the television, watching an American version of *Come Dine with Me*.

"It's just you and me tomorrow," he sat down next to her. "The others are going to chill out here. Have you got any ideas?"

Perhaps giving her a choice would be more successful. She thought about it.

"Legoland," she said, like a question.

"What, you haven't already been to Legoland?"

Anthony was surprised. It was one of San Diego's premier attractions and he had it on the itinerary for later in their stay.

"Mummy filmed there, but we never went."

Anthony was delighted. Not that Claire had filmed there. That actually unsettled him. Maybe her career was going better than he'd given her credit for. But Legoland was perfect and Jasper would be too young to enjoy it anyway, so at least Ali wouldn't feel she was missing out. Plus Ali had an aversion to theme parks. Ah-ha, suddenly another idea popped into his head. Whilst the word *Disney* made him feel slightly queasy, with all its stomach-churning rides and plastic saccharine sparkle, it might just be the answer to his prayers.

On the television screen, a hippy Californian lady was busy constructing her own homemade organic pork sausages, mincing the meat and piping it into casings. Miriam stared at the screen transfixed. Anthony was thinking why bother, it would be much easier to buy them from the butchers.

"Would you like to go to Disneyland?" he asked.

In a flash her attention shifted from the sausages to him, proof of the power of Disney.

"Really?" she asked, her eyes popping out of her head.

Anthony hadn't cleared it with Ali, but why didn't he and Miriam go to Los Angeles for a few days? Disneyland was easily reachable from there and it would offer a change of scenery. Plus, at least that was somewhere she hadn't yet been.

"Absolutely," he said.

"You bet," she said. "That would be awesome."

There was an American twang to the way Miriam now spoke. She was definitely emulating Martha and a stop needed to be put to it.

Miriam flung her arms around Anthony's neck. It was the nicest she'd been to him since he'd fetched her.

"Thank you so much Daddy," she said.

"It's a pleasure darling."

299

He grimaced over her shoulder as they hugged. Now all he needed was for Ali to agree that she and Jasper should be left behind. Much as Anthony would prefer not to go there himself, it would definitely be worth it. Because crucially, this Disney trip would definitely, unequivocally and cunningly be coinciding with Martha's party.

Sleep deprived as a result of Jasper's unsettled nights, Ali didn't fancy cooking dinner so Anthony ordered takeaway pizzas: pineapple and ham for himself, margherita for Ali and pepperoni for Miriam. Anthony raised an eyebrow at the pepperoni. "Are you sure?" he checked. When it came to pizza she always played it safe with cheese and tomato. "Martha always has pepperoni," she explained. A muted 'huh' left Anthony's throat. Of course it had something to do with Martha.

Nonetheless, the pizzas went down well and even though Anthony doubted that she would, Miriam *did* eat the pepperoni. As her father, he knew he should be delighted not only that she was broadening her culinary horizons, but that she was making new friends and seemed happy. If only it were that simple. He wanted her all to himself and was jealous. A bigger man might have been able to handle this complicated scenario better and risen above the green-eyed monster. Nobody taught you how to deal with creating new, blended families. It was hit and miss, trial and error, and a torturous journey of making it up as you went along. So far, the merger of everyone's twisted lives felt like a complicated, knotted ball of wool. Untie one knot, but then you find another. The ball of wool wouldn't and couldn't ever return to its former shape, tug, pull and try as he might. Not that he would ever admit it to her but Claire had handled everything much better than he had.

Their rented apartment wasn't huge, but it was comfortable, especially the lounge with its plush suede sofa suite and its showpiece, wall-mounted flat screen TV. Chilling in front of the television chewing pizza was a nice way to round off the day. Perhaps that's what they'd all needed. An easy-going twenty-four hours to recharge and regroup. Jasper had thankfully fallen asleep early, leaving just the three of them to enjoy some peaceful grown-up conversation. Ali was having a nice chat with Miriam, asking about her stay in San Diego. Miriam was responding and opening up. It felt like the two of them were bonding and Anthony was grateful to just sit back and flick between sports channels as they spoke, with one ear on their dialogue. He yawned and checked his watch. It was 8.55pm and they were going to LegoLand tomorrow.

"Princess," he interrupted their discussion about some funky clothes boutique in Coronado. "I think it's time for bed. We've got a big day ahead."

"Oh my God," she clapped a hand over her mouth. "I nearly forgot. What time is it?"

"Five to nine," said Anthony, laying down the remote control next to him on the sofa.

Miriam picked it back up and starting flicking through the channels until she reached ABC.

"Mummy said she might be on at 9 pm. There's this pilot for a new family-friendly food programme and she's in it."

For once Anthony resisted the temptation to guffaw and say "unlikely", even though he thought it was just that. Why on earth would Claire be on American TV, prime time, Saturday night? Miriam had surely got it wrong but he didn't dare risk the wrath of his daughter, not when everything appeared to be slowly getting back on track. Miriam kept looking at the face on Anthony's watch. 8.57….8.58….9.00….9.03…..No, it definitely wasn't going to happen, he was certain of it.

"Come on princess," he stood up, "perhaps you got the day muddled."

He offered his hand, trying to pull her up to standing, but she wriggled away from his grip and refused to budge, eyes glued to the screen. Then, sure enough, an announcer introduced a new show called *Taste of the Place.* The opening titles started running, a montage of fast-cut images which interlaced visuals of different dishes from around the globe with animated shots of both Claire and a preppy-looking all-American male TV Presenter examining food and tucking in.

"Look," Miriam started jumping up and down, finally on her feet, pointing at the television. "Did you see Mummy?"

Anthony *did* see Mummy and he was so not expecting it that his eyes nearly pinged out of their sockets. Bloody hell, what was Claire doing on American TV? It was implausible, impossible and inconceivable. Had Jonah Kennedy pulled some strings? The Presenter was called Chad Black. His name flashed up on screen as he started introducing the show, which had a studio audience and a set designed like a kitchen, with two separate work stations. The concept of the programme was to put American food under the microscope by comparing it to international cuisine. He introduced Claire. The name Claire Jackson, with the word Nutritionist written underneath it came

303

up on screen. It was strange for Anthony to see her using her maiden name. For most of his life he'd known her as Claire de Klerk. She smiled, she was calm, she was confident. Goddamn it, she was bloody radiant.

Claire: *Thanks Chad. Right, today we're going to look at hot breakfasts and we're going to pitch the American breakfast against the good old traditional British version and see which one is healthier. Do you have an opinion which one you think is better nutritionally, Chad?*

Chad: *I think I might do, but it's not for me to say. It's for viewers at home to decide and of course our studio audience. Studio audience, do you have your buzzers at the ready?*

Studio Audience: *Yes.*

The camera panned from a group of obese women towards a couple of stick-thin twenty-something girls. All of them were smiling broadly and had clearly been well 'warmed-up' prior to filming.

Chad: *Behind me is our health 'o' metre. Audience I want you to press your buzzers now, before we get cooking, to tell us which country you think makes the healthier cooked breakfast. Is it the US or the UK? You may vote now.*

A clock ticked for ten seconds whilst the camera focused on the health 'o' metre graph's two bars, one labelled US, the other UK. The green line on the bars eventually settled at a 70% to 30% vote in favour of America.

Chad: *Ok, that's the audience's first impression but, now, to help them properly make up their minds we're going to see how the dishes are prepared and to do that we've got two very special chefs. For the US team please welcome Mr. Benny from Benny's Diner.*

Studio audience: Big cheer and enthusiastic clapping as Mr. Benny enters stage left.

Claire: *And for the UK team please welcome none other than Mr. Gordon Ramsey.*

Gordon entered stage right. The audience didn't cheer for him, they positively roared. Gordon gave Claire a kiss on each cheek as he greeted her and took his place behind his cooking station. Miriam fell onto her knees and crawled right up close to the screen, just so she didn't miss anything. "Wow, I can't believe Mummy's with Gordon Ramsey," she said. Anthony's view was now partially blocked but perhaps that was just as well. The range of emotions coursing through his veins was

305

making him feel more multiple schizoid than bipolar. He was jealous. He was angry. He was scared. He was impressed. He was belittled. He was even a little in love. He was bloody, fucking confused. For the next half hour they watched Mr. Benny cook pancakes, apple sauce, syrup, waffles, cream, a couple of sausages and a couple of eggs, sunny side up. Claire and Chad asked him questions as he cooked and after he finished loading up a large oval plate with the goodies, scattering a few token blueberries on top, Claire looked into the camera, holding out her hands, smiled and said voila! Gordon Ramsay was up next. He prepared a feast of scrambled eggs, mushrooms, baked beans, bacon, sausages and black pudding. It all looked so good, it was making Anthony hungry.

"For those who don't know, what *is* black pudding?" Claire asked Gordon.

"It's a sausage which contains pork, dried pigs blood and suet. It's the dried blood which gives it its colouring."

"May I?" asked Claire, brandishing a fork.

The camera cut to someone in the audience pulling a disgusted face as Claire put a slice of sausage in her mouth.

"That's truly delicious," said Claire. "Anyone in the audience want to try?"

Chad went over to the studio audience brandishing a plate of small pieces of black pudding and a microphone, offering a morsel to anyone game enough to try and then asking what they thought of it. For the next half hour there were discussions about the nutritional content of the two breakfasts. The only remotely healthy thing on Mr Benny's plate was the few blueberries, and Claire spoke about how this was a super-food full of anti-oxidants which should be eaten plentifully. The apple sauce was apparently not even remotely healthy, despite the fact that its name sounded promising. No, it contained far too much high glucose corn syrup. By contrast, the British fry-up was packed with natural goodness in the mushrooms, baked beans and grilled tomatoes.

All in all, though it pained Anthony to admit it, it was a highly enjoyable show. If he'd been channel-hopping and had stumbled upon it, he would have stayed tuned in, if not just to watch Claire. She was irritatingly pleasing on the eye and lit up the screen. Who would have thought she had it in her? The end credits started to roll.

"I think your mummy was excellent, darling," Ali said to Miriam. "Don't you, Anthony?"

Begrudgingly Anthony nodded, but he couldn't bring himself to speak. Damn it, damn it, damn it. He rubbed the flat of a palm up and down over his forehead and right eye repeatedly, like a nervous tick. He wasn't quite sure how to process everything. It was all becoming a little bit too much. He could only hope that the rest of America thought *The Taste of the Place* was ridiculous.

As he put Miriam to bed, he consoled himself. This was just a one-off pilot, according to his daughter. It might never be commissioned as a proper series. And even if it were commissioned, there were ways and means that Anthony could prevent Claire from ever being part of it. Yes, he mustn't worry. At least now he had a better picture of the enemy, and that was all that mattered.

CHAPTER TWENTY-ONE

CLAIRE

Claire had always considered herself to be an excellent keeper of secrets. She despised gossip and if she was ever told to keep a piece of information close to her chest, then that is what she would do. A promise was a promise. As far as she could recollect, she had never divulged a secret and Georgia often told her that this was what elevated her from being not just a good friend, but a *great* friend. "I've always trusted you unconditionally," she once told her, "and I'm not sure that there's anyone else I would rely on more than you. Not even my mother."

The secret that Claire was guarding, however, was proving much harder to keep. She and Jonah had decided to wait at least another month before telling anyone about the twins. Jonah warned Claire that he had a meeting with his agent that morning and left first thing. Before departing he brought her a cup of hot water with lemon in bed and, after she heard the front door close, she sat up against the headboard and turned on her laptop to check emails. The silence in the house without either of the girls around took some getting used to but, although she felt guilty admitting it, there was something nice about it being just the two of them at the moment. It felt like the old days and she knew that these were moments to treasure. She laid a hand on her stomach. They might as well enjoy the peace whilst it lasted. In seven months time it would be mayhem.

She managed to read one email before Orlando Goodman video-called her on Skype. She was relieved to see that he looked vastly improved. Whilst she valued the power of nutrition when it came to health, she also knew it had its limitations. It would not and could not cure pancreatic cancer, much as she wished it were otherwise. And so she'd had another idea. Orlando might have eschewed conventional treatments for his illness but she'd heard good reports about an alternative therapy which involved the injection of mistletoe extracts. Again, this wouldn't be a cure, but she'd researched this plant and it seemed that it could vastly improve one's quality and length of life. Orlando had investigated further and had flown to Aberdeen in Scotland, one of the UK's leading mistletoe therapy centres, to commence treatment.

"I've got so much more energy," he told her, "and I'm sleeping far better. I feel like a new man. Thank you so much for suggesting it."

"That's what I'm here for," she said. "And I'm delighted it seems to be helping."

310

There was more colour in his face, his eyes were alive. Gone was his sickly, grey pallor. It offered hope. Perhaps miracles could come true.

"Enough of me," he said, "tell me about you. It looks like you're having a fabulous time out there from what I've seen on *Morning Cuppa.* And the California air clearly suits you. You're not going to want to come back. You're looking radiant dahling. Is there something you're not telling me?"

She hadn't meant to tell him, but withholding the information from him felt wrong. "I'm pregnant," she squealed unprofessionally, "with twins! But please don't say anything. I wasn't supposed to tell anyone yet." He was delighted for her and promised faithfully that her secret was safe with him. The problem was, however, that the moment she hung up on that call, another came in. This time it was her mother. Claire was finding it hard to concentrate. Dolores was filling her in on news about Claire's father and some grievance they were having with rowdy neighbours and all the time that Claire was politely nodding and interjecting with a smorgasbord of "oh no's" and "I can't believe it" she was thinking to herself: shall I tell my Mum?

She was desperate to. She couldn't wait to see the look on her face when she heard the news and was itching to share her excitement. Telling her would be the most natural thing in the world. Should she? Would Jonah care?

"Darling, are you actually listening to me?" asked Dolores.

The sharp tone in her mother's voice snapped Claire away from her musings.

"Of course I am. Why?"

"Because I just asked you three times to remind me what date you are coming home and you replied 'I can't believe it'."

Claire giggled, although it wasn't actually that funny. Without meaning it to be, her 'I can't believe it' response was a fair representation of how she was feeling. She couldn't believe she was going to have to go home. She didn't want to go home. It felt wrong to go home now. She didn't want to think about the fact that in three weeks she would be back in London.

"Sorry," Claire apologised, "but I've got a lot on my mind."

"Is everything ok there dear?"

"Yes…….no…….yes…..I mean-

Claire burst out crying.

"I'm sorry," Claire found herself apologising again, laughing through the tears. "I'm not even sad. I'm actually really happy."

"You don't look so happy," said Dolores uncertainly.

Claire couldn't hold it in a second longer.

"I'm pregnant," she blurted.

Just telling her mother instantly made her feel better. She wiped her eyes and beamed. Dolores shrieked so loudly that Claire covered her ears with her hands.

"That's wonderful news," squealed Dolores, once she'd finally calmed down. "When's it due?"

"*It*?" asked Claire, teasingly.

"Yes, *it*," replied Dolores. And then, thinking she'd understood why Claire was teasing, she added, "By *it* I mean the baby."

313

"That's the thing," said Claire, pausing for dramatic effect. "It's not just one baby, it's two. We're having twins."

Claire remembered breaking the pregnancy news about Miriam. Telling people you're going to have a baby is exciting stuff, but somehow telling people you're having *twins* feels even more special. Dolores shrieked again, so loud and long that Claire didn't hear Jonah entering the room. She started when he put a hand on her arm.

"Oh my God," she said, turning her attention temporarily away from her mother. "You're back. Hello."

"Yes I'm back," Jonah smiled at Dolores on the screen. "Hello Mrs J. What's with all the screaming ladies? Have I interrupted something?"

"I'm sorry Jonah," Claire admitted, "I've just told my mum."

"I hear congratulations are in order," said Dolores.

"Thank you," said Jonah, sitting down next to Claire and wrapping his arm around her shoulder. "You're the first to know other than ourselves. We're very excited."

"Twins," said Dolores, shaking her head, "I can't believe it."

314

"Yep," he grinned, "a ready made doubles tennis team."

"Oh my God," said Dolores, clapping a hand over her mouth and going straight for the jugular with her questioning. Like mother, like daughter, the same concerns floated round their heads. "But where are you two going to live? Does that mean I'm going to have to fly to America?"

"Bring a sweater with you," said Jonah an hour later, after Claire had eaten breakfast and taken a shower. "We're going out."

"But it's baking hot," Claire objected. "What will I need a sweater for?"

"It might be a bit cooler where we're going."

"Where are we going?"

Claire loved Jonah's spontaneity and the fact he liked to surprise her. Anthony had rarely done anything on a whim. In fact, it was always she who made the plans and he just fell in with whatever she'd organised. It made a pleasant change to have someone else taking charge of her social diary. Although with Jonah, she didn't much mind about social arrangements. She could stay at home with him all day every day and it would be heavenly.

"We're going to the mountains."

"The *mountains* – do I need to pack?"

In all the times that Claire had been to San Diego Jonah had never taken her to the mountains. She wasn't even sure where they were.

"No," Jonah chuckled, "it's only an hour away."

Claire's black cardigan was draped over the back of one of the dining room chairs. She pulled it off and followed Jonah to the front door.

"Why are we going there?"

"I thought the air would do you good. And getting away from here will at least stop you from telling any *more* people about our secret," he reprimanded, kissing the tip of her nose.

"Sorry," she apologised again, as he closed the front door behind them.

"It really doesn't matter," he said, pointing the car key at the Porsche Cayenne and clicking it. "I actually don't care who knows. It was you who minded. And look how much happiness it gave your mother."

Claire sat back and relaxed in the car as Jonah drove them along the scenic twists of the Sunrise Highway. The narrow, gentle road somehow mirrored Claire's mood. She was feeling calmer about the pregnancy now, even excited. Jonah was right. They would and could work it all out. And the fact that it was two babies and not just one somehow seemed to make up for the past. It all felt like it was meant to be. Claire stroked the back of his neck as they wound through forests which eventually thinned out into desert down on her right. Pharrell Williams' *Happy* started playing on the radio. Claire was about to say that despite how much she loved the song, she thought the radio station was playing it too much when her phone rang.

"Don't answer," said Jonah. "Today is now about you and me."

Claire looked down at the screen.

"It's Will Ryan from ABC," she said.

"That call you *answer* woman," he barked, smiling. "Quick. And whatever you do, *don't* tell him you're pregnant."

Welcome to Julian. That's what the sign said as they approached a remote and achingly pretty mountain village. Parking up outside the Café and Bakery, which resembled a Western-style saloon with a wooden clapboard façade, Claire finally ended the call to Will Ryan. She turned to Jonah, eyes wide and took a deep breath.

"Oh, my God," she whispered.

"Good news, huh?" he grinned.

"It's been commissioned. The powers that be loved *Taste of the Place* and they've ordered a series of twelve hour-long shows with me in it and, apparently, Gordon Ramsey is going to feature in each episode too. They love the whole British vibe thing going on. I'm in shock."

"I'm so proud of you," Jonah leaned across to kiss her, planting a hand on her abdomen as he did so. "I'm so proud of all of you."

"Filming starts at the beginning of October. I'll definitely be showing by then, perhaps even earlier because its twins but you told me not to tell them I was pregnant. Don't you think I should call back and come clean?"

"I think," said Jonah, moving to get out the car, "that we should go for a walk and think about it and then we can discuss it over lunch. Good plan?"

"Good plan," she agreed, standing up and slamming the car door behind her. "Mm, something here smells delicious."

"This bakery is famous for its apple pie. In fact, the whole of Julian is famous for its apples as well as its pies."

"Is that why you've brought me here?"

"No," Jonah smirked, "I just fancied a change of scenery."

He linked her hand in his and they started ambling towards a mountain lake. The narrow lanes and rickety shops felt like they were from a bygone era. Some horses and carriages even trotted by. They swung their clasped hands and breathed in the pure air.

"I didn't see my agent this morning by the way," Jonah started, "I met with an attorney."

"You met with an attorney?"

Claire was slightly alarmed. She'd spent years married to a lawyer and between Anthony and the divorce she'd had enough of attorneys to last a lifetime.

"Duchess," Jonah's voice was serious. "We've got two babies on the way and a lot of decisions which need to be made. Whether you like it or not, I have a feeling that we will need help from a professional. I'm not convinced your ex-husband is going to like what we've got planned."

Claire knew that Jonah was right. In fact, he was more than right. And they didn't need any old attorney. They needed the best. Anthony was no pushover.

"Is your lawyer good?"

"My lawyer has put me in touch with an expert in the field and that's who I met today."

"Go on," Claire whispered, her mouth turning dry. "Tell me what he said?"

Julian is a historic mining town. After a long leisurely walk during which they chatted about their future as they circled a sparkling blue lake surrounded by foothills, Claire and Jonah passed a place where you could pan for gold.

"Want to try?" Jonah joked.

"Nah," said Claire, "I'm more a silver kind of gal."

He nodded and seemed pleased by her response. A few minutes later they were back at their car outside the Café and Bakery where the aroma of fresh baking engulfed them tantalisingly. Claire peered through the glass shop front at the trays of pastries.

"Shouldn't we get some?" Claire suggested. "That apple pie smells and looks amazing."

"No," said Jonah. "Save yourself for lunch. I'm taking you to the hottest place in town."

They returned to the car and drove a few miles down the road until they arrived at a bistro called Jeremy's On the Hill. Claire had never seen something quite so un-American in America. It was more akin to a quaint farmhouse in the French countryside. The inside was cosy and romantic. White linen tablecloths

321

were dressed with wine glasses to accompany every course. But Jonah had a different plan. He'd reserved a table on the pretty outdoor patio. "It's more private," he said as they sat down and the waitress handed them menus.

"Would you like an aperitif?" the waitress asked.

"Yes," Jonah was quick to answer. "Two glasses of champagne please."

"And a bottle of sparkling water," added Claire.

Once the waitress had gone, Claire reminded Jonah that she wasn't allowed alcohol.

"A little bit won't hurt," he said.

She began perusing the menu - gourmet burgers and salads, with lots of interesting starters and sides, one of which, impressively, was crispy Brussels sprouts. Claire had long been extolling the virtues of this humble vegetable to her clients, but in England she'd never seen it on a cordon bleu menu.

"Wow," she spoke out loud. "Brussels sprouts?"

"It's their signature dish. You've got to try them. They're sensational. And the lobster bisque is good too."

The waitress returned with two flutes of champagne and a pad to take their order. Jonah asked for Bison burger with garlic herb fries and Claire chose two starters instead of a main course, with Jonah promising to let her have a taste of his Bison. Once the waitress had gone, Jonah stared at her strangely, furrowing his brow. It was unsettling.

"What's the matter?" she asked, self-consciously touching her face, wondering which part of it was bothering him.

"You've got a weird rash," he said, "across your nose and cheeks."

She ran a finger over the area in question, expecting to feel bumps or soreness, but nothing. It didn't remotely hurt. Perhaps pregnancy was starting to do weird things to her body.

"You sure it's not the light?"

"If you don't trust me, go look in a mirror."

Claire scraped back her chair and headed indoors, asking for directions to the Restrooms. Once there, she stared intensely at her reflection but, in her opinion, she looked completely normal. Perhaps a few more freckles since she'd arrived in California but nothing more sinister. She washed her hands and headed back outside.

"I can't see anything," she said.

He eyed her intensely.

"Wow, that's strange. It's completely gone. Weird."

Something wasn't right. Jonah wasn't right. He was acting strangely. How could a rash just vanish? He wrapped his fingers round the long stem of his glass.

"To your new job," he toasted, "and to our ready made mixed doubles tennis pair."

He raised his glass.

"Oh," Claire retorted, "you're convinced it's a boy *and* a girl now?"

"Absolutely," he grinned, looking at her glass and motioning that she should raise it to the toast too. She picked it up and tinkled his glass with hers.

"Thank you for making me the happiest woman in the world," she whispered.

"No," he was adamant. "Thank *you* for making *me* the happiest man alive."

He lifted his glass to his lips and watched her do the same.

"Ugh," she said as she took a sip, slamming the glass straight back down on the table.

"What, you can't take the alcohol?"

"No," she said, staring at the glass. "There's something in my drink."

Her eyes grew wide as she fished her fingers into the champagne and drew out the article in question. She stared wordlessly at the object she was now holding between her fingers, a thick silver band topped with a large square diamond which was sparkling like a kaleidoscope in the sunlight.

"Will you marry me?" he whispered.

"Oh," she gasped, clapping a hand over her chest. She burst out crying as she nodded.

"Your signals are a little confusing," Jonah murmured, eyes twinkling. "Is that a yes or a no?"

"Yes," she laughed through her tears. And then, a little louder, "yes."

They stood up, hugging and kissing and then Claire pulled away, to slide the ring onto her fourth left finger. It was the perfect fit, the perfect taste.

"Silver," she said. "You knew I liked silver better than gold."

"It's actually white gold which just looks like silver."

She kissed him hard and long and deep. It was a kiss so full of passion and intent that, had there been other diners on the patio, they might have averted their gaze.

"I've always wanted to marry a Kennedy," she whispered into his lips, a half-joke.

"And I," said Jonah, "have always wanted to marry a Duchess."

326

CHAPTER TWENTY-TWO

ANTHONY

"Good morning sir," welcomed Jon the clerk as Anthony entered his law chambers. "Did you have a good holiday?"

"Yes thank you, Jon," Anthony replied before sprinting up the narrow spiral staircase which wound to his office.

"I've left your mail on your desk," Jon called behind him.

Anthony wasn't certain why he tried to sprint the stairs. It's not as if he was infused with energy and zest. Perhaps he was just trying to convince himself that he was feeling brighter than he actually was. Half the battle against fatigue and depression lay in the mind, he was convinced of it. So, if he could think himself positive then he might actually start to feel positive. And, fond though he was of the clerk, he certainly didn't want Jon to suspect there was anything troubling him. Jon was one of the biggest gossips he knew. No, Anthony's private business needed to stay just that: private.

Anthony had always looked forward to his holidays. One of the rewards for working so hard, which he did, was to play hard too. Vacationing gave him the chance to unwind and recharge, to prepare himself for the harsher months which lay ahead. It was only September 1st but already it felt like winter. A brief hailstorm rained down on him as he made his way from the tube station to his Chambers, the sharp hail stones pricking his skin. He prayed it wasn't an omen of what was to come. Whilst he was pleased to be back in London and Jasper certainly appeared to be happier at home, what *would* be missed was the wall-to-wall California sunshine. That was definitely something Anthony could get used to. In all other respects, however, their holiday had been far from a hit. It hadn't been a total whitewash. There were some high points. They had a great time in Los Angeles where they found a new hotel in a district called Korea Town, whose streets felt so authentic that Miriam kept asking if he was sure they weren't in Asia. Then there was their road trip to the Joshua Tree National Park in the desert. On a sunrise trek they were greeted by a snake wrapping its sinewy body around a rock, flicking out its venomous tongue, daring them to approach. Thankfully nobody was hurt and it was an event whose story had grown like Chinese whispers so that now, when they spoke of it, what began as a distant sighting had morphed into a description of their scary brush with death. A few days later they hopped across the border into Tijuana, Mexico. So yes, they'd brought back with them several outstanding memories but even these highlights were somewhat fraught. Either Jasper had been fussing or Miriam was complaining. "It's too hot." "I don't like the food." "Shut up, Jasper." Plus Anthony and Ali, who were normally solid as a team, were bickering far too much for his liking. The dynamic of the trip hadn't been good and, now that they were home, Anthony very much hoped things would settle down.

He ran a hand through his hair as he surveyed the pile of mail on his desk. It wasn't a pile, it was a tower. That was another downside of going away. There was all the catching up to do on the return. He set down his briefcase by the side of his desk and picked up the wedge of letters. One by one he examined their exteriors. Junk mail went straight in the bin. Boring brown envelopes were siphoned into a separate pile to be looked at later. Anything that looked interesting or important he tore open. A bank statement; an order for a new wig and gown from Ede & Ravenscroft; correspondence from the Old Bailey regarding a date change for a trial and a rich cream A3 envelope bearing an American stamp and postmark. He hesitated before opening the letter from America. Could it be a bill? Had he incurred a speeding fine without realising it? He felt uneasy. In the right hand corner in bold black italics was the name of the firm it was sent from: **Quinn, Sullivan & Pentecost**.

The paper was expensive and excellent quality. Ridiculous though it might sound to the layman, in terms of legal stature, quality of paper means everything. This paper told Anthony that the sender was a force to be reckoned with. He tore at the envelope furiously, but the paper was so thick that it was hard to open. Or was it just that his hands were shaking? Eventually he created a big enough tear for the letter to be extracted.

Dear Mr. Anthony Aidan de Klerk

We hereby inform you that an emergency application has been filed by Claire Ruth Sarah Jackson, formerly known as Mrs Anthony Aidan de Klerk, for leave to remove your daughter Miriam Anisia de Klerk from the British jurisdiction to reside with her in San Diego, California, USA.

An emergency hearing has become necessary due to a change in Claire Jackson's circumstances. She has recently learned that she is with child and is engaged to be married to California resident Mr Jonah Stephan Kennedy. She also has work commitments in the USA which will commence in October.

A date for the hearing has been set for September 15th. Attached are forms to be filled in at your earliest convenience and filed to ... ...

Blah, blah and bloody, fucking blah – Anthony tossed the letter face down on the table and buried his face in his hands, trying to process it all. Claire was pregnant? Claire was getting married? *Claire wanted to live in the US?* Anger began bubbling dangerously in his belly, like the core of a volcano building towards eruption. He wanted to spew, to shout, to pierce the wall with his fist. He'd feared this might happen, but not quite this fast. Claire was daring to take Miriam away from him to live in America? Instead of finding the wall with his fist, he found it with his cranium. Four words came from his mouth and he accentuated each one with a head butt. "No – bloody – fucking - way."

As he nursed his bruised brow, his first thought was to call Ali. But then he remembered that she was also returning to work today after a period of maternity leave and the only reason that they hadn't come in together was because she was busy setting things up with the childminder to make the transition for Jasper as smooth as possible. Ali had been extremely stressed these last few days. She was jet lagged, she'd been weaning Jasper off the breast, she was nervous about coming back to work and about leaving the baby. He'd tried to be as supportive as possible, reassuring her that she was doing the right thing by going back to work but, nonetheless, cutting the cord from

331

Jasper made her feel like she was being a bad mother. So no, Ali almost certainly wouldn't want to hear his woes about Miriam, not right now.

Anthony paused to consider what she'd say to him if he did ask for her advice. He wasn't even certain she was capable of being impartial. Ali liked Miriam and had always done her best to be compassionate and treat her well, but would she miss it if Miriam weren't there, if the court granted Claire permission to take her to the States? In many ways Miriam's absence would make Ali's life easier. Many of the problems they'd faced in the last couple of months had been *because* of Miriam. But perhaps Anthony was being unfair. Despite these troubles, Ali would always want the best for Anthony. And the best for him was most certainly not having his daughter spirited away to the other side of the world? When would he see her? Flying back and forth across the Atlantic on a regular basis wasn't cheap. It was also exhausting. Was this what was to become of his life?

No, no, no. This wasn't what was to become of his life because he wasn't going to let it. He had an important murder trial to prepare for and conferences set up for most of the morning but all that would have to wait. This was much more important. His children meant more to him than anything and he would fight tooth and nail to keep them close by. Claire was free to live wherever she wanted but that didn't mean she was going to be able to take Miriam with her. Over his dead body would he ever allow that to happen! He tapped his lips with an index finger, contemplating. If Claire was going to use the pompous-sounding **Quinn, Sullivan & Pentecost,** then he needed to better it. That American firm probably wasn't even specialised in family law at all, let alone the vagaries of *British* family law, but Anthony knew someone who was. And they were the best. If anyone could make sure that Miriam would never be taken from the country then David Sherwood QC could. He picked up his handset and called down to the clerks' office. "Hello, Jon," he said, "Could you get me the number for David Sherwood please?"

Half an hour later, after a long conversation with David Sherwood QC, Anthony was feeling much more positive about his situation. "Well done, well done, excellent work," David praised when Anthony talked through the evidence he'd so far managed to compile against Jonah and Claire. "That's all looking extremely promising."

"Do you think I've got a strong case?" asked Anthony.

It was odd having the tables reversed. It was usually clients who asked *him* that question.

"I'm sure you're aware that the law leans very heavily in favour of keeping a child with their mother but you do have some very compelling evidence and there have been a few surprise cases more recently where judges seem to be leaning towards the father."

Anthony could feel a weight lifting from his shoulders. This was exactly what he needed to hear. That there was still hope and that he could make this happen. David Sherwood paused for a moment and then restarted.

"But I must warn you, there is more to consider. From what you have told me, you and your ex-wife have had an extremely amicable arrangement to date. If we do win the case there will be a lot of bitterness towards you because you will be preventing her from leading her life, or at least making it very difficult to do so. What you have to decide is whether you are ready for that kind of resentment. It could also turn your daughter against you long term. Have you considered what she might want? Do you think she would prefer to go to America and be with a happy mother or to stay at home and be with a mother who feels straight-jacketed?"

It was all so damn complicated, but surely Miriam wouldn't want to leave her father behind if she had a choice.

"Miriam and I are very close," Anthony insisted. "I'm sure she'd rather stay in London than live in San Diego. Her friends are all here. Her family is all here."

He didn't bother mentioning that actually neither of his parents lived in the UK.

"How do you feel about social services interviewing your daughter?"

David Sherwood said this like a statement, but its content felt loaded. Was it right to involve Miriam in this? Should her opinion count? Should she be put in the unenviable situation of choosing?

"I'm sure that would be fine," he decided.

The phone line crackled as the discussion ceased.

"Right then," said David Sherwood, "we are pressed for time, so if you could furnish me with all the documentation and supporting evidence as soon as possible, that would help expedite matters."

"But you do think I have a solid case?" Anthony checked again, anxious for reassurance.

"It could get a bit ugly, but I most certainly do believe that the evidence you have garnered might well turn the odds in your favour."

Phew, that's all Anthony needed to hear. As he put the phone down, shards of sunlight beamed through the window. From hailstones to sunshine, perhaps this was a sign of things to come. Jonah Kennedy, Anthony thought to himself, you better watch out. You have no idea what's coming your way. By the time I've finished with you, your character assassination will be complete. I'll expose you to the world for the man you really are. Even Claire won't come out of this unscathed. But who cares? It was their fault. They asked for it. They pushed me too far, trying to take Miriam away from me. Ah yes, and before the hearing there was one more thing that Anthony needed to do. He hadn't discussed it with David Sherwood QC, but he didn't need to. This was a little something he planned even before he received that damned letter from **Quinn, Sullivan & Pentecost.** If Claire was going to play dirty, then so could he. He picked up the phone again and called the clerks office.

"Hello again, Jon," he said, a smile finally returning to his voice. "Could you get me the telephone number for ABC Television's head office in America please?"

CHAPTER TWENTY-THREE

CLAIRE

It was only a few days since Claire had left Jonah and San Diego behind but his absence was already an aching void in her chest. Even though he'd never lived with her in 77 Gladstone Road, she missed his presence in every nook and cranny of the house as if he were a permanent fixture that had been removed. She was counting down the days that they'd be together again, even if the purpose for him being there *was* for what had the potential to be the most unsavoury episode of her life: the court case. The anxiety about the imminent hearing was hovering over her like a black cloud. Without Jonah's reassuring presence, doubt crept into her mind like an unwelcome parasite.

Keeping busy helped keep the demons at bay. She was currently en route to visit Orlando Goodman and after that she was heading to *Morning Cuppa* for a meeting with Editor Richard followed by lunch with Georgia. And then tonight was the night. Tonight she would tell Miriam not just about the babies but about her plans to relocate to America. Three key conversations would take place in just one day. She was apprehensive about all of them but it was the one which would happen at home, later, that filled her with the most dread. What if Miriam hated the idea of bidding farewell to her friends? What if she hated the concept of yet another new sibling, let alone that two of them would arrive simultaneously? What if she blamed her mother for ruining her life? Thankfully the cycle of torturous 'what-ifs' was broken by her arrival at Orlando's Kings Cross maisonette. As she stepped out of her car she soberly reminded herself how insignificant her troubles were compared to Orlando's.

She tugged at the doorbell pulley, smiling at the church bell peels which rang out in response. Orlando opened the door. Despite the fact that he was beaming, he looked ghostly. How on earth was he carrying on performing in the theatre?

"Finally," she picked her words carefully. "It's wonderful to be with you in the flesh instead of seeing you on a screen,"

She felt this even more acutely with Jonah, who she'd spoken to on Skype several times since returning to London. Granted, it was miraculous that technology allowed you to see a person as you spoke to them on the other side of the world but that's where the magic ended. She now considered that seeing someone you love frozen behind a glass panel was a cruel tease. It reminded you of quite how far away and untouchable they were. Orlando closed the front door and pulled her in for a hug, instead of his usual double kiss air greeting.

"Dahling, you're looking more radiant than ever. May I?"

His hand hovered above her stomach, waiting for permission. She nodded. He closed his eyes as the flat of his palm met her lower abdomen which was covered loosely in a thin white muslin shirt. About a half minute passed until he raised his hand and opened his eyes.

"I know what you're going to have," he said.

"Excuse me?"

"There's a psychic gene running through my family. Disbelieve me if you will, but I can tell the sex of your babies."

Claire rolled her eyes, chuckling.

"Jonah's latest guess is that it's a boy and a girl."

Or was it two girls? He changed his mind the whole time. Orlando led her into the kitchen where he found a pad of yellow post-its and started writing. Once finished, he tore off the slip of paper and handed it to her. The note was signed and dated.

I predict you're having two boys.

"We'll see," she laughed.

Claire slipped the note into her bag and swapped it for a small carton which she handed over.

"This is for you."

"Salty Sisters?" read Orlando, perusing the box.

"I bought you these in San Diego," she explained. "Salty Sisters are two Californian women who started up a company which makes salted toffees. They are the most sensational thing you will ever put in your mouth and dangerously addictive."

She'd been with Miriam and Martha shopping in Whole Foods when one of the Salty Sisters offered them samples to taste: salted toffees, salted caramels, some coated in chocolate, others iced in coffee. Whilst the salty sister and Claire chatted, the girls quietly gorged on the samples, practically depleting supplies. Partly because she was embarrassed and partly

340

because Claire herself found the confectionary divine, she bought more than a dozen boxes back to the UK as presents.

"They're packed with sugar," Orlando read the label. "I thought I wasn't allowed sugar."

She wondered if what she was about to say was breaking the Nutritionist's code of conduct.

"Some things," she said "are worth breaking rules for. At least they're gluten-free and I'm sure a little a day won't hurt you."

Orlando sat down at the table and patted the bench next to him.

"I wanted to thank you so much," he said as she sat down. "I really value all that you've done for me. You've been a real source of support and comfort, even from the other side of the Atlantic."

"It's been my pleasure," she said, taking out her notebook. "So tell me, how are things? Is the mistletoe therapy still working for you? Do you feel as if you're improving?"

He shook his head and removed the pen and notebook from her clasp, laying them on the table.

"There's nothing more you can do for me Claire," he said. "I'm literally riddled with the stuff. Every day that I'm here is borrowed time. I'd prefer to hear about those little boys growing inside of you as well as that not so little boy of yours that lives in America. What does the future hold for you? And before you go, we must put a date in the diary for me to meet him."

Three hours later, Claire and Georgia were sitting in Gourmet Pizza, a bustling artisan restaurant on the South Bank, overlooking the Thames. Georgia was tucking hungrily into her Hawaiian pizza whilst Claire toyed with her avocado and bacon salad.

"I'm not hungry," Claire complained. "I don't know if it's the jet lag or because seeing Orlando was so upsetting, or the hormones -

"The *hormones?*" Georgia quizzed.

Oops, Claire had forgotten that her pregnancy was still a secret. Damn, she hated lying, but she shouldn't tell Georgia when even Miriam wasn't yet aware.

"Um, yes," she forked a tiny cube of avocado into her mouth, "I'm premenstrual."

Georgia screwed up her eyes and looked down at Claire's belly.

"I'm a witch too," she said.

"What do you mean?"

"I know that you're pregnant."

"What are you talking about?"

"Every time I suggested that you order something which contained goats cheese you straight away snapped 'no'. I know that you normally *love* goat's cheese. So I can only deduce that means you're pregnant. See, now that *I'm* pregnant, I know the things that you're not supposed to eat."

Georgia smiled smugly, displaying pride in her detective skills.

"That's really not it at all," Claire stuttered.

"Oh, come on," Georgia wouldn't let it go. "I can *see* that you're pregnant. You're showing."

"How do you know I haven't just got fat and am now very insulted?"

"Because your boobs are enormous," Georgia whispered, illustrating quite how big they were with her hands.

Claire knew she couldn't keep up the pretence.

"That's because there are two," she whispered back.

"Thankfully there are two," Georgia was confused. She still thought they were talking about breasts.

"Two *babies*," Claire hissed.

Georgia's eyes widened.

"Twins?" she mouthed.

Claire nodded. And then she started crying.

"I'm sorry," she apologised. "I'm tired and seem to be crying at everything at the moment. And I miss Jonah."

She'd put a date in the diary for Jonah to meet Orlando just before the court case. At the back of her mind now was the thought: I hope he makes it. Georgia got up to hug her.

"That's wonderful news. Our children will be the same age and can grow up together."

"Oh Georgia," Claire touched her friends arm, suddenly piqued by the thought that if all went as planned, her best friend Georgia wouldn't be round the corner any more. Miriam wasn't the only one who would lose out. There would be adjustments for them all. "There's so much to tell you."

"So tell me, that's what I'm here for."

The next hour was pure catharsis as Georgia listened to her friend's American escapades. "I often think about the fact that if you and Jonah hadn't crossed paths in that studio, none of this would be happening. I've got you and fate to thank for that," said Claire, patting a hand on her stomach and adding: "and these." She paused a second, contemplating. "And I've got you to thank for me getting that job at ABC. Without you I wouldn't even be working in TV. Georgia, you *are* a witch. You have single-handedly helped turn my life around. What am I going to do without you?"

"I'm not going anywhere," Georgia said.

Claire stilled and laid down her fork.

"No, but *I* probably am."

Claire admitted this with a hint of sadness, but Georgia insisted it was the right thing to do, reminding her that the world wasn't such a big place anymore. There were holidays and Georgia promised resolutely that, from now on, she would always spend hers in America.

"I'm jumping the gun," Claire became pensive. "I've asked for permission to take Miriam out the country. There's a hearing on September 15th but there's every possibility that the Judge will say 'no'. I'm sure Anthony won't give up without a fight."

Georgia reassured Claire that the law always favoured keeping children with their mother. Claire hadn't yet mentioned Jonah's marriage proposal but at this point Georgia picked up her friend's finger and admired the sizeable diamond perched on it. "And if the mother has an American husband and a job in America to boot," she smiled, "then I can't see how they could make you stay here."

Claire told her that as well as the ABC show, when she'd mentioned to Richard from *Morning Cuppa* that there was a chance she might be relocating to the States, he promised that she could keep her job on the programme and would continue as she'd done over the summer, as their star US-based correspondent. "You're wonderful for our ratings," he told her. "Your American segments were a hit. The public seem to love you." Claire didn't mention anything about the pregnancy to him. She decided not to tell anyone else until after the first trimester. That is except for Miriam. Claire pushed her plate away. She couldn't bear to have the food close to her. The smell was making her feel nauseous, or was it the thought of tonight's tête-à-tête?

"It will all be ok, won't it?" Claire asked her friend.

"Of course it will," Georgia promised, before stuffing her final piece of pizza into her mouth.

Claire picked Miriam up from school and once they were back at home she began searching for the 'right' time for that conversation. Miriam was so happily making rainbow loom bracelets that Claire hadn't the heart to disturb her and then the thought of doing it over dinner felt too contrived. Bath time came and went, homework was completed. It wasn't until Miriam scrambled under the duvet waiting for her mother to read her a story that Claire's cheeks began to flush hot from nerves, her heart started pounding and she counted down from three to one in her head before opening her mouth.

"Darling, do you know how much I love you?"

Claire stroked Miriam's hair back off her face. The love she felt for her daughter was so immense that she was scared what she was about to say would hurt her.

"I love you more," said Miriam.

"Not possible."

"Yes it is."

They giggled and shook their heads furiously. Then Claire turned serious.

"Sweetie, there's a couple of things I need to discuss with you."

Which 'thing' should she start with?

"I hope this doesn't come as too much of a shock to you, but I wanted you to know that you're going to have another brother or sister.......actually, you're going to have two of them."

"Two? You mean Jasper and yours?"

"No sweetie, I mean that I have two tiny little babies growing inside my tummy at the moment." And then, to clarify, she added: "Jonah's the father."

Miriam sat bolt upright in bed, eyes wide.

"You're having *twins*?"

Claire wasn't sure if Miriam looked thrilled or pained.

"Yes, all being well."

Claire knew there were complications involved with carrying twins, so she didn't want to tempt fate.

"Cool," beamed Miriam.

"That's really ok with you?" checked Claire.

"As long as they're not as annoying as Jasper, then yes, that's fine with me."

Crikey, Claire suddenly feared they might be *more* annoying than Jasper. Two sets of lungs, two sets of crying and two mouths to feed.

"It might not always be easy," Claire stroked her daughter's face, "but you know that you'll always be my very special big girl."

Miriam nodded, leaning her cheek into her mother's caress.

"Where will we live?" she asked. "Is this house going to be big enough for everyone?"

Claire sucked in her breath.

"That's the other thing sweetheart. Jonah has asked us if we'd like to go and live with him in America, permanently. How would you feel about that?"

Damn, she shouldn't have asked a question. She should have delivered the information as a fait accompli.

"When would we go? When the babies come?"

"No honey, I was hoping to go a little sooner; perhaps in the next few weeks. My job with ABC Television starts soon and it would be much easier if we were living there than if I had to keep flying back and forth."

Miriam was quiet, digesting all the information.

"What school would I go to?"

"Jonah's already managed to get you a place at Martha's school."

Claire was about to ask if that sounded ok, but what if it *wasn't* ok with her daughter?

Miriam remained taciturn. Claire felt certain there was a myriad of questions buzzing inside her daughter's head.

"What about all my friends?"

"You can still stay in contact with them if you want to by email and Skype. And we'll definitely be coming back to London from time to time. I'm hoping to even keep this house."

"Ok then," said Miriam, as she lay back down.

"Ok?"

"Yes, it all sounds ok."

Claire was waiting for and expecting Miriam to bring up the subject of her father, but perhaps she hadn't yet quite worked out that their move would result in her seeing her daddy less.

"If there's anything you ever want to ask or if you feel sad or worried, then please talk to me darling. I'm here and I want you to be happy. Nothing you can say will upset me. I'd be more upset if you *didn't* tell me about something important which was on your mind."

"What about grandma?" Miriam asked. "How will she come to see us?"

"Grandma has booked herself onto a course which will hopefully get rid of her fear of flying."

Claire laughed, but actually the prospect of seeing her mother less did make her sad. Transatlantic air fares were costly. Nobody would be making that journey on a regular basis. Miriam took the book out of Claire's hands and opened it. It was *Matilda* by Roald Dahl.

"Can you read to me now?"

"Of course I can darling."

CHAPTER TWENTY-FOUR

CLAIRE AND JONAH

Claire took a left off Fleet Street and entered a twisted warren of cobbled pedestrian streets called Middle Temple. This was a little-known part of central London which Claire was only familiar with because she'd been married to Anthony. The terraced Dickensian buildings lining the narrow lanes housed hundreds of barristers' offices, which were called chambers. Near to where she was the alleys opened up into a pretty square with a fountain and a church on the side. This was where they had got married, in a grand Elizabethan hall whose high-beamed timber ceiling and dark oak walls had made it look like a set from *Shakespeare in Love*. They'd chosen bowls of green apples and gothic candelabra to dress the tables instead of flowers. Claire paused for a moment to recall this better time in their marriage and then picked up her pace. Anthony's set of chambers wasn't far from where she was now headed and she was petrified that she might bump into him. It made her feel very uncomfortable, but Jonah's US-based law firm Quinn, Sullivan & Pentecost had recommended the best family lawyer to represent their case in the UK and, if the 'best' worked round the corner from her ex-husband, then so be it.

She'd spoken to Jonah the night before and those had been his words. *So be it.* "We need to win this thing, baby," his dulcet tones soothed her, "so don't worry if you bump into your ex-hubby. In fact, if you do, just smile and tell him 'hey'. Don't let him think for one second that you're nervous." They both giggled at the thought of her casually telling him 'hey'. She touched the glass screen and he met her hand with his, their fingers meeting in a blurry pink mass of pixels. She hated how he was so far away, how when she reached out to him, all she got back was cold, un-giving LCD. "I wish you were coming with me," Claire said in a small voice. It felt odd and wrong being here in London, pregnant and without the father around. How on earth did army wives cope with that kind of agony, let alone with much longer absences than this? Hell, she needed to man up and be brave. She'd been a single mother and coped just fine before Jonah had reappeared on the scene, so she knew full-well that she *could* do it alone. It's just that she no longer *wanted* to do it alone. Jonah planned to fly to the UK a couple of days before the hearing. She asked if he could maybe come a little earlier but he said that wasn't possible. "There's this work thing that I've got to do," he told her, "plus Martha's Mom is having an operation and I promised to have Martha for a few extra days." It took all of Claire's willpower not to pout and wallow in self-pity; right this second, should she not be his priority? *Get over it.* There would be plenty of other times in the future when Martha or Miriam would be put first so she needed to get used to it now.

She told Jonah about her conversation with Miriam and how well it had gone. He was jealous that she'd got it over and done with and vowed that when he picked up Martha that afternoon, he, too, would have the 'conversation'. In fact, it might well have been done by now. This is what Claire was thinking as she saw the name of the barrister she'd come to meet, Benedict Pendleton, engraved on a brass plaque outside 10, Temple Gardens.

The clerk called up to Mr. Pendleton's office to announce Claire's arrival and then led her up a spiral stone staircase. Benedict was standing at his open door waiting, hand extended.

"Benedict Pendleton," he introduced.

"Claire Jackson."

He motioned that she should enter and take a seat in the area next to his desk where there was a cosy selection of burgundy leather armchairs assembled round a coffee table. His office felt homely and comfortable, far less austere than Anthony's. But then again, Anthony was usually meeting with hardened criminals, not divorcees. Perhaps that's what people going through messy family disputes needed - a milieu which dampened the blow of acrimony. Benedict picked a file of papers off his desk and came to join Claire, sitting down in one of the chairs opposite, leaning forward.

"Ms Jackson," he started.

"Please, call me Claire."

Benedict smiled and cleared his throat. He reminded her of a younger and taller Robert de Niro.

"Claire," he smiled warmly. "Let me start by saying congratulations."

"Thank you," she said.

She wasn't sure if he was referring to the pregnancy or the fact that she was getting married. Or that she'd snared one of America's most eligible suitors.

"How far along are you?"

Now she knew.

"Nearly three months."

"And have you gone public with it yet?"

"No, why?" she asked, suspicion creeping into her tone.

He threw the papers on the table and looked her straight in the eye.

"I'm not sure if you are aware, but normally this type of hearing would take place behind closed doors. But due to the nature of your application and the fact that it's been expedited, I received news this morning that this case will be heard in an open family court."

Claire wasn't sure what he was getting at.

"Should that be worrying me?"

"Well, it just means that your dirty laundry will be aired in public. There could even be members of the press present, although they're not permitted to actually report it."

"Surely the press wouldn't be interested in me?"

Claire still didn't think of herself as someone in the limelight and would the British press be that interested in Jonah? Or was

Benedict suggesting that the American media could be there too? No, that was ridiculous. Who on earth would be interested in the fact that she was moving to America to live with Jonah? It was no big deal. People did it the whole time. Was she being naïve?

"My wife loves your slots on *Morning Cuppa,* so much that not only has she made several of your recipes - and let me tell you, she hates cooking normally - but she's also now bugging me to spend next summer in California. And I don't think she's alone. That show has millions of viewers and your partner, Mr Kennedy, would definitely still be of interest to the media, especially in a situation like this."

"But I, I mean we, don't have any dirty laundry to air. Won't the hearing just be a formality?"

Claire could feel her hands turning clammy. There were several small bottles of sparkling water on the table. She leaned forward to open one and half-filled a glass. Mr Pendleton waited until she'd taken a sip.

"I haven't yet received full disclosure of documents but it would surprise me greatly if your ex-husband didn't put up a strong fight."

"Do you know my ex-husband?"

"I don't personally know him but he has a reputation. And he's got one of the best family lawyers representing him."

"But Quinn, Sullivan & Pentecost claim that *you're* the best."

Claire said it as a half-joke and Mr. Pendleton smiled but suddenly nothing about any of this felt in the least amusing.

"We'll be good adversaries and your case is strong but don't be fooled into believing this will be a walkover. In normal situations it would be, but your ex-husband is likely to throw everything he's got at this."

"But I don't *have* any dirty laundry," Claire repeated.

"You might think you don't but he'll dig it out, of that I'm sure. So it's quid pro quo. You need to go away and think hard about every bad parenting decision he's ever made and any unsavoury characteristics he might have. Does he have a temper? Has he ever been violent or physically attacked your daughter or any of her friends? How present has he been as a father? We need independent character references for yourself and Mr. Kennedy also, to prove that you're both excellent parents who have never put a foot wrong, that kind of thing."

360

Claire could feel her palms moistening and her head was starting to spin. She took another sip of water. She hated confrontation and she didn't want to be vindictive towards Anthony. She didn't want to ruin his reputation or suggest to the world that he was a bad father.

"So your strategy is to tear my ex-husband's credibility to shreds?"

Mr. Pendleton opened his hands in a gesture of apology.

"I'm afraid we can't afford to sugar coat the situation. If necessary, fire will need to be met with fire."

"Anything else I should know?" Claire attempted a weak smile.

Mr. Pendleton picked up the papers again and flicked through them.

"Yes," he acknowledged, "I thought so. Your ex-husband has also asked for a social worker to interview your daughter."

This information hit Claire like a vertiginous blow. Damn Anthony. It was one matter throwing sticks and stones at Claire, it was quite another to involve Miriam. Or worse still,

361

to try to get her to choose. Claire's legs were turning to jelly. She doubted she'd be able to stand if she tried.

"I'm starting to think this is all a bad idea."

"This is all par for the course, trust me. But that doesn't mean that we won't win. That's why your ex-husband has to play it dirty, because he knows like I know that nine times out of ten this kind of case will sway in the mother's favour."

"And what happens the other ten per cent of the time?"

Benedict Pendleton's demeanour oozed quiet confidence and professionalism.

"We're not going to think about that. We're only going to think positively. So your job is to go home, get yourself and your partner some sparkling character references and think hard about your ex-husband's bad points. He's a man," Mr Pendleton eyes sparkled as he winked, "he must have lots of them!"

Claire took a double decker red bus to get home, sitting at the front on top, opening one of the little side-panel windows to let in some air. All of a sudden her throat felt tight. She reminded herself to breathe and her inhalations took on a laboured heaviness as she sought cooler, fresher oxygen to replenish her lungs. Now she really did wish Jonah was here with her. She looked at her watch. It was only 11 am in the UK, 3 am in California. She would dearly love to call him to discuss Mr. Benedict Pendleton's pearls of wisdom, but she didn't dare. Better to let him sleep and spare him from the news for a while longer. Lord knows, she wished she'd been spared. Back in the US, when they hatched this plan, it all felt so simple and made complete and utter sense. Now there were ugly hurdles to jump and an uneasiness spread through her chest like heartburn.

She absent-mindedly flicked open her I-phone and glanced at her emails as a distraction. There was one from Will Ryan, ABC.

I received an anonymous letter informing me that you're pregnant. If that's not true, then please ignore this. If it is true then the team at ABC send you heartfelt congratulations. Pregnant presenters are always a ratings winner here in the US, the bigger the bump, the better! Just finalising the filming schedule our end, will be in touch very soon.
Best
Will

On the one hand, this mail delighted Claire. On the other hand, what was all this about an anonymous letter? Who on earth would send something like that and why? And who even knew that she was pregnant in America? The only people she could think of were the doctors at the hospital. But what would they have to gain by sending a letter to ABC? Claire started trying to work out who else might send Will Ryan a tip-off but quickly gave up. It didn't really matter. No harm had been done. Much more worrying were today's enlightenments.

Everything was so complicated - love, divorce, children, happiness. Perhaps if it all came too easily the victories wouldn't taste quite so sweet. But, for every victory, there was a flip side, someone who lost or suffered. Transatlantic relationships were problematic. Claire thought about Madonna and Guy Ritchie, Gwyneth and Chris Martin. When everything's good, it's great, but when the parents either consciously or unconsciously uncouple, it's the children and parent left behind who suffer. Claire couldn't help that Jonah lived in America, but was she being selfish in wanting to emigrate and take Miriam with her? What was the alternative? If Jonah came to the UK, when would he see Martha? Someone would lose out whichever way you looked at it. It was an imperfect world. She leaned her head on the rail in front of her and closed her eyes.

Jonah was tossing and turning on his mattress. He reached a hand over to the side of the bed where Claire normally slept and was met by cool sheets. It was a cruel reminder that Claire wasn't there. He opened his eye a fraction. He groaned when he saw the red digits on his digital alarm clock. 02.59. His talk with Martha had gone well so why wasn't he sleeping? She was wowed by the news that she would have twin brothers or sisters. The only thing that upset her was that Miriam and the twins would be with Jonah *all* the time and Martha wouldn't. "That's not fair," she stamped her foot. "Come on angel," he rationalised. "You want to spend time with your mom, don't you?" There was a long silence and then a capitulation. "I guess," she begrudgingly admitted. And then she moved on. "Can we be the bridesmaids at your wedding?" He hugged her tight. "Absolutely you can, Princess. Claire and I haven't discussed it but I know she'll love the idea. You'll be the two prettiest bridesmaids in the world."

He allowed his mind to wander towards the wedding. They hadn't set a date yet, but why wait? Perhaps they should do it before Claire started properly showing and complained about being a fat bride. He knew the way her mind worked. His thoughts drifted back to his proposal. How he wished he'd hired someone to hide and film that moment with a video camera. The expression on her face as she nearly drank the ring

365

he'd popped into her glass of champagne was priceless. Her nostrils flared and one eyebrow raised itself a good inch higher than the other, as if shock could encourage it to part from its foundations. What she didn't know and couldn't have known was that he'd been holding onto this ring for nearly fourteen years. He'd been planning to propose the evening they found out they were having a baby and somehow, after that, the moment had never re-presented itself. He'd known all those years ago that she was the person he wanted to spend the rest of his life with. He just hadn't yet felt ready to start a family. He could have offered that ring to his ex-wife, but it felt wrong. He could have sold it or got rid of it, but instead he stuffed it to the far back of the top drawer of his bedside table, unable to let go of it, despite the pain it caused him on the odd occasion that his fingers brushed against the little square jewellery box inside which it was cushioned. He'd bought white gold because he knew full well that Claire didn't like the look of yellow gold against her skin, complaining that it made her look even paler.

03.14. If only Claire was here. He knew the perfect cure for insomnia. That would definitely make him feel better. He lay on his back, eyes wide open, staring at the whirring ceiling fan. Why was everything so complicated? He had no doubt that all would be well in the end, but when he and Claire had spoken on Skype that morning he saw how much she was missing him and ached to take her in his arms, to hold her tight and safe.

Perhaps he should go to London earlier? Perhaps it wasn't fair to leave her alone to cope with all of this? Perhaps it was too much. They were in this together which meant that he should be there too. But then what would he do with Martha? He could take her with him to London but that would involve her missing school which set a bad precedent. Or he could perhaps ask his mother if she could stay there instead? If he did that though, there was a danger that Martha could start feeling like a spare part, being passed from pillar to post, and seeing as this was a sensitive time, that was the last thing he wanted.

Jonah sighed. No, there was no easy solution. And even if Martha *did* stay with his mom, he still had that screen test coming up which he now knew it would be foolhardy to miss. He hadn't wanted to burden Claire any more than necessary because she already had enough on her plate, but he'd had another meeting with an attorney at Quinn, Sullivan & Pentecost today and the situation was made very clear to him. They claimed that at the moment there was a slightly better than 50/50 chance of Claire being granted permission to take Miriam out of the country. Not helping their cause was the fact that Jonah's life was peripatetic. He was moving around the world, commentating, and it didn't matter if his fixed abode was in California or the UK. What could tip the balance, however, was if Jonah had a job that tied him to the US. And so Jonah had given the green light to his agent to pursue an offer that was already on the table. It wasn't something that struck Jonah as the perfect fit but NBC San Diego had watched a tape of him commentating and liked what they saw. He was a local personality and they thought he would be perfect as the news anchor for their five day a week morning breakfast show. The screen test was scheduled for three days time. Jonah didn't really want to do it. It was a regional show, which hardly felt like hitting the big time. The pay they were offering wasn't much of an incentive either and the early morning rises were even more of a turn-off. But if this is what would help Claire win her case then he would do it, for her, for them, for their future.

03.33. Jonah rubbed his eyes and sat up in bed. It was clear that sleep was going to elude him. He calculated eight hours ahead. It would be 11.33 in London. Claire's meeting with the barrister might well be finished by now. He reached for his mobile and found her number. It rang five times before she answered.

"I'm so pleased you called. I was desperate to speak to you, but didn't want to wake you up. It's the middle of the night. Why aren't you sleeping?"

"Hey babe," he said, "I couldn't sleep because this bed's lonely without you. So tell me, how did it go today?"

CHAPTER TWENTY-FIVE

MIRIAM

It was Saturday and finally, because there was no school, Miriam was free to lie in. Coping with jet lag after coming back from America was hard. Every morning her mother tried to wake her by opening the curtains, turning on the lights and peeling back her duvet but still she didn't stir. In the end her mum resorted to rolling her body from side to side. When that didn't work, she tickled her feet. Miriam was hellishly ticklish so there wasn't even the remotest chance that she'd sleep through that. This morning, however, it was lovely to finally be allowed to wake up naturally, without being pushed or prodded or cajoled. With one eye open she realised why she felt so euphoric. It was 09.37, which meant she'd had nearly thirteen hours sleep. Epic!

Miriam was equally ecstatic about being able to stay put this weekend. It was her father's 'turn', but he called the day before to say that he, Ali and Jasper had all come down with a bad case of the vomiting bug which he didn't want to inflict on his daughter. That was the most selfless he'd been in a long time. That's what Miriam was thinking as she reached underneath her bed to pick up her favourite new toy which her dad had bought her in Los Angeles. She'd been grumpy up until the time of its purchase mainly because, when her father had asked whether she'd like to go to Disneyland, he had promised that they'd go just the two of them together and that was what clinched the deal. Somewhere along the line, however, the plans changed and Ali and Jasper had gate-crashed this special father-and-daughter trip. Despite the fact that she loved Disneyland and that Jasper was significantly better behaved than before, gurgling and cooing and smiling for pictures with Mickey, Miriam was still irritated by his presence. The next day Ali insisted they visit a place called The Grove which she described as an amazing outdoor shopping centre. "I don't want to go to a shopping centre," Miriam whined. "I *hate* shopping." It was true, she wasn't a massive fan of shopping but that's not why she made a fuss. She just wanted to annoy Ali. It was payback for her having come with them to LA in the first place. "There's a fabulous old-fashioned tram there," Ali patiently tried to convince her, "and this musical fountain. My sister's been. She said we have to go." "I don't care about a stupid fountain," Miriam stood her ground. There was so much more on the tip of her tongue. Like 'I don't want you here', 'why did you come', 'you're not welcome', 'Jasper's a whingeing brat', but she restrained herself. None of this was strictly speaking Ali's fault. It wasn't even her father's fault. It was just the way it was. That didn't make it any better though.

370

Sometimes it's nice to be able to lay the blame on someone else for your own disappointment.

In the end Anthony intervened and they *had* gone to The Grove. Miriam was reluctant to admit it but it actually was kind of a cool place. It looked like a film set. Upscale shops like Abercrombie & Fitch and Nordstrom lined pedestrian streets so clean and perfect they looked unreal, as did the bright green patches of grass peppered with people lazing in the sun and sipping cups of takeaway coffee. At its heart the 'musical fountain' erupted into a choreographed water show set to music. Miriam was transfixed by a fish at the bottom of the pond that seemed to be stunned immobile, caught in the line of fire from the jettisoning spray. She insisted on waiting till the very end, to ensure that the fish was still alive. Satisfied that it was swimming again they moved away and that's when she saw it, the shop it felt like she'd dreamed about forever: American Girl. Her best friend Gabriella was given one of their dolls for Christmas and Miriam had been so envious. It wasn't any old doll. It was a deluxe version, like a *real* mini person whom you could dress and groom and with a life history – called a "back story" - provided by the manufacturer. You could only buy them in America, according to Gabriella, and hers had been bought for her by a relative. The dolls were very expensive. Miriam's father hadn't been keen and complained that the dolls were so big that there wasn't room in the suitcase

371

to bring one back but in the end he gave in. There were dozens to choose from and she selected Isabelle, a blonde beauty with long golden tresses and pretty silver ballet pumps. That's who Miriam was cradling now, admiring her delicate black lashes and how her green eyes closed if she was laid horizontally.

Ever since her mother mentioned that they were going to live in America she started talking to Isabelle about it. Isabelle was a great listener, always so positive, unfailingly smiley and calm in response.

"I know what America's like Isabelle, because I've already been there. But what's it like to live there the whole time?"

Isabelle beamed. Of course she liked living there, it was her home. There was no place like it.

"What's your school like Izzie? Do you have lots of friends and do you think I would like your school too?"

Her favourite toy fluttered her eye lashes. According to Isabelle's back story she loved designing clothes and dancing, both things which Miriam liked herself.

372

"It's not that I love my school *that* much Izzie, it's just that I know it and am familiar with it. It feels safe. I'm not explaining it very well but do you understand what I'm trying to say?"

Miriam sat Isabelle upright and rocked her gently backwards and forwards, which gave the impression that she was nodding. Miriam picked up the doll's miniature hairbrush from her bedside table and started combing the golden mane, wondering what hairdo to give her today. In the end she decided on a wraparound braid, kind of like a halo. She took a thin clump of hair from one side and began to plait it.

"I'm sure everything will be just fine when we get there," she whispered conspiratorially, leaning close to Isabelle's ear so that nobody might overhear, "it's just that I'm a bit scared."

Isabelle smiled calmly at her. Miriam swore that she heard Izzie tell her: "you're going to be just fine."

Was Isabelle delighted at the prospect that she would be going home back to the States or was she a tiny bit disappointed that her exciting sojourn in London had been cut short? Or maybe it was a bit of both, just like her owner.

Miriam sat Isabelle on her lap. It was strange. Fifteen minutes ago she'd gently stirred from slumber with her mind void of all thought bar how amazing it was that she'd slept for nearly thirteen hours. And now anxieties were careering through her brain so fast that she half expected some of them to crash into one another, creating a mass explosion in her skull. Her mother kept asking if she was ok with the whole America thing and she really was. Mostly she was actually very excited. In the US, all she could think was how much more fun it would be to live *there* instead of London. But now that was soon to become her reality she was beginning to think a little more about her father. Yes, there were things he did which upset and annoyed her. He wasn't all bad though. He couldn't be all bad. He'd given her Isabelle. She bent over to kiss Isabelle's smooth pink cheek. She couldn't imagine a life *without* Isabelle anymore. She wondered what Martha would make of her.

"What's your father like Izzy?" Miriam turned her doll to look at her.

Izzy smiled.

"Do you miss him now you're in London?"

Izzy stayed smiling.

"Does it mean that it's not that bad if you don't see your father a whole lot?"

Miriam was used to not seeing her father much. An 'absent wee father', that's what her mother had accused him of being when they were still married. Miriam had once overheard an argument. And even now she only saw him every other weekend and one night during the week. That was plenty enough. She didn't feel as if she was missing out by not seeing him more. But if she was in America, would she see him at all? How would that work? Her mother hadn't mentioned it. Should she speak to her mother about it or should she just leave it alone. It wasn't as if she didn't like Jonah or anything. She *loved* Jonah. At Lily Beach she was jealous that Martha had him as her dad and she didn't. So why was she even worrying about how and when she'd see her real father? She pulled Isabelle up to her mouth and gave her a huge, loud kiss to try and lighten the mood, but it didn't. Ugh, this was all so horribly confusing.

Early afternoon, Miriam was sitting amidst a sea of cut up pieces of cardboard in her bedroom. There was so much debris scattered around that the carpet underneath was barely visible. She was busy constructing a house for Isabelle with furniture fashioned from empty cardboard boxes and was putting the finishing touches to a small table.

"Darling," her mother called up from downstairs. "Martha would like to speak to you."

Miriam shot to her feet. She hadn't spoken to Martha since the day her father retrieved her from Lily Beach and, since her return to London, the eight hour time difference had made it difficult. Whenever Martha was waking up in the US, Miriam was at school. And by the time Martha got back from school, Miriam was in bed. There were a trillion questions she wanted to ask her sort of step-sister. If there was anyone who came remotely close to understanding how she was feeling, it was Martha. She ran down to the kitchen where she found her mother seated in front of her open laptop and saw both Jonah and Martha smiling on the screen.

"Daddy, daddy," squealed Martha, "can I take your computer up to my room to speak in private?"

"Sure honey, but let me just say hey-

Too late, Martha had taken hold of the computer and was already running with it up the stairs. Miriam snatched her mother's laptop away with a cheeky grin and did the same.

"You've got five minutes," Claire called out as her daughter scampered off. "We've got to go to town for some stupid meeting your father's set up."

Miriam reached her room, shut the door behind her and planted herself cross-legged on the floor in front of the computer. She held up Isabelle.

"Do you know what this is?"

"It's an American Girl. I've got one."

If there was any physical way that Miriam's lower jaw could have reached the floor, it would have. She couldn't believe what she'd just heard.

"*You've* got one? I've never seen it."

"That's because it's at my mom's. She's called Julie."

"Wow, that means Isabelle and Julie can play together when I come," chattered Miriam excitedly.

"Dad says we can be bridesmaids at their wedding. Isn't that cool?"

Wedding? Miriam didn't know about any wedding. Her mother hadn't mentioned it. But that was brilliant. She was delighted. She'd *dreamed* of being a bridesmaid.

"Are you sure they're getting married?" she checked.

"Yes, Dad told me. And he also said he'd like to do it before the babies come. Can you believe we're going to have baby brothers or sisters?"

"I can't believe it's going to be twins."

"We can totally boss them around," laughed Martha.

The girls giggled.

"And I can't believe you're going to be coming to my school," said Martha. "That's even cooler than us being bridesmaids."

Miriam beamed. Speaking to Martha felt very reassuring.

"I will like it, won't I?" she asked tentatively.

"Sure you will. It's really fun and you don't have to wear uniform like you do at your school."

That definitely appealed to Miriam. She hated her stupid school uniform. The kilt was so itchy and the blazer felt like a straightjacket.

"And I promise I'll look after you," Martha added.

"So we really *are* going to be like sisters?" asked Miriam.

"Looks like."

Miriam nibbled the skin around a finger nail, contemplating. If Martha knew about the wedding, what else might she know about? Her mother was somewhat vague about timings.

"Do you know when I'm meant to be coming to the States?"

"Sure," grinned Martha. "Dad's coming over to join you in a couple of days just in time for the court case. And after that you're going to come."

"Court case -?

Miriam stopped mid-speech as her door creaked opened. Her mother was standing at its entrance.

"Darling, I'm sorry but we've got to go," said Claire. "I promise we can call them as soon as we get back."

In the car on the way to town Miriam gazed out the window. People were carrying on with their everyday business. A young couple sauntered along holding hands and laughing. A mother pushed a pram inside which a strapped toddler was wriggling and fussing and throwing a mega tantrum. Two businessmen carrying leather briefcases passed by engaged in a heated discussion. But inside the car, everything felt far from normal. There was tension in the air. Her mother's back was ramrod straight and the smile she wore on her face was fake. Miriam could spot the difference between her mother's genuine smiles versus the forced ones and what had been lovely about America is that there her mother had smiled real, proper smiles *all* the time. But since they'd got home her mother was smiling more of her forced, tight smiles again, especially in the last couple of days. Miriam asked on several occasions whether everything was alright and in response her mother managed to pull a more honest expression, reassuring her that she was just tired from the jet lag and perhaps from there being two babies growing inside her tummy. Miriam turned now to look at her mum. She was rigid as a robot, as if her limbs and skin had formed a metallic shatter-proof barrier behind which every conceivable emotion was being kept guarded.

"Where are we going?" asked Miriam.

"Oh, to some irritating meeting which I shouldn't be taking you to."

Miriam's mother kept her eyes on the road in front. She was barely blinking.

"Then why are you?"

Her mum pursed her lips into a thin line.

"Your father arranged it and it has to be today. Because he's sick I have to take you."

Her tone was sharp. Miriam thought she almost sounded angry. Her mother rarely got angry. And her mother rarely spoke ill of her father either.

"Who am I meeting?"

Her mother opened her mouth as if to speak but then closed it without formulating a single word. A tear slithered down her left cheek. Miriam hated seeing her mother sad.

"Is this anything to do with the court case?" Miriam asked quietly.

Her mother blinked, once, twice and then her eyelashes suddenly started fluttering uncontrollably.

"Court case? I never told you there was any court case."

"No, but Martha did."

The two of them were silent as they sat at red traffic lights, lost in their own thoughts. The light turning to green broke their reverie and after they'd driven through, her mother clicked the left indicator and pulled into the curb to park. She turned off the engine and removed her seat belt.

"Darling, I'm sorry I didn't tell you about the court case. I didn't want to get you involved. I was trying to protect you."

"I don't need protecting," Miriam insisted. "I want to protect *you*."

A few more tears spilled out of Claire's eyes. Miriam dug in the pockets of her sweatpants hopeful that there might be a clean tissue inside but the only object she pulled out was an empty sweet wrapper. Claire leaned over and kissed Miriam on her head.

"You are such a special girl. Do you know that?"

Miriam nodded, but her mother's platitudes weren't going to make her drop the subject. She instinctively felt that there was something about what was happening this afternoon which was very important for them all.

"What is the court case about?" she asked.

"It's about whether we can all go to live in America."

"And why can't we just go?"

Claire faltered a minute and then decided to answer, looking her daughter directly in the eye.

"Because your father doesn't want you to go."

"So he's trying to stop you taking me?"

Claire nodded.

"And who will decide?"

"A Judge and -

"And who?"

"And the person you're meeting today."

"And if they decide we can't go, what then?"

Claire's hand moved protectively to cover her belly.

"I guess then we'd just have to divide our time somehow between the two countries. Jonah would live here when he's able and we would go there when we were able. It wouldn't be perfect but we'd work around it. But I really don't want you to worry yourself about this."

"Would you and Jonah still get married?"

Claire's eyes opened wide, as if to say 'how did you know'?

"Did Martha tell you that too?" Claire asked.

Miriam nodded, relieved that her mother didn't look angry. In fact, it was a relief to see that her lips were curled in a genuine smile.

384

"I can see that there's no secrets shared between you two," she reprimanded. "And yes, I'm sure we'd still get married."

"And we can be bridesmaids?"

"Absolutely you can, if that's what you'd like."

Silence fell between them again. Miriam's mother pulled a tissue out of her purse and blew her nose.

"What do *you* want Mummy?" asked Miriam.

Claire hesitated, before taking a deep, audible breath. She spoke as she slowly exhaled.

"In an ideal world I would like to go to America, for a fresh start and to live in one place full-time as a family rather than going back and forth constantly. But only if that would make you happy too."

Miriam nodded. Grown-ups often thought that children couldn't understand complicated situations but they could. She understood it perfectly. Her mother loved Jonah. They were happy. They were getting married and were having babies together but still her father was being mean. She hated how her father was always thinking of himself and not of others. If the Judge told them that they had to stay in London, Miriam could tell that that would make her mother miserable. Is that really what her father wanted? Her mother was the opposite of him in every way. She only wanted the best for everybody. She'd been so nice to her father when he had a baby and got together with Ali. She never put herself first. She was always conscious of not wanting to upset anybody. So if this person that Miriam was meeting today was going to ask her opinion on the matter, she would tell them straight. She wanted to go to America to live. She was starting to intensely dislike her father. He was a selfish man who always wanted to win, whatever the cost. If it was in her power, then she wanted to give the gift of a new life and fresh start to her mother. That was exactly what she wanted. End of.

CHAPTER TWENTY-SIX

CLAIRE AND JONAH

The next evening, after Miriam was in bed, the doorbell rang. Claire had been anticipating this moment for the last twelve days and couldn't contain her excitement. She ran downstairs, taking the steps two at a time, only slowing when she reminded herself that there were two babies in her stomach and she should take care. The door opened to reveal Jonah. She jumped into his arms and pressed her lips into his, not allowing their conjoined mouths to part as she pulled them both into the house and closed the door behind them, leaning his body up against the wall.

"Promise you won't leave me ever again," she whispered.

"I promise," he murmured through a smile, "but strictly speaking it was you who left me."

She'd been warding off a cocktail of anxieties over the last few days but the moment his arms wrapped around her they all dissipated. He'd been drinking beer on the plane and definitely more than one! The taste of him combined with his musky scent stirred altogether different feelings inside of her. Jonah finally pulled away. A few strands of her hair had become tangled in their kiss and he gently pushed these back from her face, stroking her cheek.

"Do you know how much I've missed you?" he asked.

"And do you know how much I've missed you?"

Jonah leaned his forehead into hers.

"Do you know what I'd really like right now?"

It was dinner time, so Claire had prepared something easy and light.

"You must be starving after your journey. I've made your favourite.....shepherd's pie."

Jonah grinned one of his electric smiles, creasing the dimple to the side of his mouth.

"Delicious though I know your shepherd's pie is, what I'd really like right now, more than anything, is a shower, to freshen up."

He was wearing a lovely dark chocolate suede jacket Claire had never seen before. Once he'd taken it off and hung it on the coat stand by the front door, Claire took one of his hands in hers and led him up two flights of stairs to her bedroom in the loft. Whilst he began to undress, she turned on the water in the bathroom to test its temperature. By the time she padded back into the bedroom he was already down to his Calvin Klein's.

"I'll go get you a towel," she said shyly.

It was ridiculous how this man still had the power to render her coy. Her cheeks slightly rouged as she opened a drawer and pulled out the largest, fluffiest towel she possessed, thick, soft and baby blue. When she turned around to proffer the contents in her clasp he was standing completely naked in front of her. She loved him so much that sometimes, just looking at him made her body ache with longing.

"Right," she said, "I'll leave you to it."

Jonah took a step towards her, placing a hand on her backside and pulling her close.

"Where do you think you're going?"

His breath was hot on her neck.

"To get dinner ready?" she whispered.

"The hell you are," he whispered back. "You're getting in the shower with me."

"Is this another jet lag cure?"

"This is a cure for everything."

His fingers tickled her neck as he found the zipper on the back of the long-sleeved black dress she was wearing and tugged it down. This was one of the few dresses that still fitted her. The material was soft and stretchy enough to expand with her figure.

"Mm," he said appreciatively, once she was down to nothing but her panties and bra. He placed one hand over her breasts and another on her stomach. "You've been doing some excellent nurturing since I last saw you," he murmured.

"You mean I've become fat."

Jonah unclipped her bra and kneeled down, kissing her stomach tenderly as he slowly pulled down her panties.

"I prefer to call it pregnant," he murmured. "Duchess, you're looking fabulously fecund."

As he stood he scooped her up with him, cradling her effortlessly into his arms as if she were light as a feather as opposed to the swollen human incubator that Claire was beginning to feel like. He walked them towards the shower, gently depositing her under the deliciously warm spray. The water soothed Claire whilst Jonah's touch melted her from the outside in, washing away the fears she'd bottled up. Benedict Pendleton and Anthony were doing a sterling job in unsettling her, forcing her to wonder if perhaps now wasn't hers and Jonah's time. If getting what she wanted was so hard to achieve then perhaps it wasn't the right thing to do. But now, as Jonah lathered the soap and started washing and kissing her and sliding his hands deliciously all over her, it was a timely reminder that this is what was right. Good things are worth fighting for.

Jonah had mixed reservations about this trip. Obviously he was desperate to see Claire but, more than anything, he wanted to be able to provide her with a perfect happy ending. Unfortunately, it would appear that however much money he was willing to throw at the situation, it still couldn't guarantee that their day in court would be successful. It could only give them the best possible chance. He didn't want to worry Claire but, as he tucked into her shepherd's pie, he knew he had to be one hundred per cent honest. She deserved nothing less. He'd had a meeting with his own attorney and there were several avenues now being explored, just in case.

"I've got good news," said Jonah.

Claire was dressing her salad and looked up.

"I love good news."

Jonah grinned.

"I'm going to be a television superstar just like you," he joked. He knew that's how Miriam referred to her mom. "I've been hired to anchor NBC San Diego's breakfast program."

Claire raised an eyebrow.

"I thought you were enjoying the commentating?"

"I was," admitted Jonah, "but my attorney said it would be in our best interests if I got a job that tied me to one place. It should help with your court case."

Jonah referred to it as *her* court case, but actually it felt every inch like they were in this together. Claire laid a hand on his, tears filling her eyes.

"You'd do that for me?"

Jonah laid down his cutlery and lifted her hand to his lips.

"I'd do anything for you, you know that. Including moving here if that's what it takes."

He wanted Claire to feel safe in the knowledge that if they lost the court case, that would not be the end of the story. Staying in London wasn't first choice for either of them, but it might have to be considered. He'd looked into whether it would be remotely possible for him to bring Martha to live in London full-time if all else failed but his attorney had said it was highly unlikely.

Tears spilled out of Claire's eyes, so many of them simultaneously that it gave the impression of a sheet of water falling over a precipice.

"Sorry," she apologised. "I don't know what the matter with me is at the moment. I feel so emotional the whole time."

393

"Duchess," Jonah wiped away her tears with a piece of kitchen paper. "You've got a lot going on, not to mention the hormones."

"Are the hormones why I've been feeling so angry of late?"

"You, angry? I don't believe it."

Jonah wouldn't say that Claire was *never* angry, only that it was extremely rare. In all the time they'd been together she'd raised her voice just a couple of times. Even when they'd done that regretful thing all those years ago - which they preferred not to think about - she'd held it all in. That was her way. She used to tell him that she didn't need to be angry. He was fired up enough for them both.

"Yes," she half spat, half-smiled, "would you believe that I have been angry of late. Very angry, angry enough that I'd like to punch him in the face with this."

She balled her right hand into a fist, wearing a mean look in her eye as she punched the air.

"Who exactly do you want to punch?" asked Jonah.

"Anthony," she punched the air again. "I hate him, I hate him. I *hate* him."

She punched the air three more times just to prove the point and then took a gulp from Jonah's glass of Merlot.

"Firecracker, I love your new attitude," quipped Jonah. "It's turning me on."

It really was. There was something very sexy about Claire's rage. It was cute and hot and only very slightly scary all rolled into one. Plus he hated Anthony anyway, so the thought that she'd like to do him harm was appealing.

"Anything else specific he's done?"

Claire put down her fork and started telling Jonah exactly what that horrible ex-husband of hers had done. How he hadn't needed to involve Miriam in any of this but he'd elected to do so anyway. How most kind, caring parents would put their child first and not place them in the unenviable position of having to choose. But no, odious Anthony had gone one step further by arranging for Miriam to be 'assessed' by one of the court's approved child psychologists to see what she wanted out of all of this.

Claire's face flushed red and her speech gathered pace as she reached the denouement.

"And worse than that, because he was ill last weekend, he had the audacity to ask *me* to take her to the psychologist's appointment instead. I wanted to say no, but I checked with Benedict Pendleton and he said it would be better for our case if I were seen as 'compliant'. So I ended up having to take her. What kind of warped world am I living in?"

Her cheeks matched the shade of her hair.

"Get it out baby," smiled Jonah, feeling a weird mix of both amusement and fury. Jonah also liked to win but he would never have used his child as a pawn in this particular game. Then again, being a father himself, it was hard for Jonah not to empathise. Anthony was doing everything he could to keep his daughter close. There are two sides to every story.

Jonah was paying the price for having been absent for the last twelve days. In the time that Claire had been alone, a battery of thoughts had been stewing in her mind and she was now trying to purge them from her system.

"So, what did Miriam say to the psychologist?" he asked.

"I don't know," she admitted. "I tried to get her to open up about it afterwards but it was clear she didn't want to discuss it, so I let the subject go."

Claire sat back in her seat and downed in one a tall glass of water. It looked, to all intents and purposes, as if she'd finally got everything out of her system, but then another thought suddenly hit her.

"And also, before I forget," she wagged a finger, "on a completely different subject you and I need to get our stories straight in future. Your daughter told my daughter that we were getting married *and* about the court case. I hadn't mentioned either of those things to Miriam."

Jonah cocked his head with a half-grin.

"Fiery Duchess, I'm sorry, but I hadn't realised that either of those topics were taboo."

A silence fell between them and Jonah returned to his shepherd's pie.

"Are you done yet?" he asked.

"Yes, I'm full," said Claire.

"No, I meant have you finished with your diatribe. Anything else you want to get off your chest?"

"Nope," smiled Claire, holding up her hands conciliatorily. "I'm done."

"Just to check, though, can the girls be bridesmaids?"

Claire was quick to answer. She loved the idea.

"Yes."

"That's good, because I already promised Martha."

"And I promised Miriam."

Jonah finished his plate.

"Great that we're done then, because you going on that way has made me hot," he winked. "What do you reckon? Any chance this old man might get a second innings?"

"Sweetheart, I'm pregnant, I'm angry, I feel ever so slightly nauseous, we've just done it in the shower and I'm tired."

"Is that a yes then?" asked Jonah hopefully.

Two hours later they were lying in Claire's bed, their limbs so intertwined that it was hard to detect where one body ended and the other started. Jonah was spooning her from behind, his palm gently spread wide across her lower abdomen, desperate not to miss out a single spot of her skin where one of their babies might be lying underneath. Despite her protestations, Claire couldn't resist Jonah's advances. He had cleared up after dinner and when she started yawning he had insisted she go to bed. "But I want to wait up with you," she said, "otherwise you're going to be lonely." "Don't worry about me," he had reassured." She brushed her teeth, slipped into a silky short negligee and clambered under the duvet, sighing with gratitude as her back settled flat on the mattress. "Don't go getting any ideas," she warned him when he came to join her, removing his clothes. But then he started stroking her and the sensuality of his touch was enough to make her turn onto her side to face him and succumb to his well-patented jet lag cure. She now wore a peaceful smile on her face as Jonah held her close, stroking his splayed hand gently across her stomach.

"Do you feel them moving yet?" he nuzzled into her ear.

399

"I thought I did yesterday. It was a weird fluttery feeling, but I'm not sure if it was nerves or the babies moving. It's a little bit early yet."

"I can't wait to see them again tomorrow," said Jonah.

Claire had booked up a scan for the following afternoon and they were both excited about it.

"Me either," Claire agreed. Her eyes were starting to close. "I've got to sleep darling, I'm sorry. What are you going to do?"

Jonah gently leaned over Claire and grabbed the remote control lying on her bedside table.

"Do you mind if I turn on the television?" he asked.

"Uh-uh."

He pressed the power button and the *BBC News at Ten* opening credits started to roll. A very attractive lady called Fiona Bruce came up on screen. Jonah propped two pillows behind him and manoeuvred to sitting. *A large region of South-Western France has been devastated by floods. Hundreds of people have been forced to leave their homes.* Jonah had an ear on the news, but it was Claire whom he couldn't take his eyes off, observing her fiery ringlets fanned over the pillow and the delicate freckles that decorated her bijou nose. Her nostrils were gently flaring as she inhaled and exhaled. He fervently hoped that their children inherited her perfect nose instead of his oversized one, which was probably the least favourite part of his body. Claire always referred to it as being 'Roman' which made him laugh. *A helicopter has crashed into a pub in Scotland, leaving eight people dead and two dozen unaccounted for.* Would their children end up having red hair or blond? Or perhaps their combined gene pool might create a colour all of its own? He knew that Claire would prefer they had his complexion. She hated that she didn't tan and was jealous of Jonah's olive skin. But he rather liked the idea of his children being red-heads. He saw it as something unique, an honour only bestowed on approximately two per cent of the population. Jonah leaned over to kiss Claire's head. The smell of her hair was divine. She'd washed it in the shower. Well, actually, he'd washed it for her, and then it just dried naturally and pinged back into perfect shape within minutes. Many women would kill for hair like Claire's. *Tributes have been pouring in for the actor Orlando Goodman who died tonight, age 52. He was best known for his work at the Royal Shakespeare Company.........*

401

Jonah turned sharply towards the television. Claire had told him that Orlando was doing better recently and that she'd arranged for them to meet.

"Oh, my God," Jonah cried.

Claire had been dozing off but Jonah's tone disturbed her.

"What's up?" she said, eyes still closed.

Jonah hesitated. Claire was nearly asleep. This news would surely upset her. Perhaps it was best to leave it till morning.

Orlando Goodman was taken ill while performing at the Adelphi Theatre tonight and died shortly after he was taken to hospital.

In a flash Claire sat bolt upright, the force of her movement causing the bed to lurch, as if there'd been an earthquake. Footage of Orlando playing the role of Willy Wonka in *Charlie and the Chocolate Factory* filled the screen and then it cut to theatregoers in the foyer at the Adelphi being asked their opinion of him. *He was so versatile and such a commanding presence on the British stage,* said one. *It's so sad. I think I'm in shock,* said another.

Claire gasped as she watched and then clapped a hand over her mouth.

"Oh, no," she cried, tears already pricking her eyes. "I don't believe it."

CHAPTER TWENTY-SEVEN

CLAIRE

Claire was feeling tired. The kind of tired where it's hard to put one foot in front of the other; the kind of tired which seeps into your bones and makes them feel like they belong to the Tin Man; the kind of tired which makes you want to curl up and hibernate to avoid the harsh conditions which lie ahead. It wasn't just physical fatigue. She was emotionally drained from worry, from grief and from nourishing two growing babies. It was seeing these babies again the other day which sustained her. The sight of them somersaulting whilst she was being scanned had served as much-needed fortification after hearing the news that Orlando had died. One door closes and another one opens, so goes the circle of life. On this point Orlando would have been philosophical, she was sure of it. That had formed the subject of their final conversation, when he'd been eager to learn all about the twins.

According to the statistics, four people are born into the world every second with half that number dying during the same time. To make space for the twins to arrive, another soul would have to depart. Perhaps Orlando was that person. She still had in her bag the post-it on which he'd marked his prophecy. *I predict you're having two boys*. Jonah hadn't wanted to know, but Claire privately asked the sonographer after the recent scan if she was able to determine their sex. Apparently it was too soon to tell.

Benedict Pendleton escorted her as she walked hand-in-hand with Jonah along Fleet Street towards the Royal Courts of Justice. He'd warned her to expect that a few select journalists would attend. What she hadn't expected was a media circus. There were television satellite trucks lining the road and in front of them stood a wall of flashing lenses and hands holding up long stick-mikes which resembled fluffy brooms. "Show us your ring!" "Congratulations." "Give us a smile." "Jonah Kennedy, we've heard a rumour that you might come out of retirement?" "Give us your 'et voila'!" A shower of innocuous comments floated towards them. "Put your head down," said Jonah. So she did. She stared at her feet and allowed Benedict Pendleton to steer her towards the court's entrance, all the while trying to focus on the babies inside of her tummy and the reason why they were doing this in the first place. "I don't think this lot are actually here for you two," said Benedict. "It's just bad timing. There's another much bigger case going on here today."

The courtroom into which they were ushered was actually fairly low key. There was no intimidating dock for the witnesses or defendant to stand behind. It was more just a grand room. Benches and chairs for both parties were laid out facing a large desk and red leather throne, which Claire presumed was for the Judge. Anthony and his lawyer were already in situ and barely acknowledged Claire and Jonah as they entered. *How sad that it's come to this*. Once seated Jonah took Claire's hand in his and squeezed it tight for Dutch courage.

"Anthony's playing a game," whispered Benedict Pendleton as he readjusted his curly white barrister's wig. "He wants to unnerve you. Don't let him get to you."

Following Benedict's advice, Jonah had dressed in a smart dark suit and Claire was wearing a navy skirt and white blouse, respectful yet casual, not too prim and proper. The message her outfit had to send out was 'great mother, in control, wants the best for their child'. Benedict had discussed whether or not she should wear a jacket but, in the end, they decided against it preferring instead to show off her ever-swelling stomach, proof of life growing inside. Miriam wasn't here thankfully and, should events drag on today, Claire had arranged for her mother to pick her up from school. Turning at the sound of a door creaking loudly to the side of them, they saw some media representatives filing into the press box. *Go away*. Claire started fiddling nervously with her fingers. She wanted to be anywhere but here under the microscope in what were very personal circumstances.

A court usher came in brandishing a gavel which she banged down on the table.

"All rise."

Everyone in court, including the posse in the press box, rose to their feet. Benedict promised that they shouldn't need to speak today, that the argument could all be battled out by the legal representatives. Claire glanced across at Anthony's lawyer to check him out. David Sherwood QC appeared very confident. So frighteningly confident that Claire wondered if Anthony had been giving him lessons in 'the look'.

The Judge entered through a door at the rear of the court, a man in his late fifties at a guess. He was unremarkable looking, of medium height, sporting grey hair and a sizeable beer belly. Claire imagined that a woman judge might have been more sympathetic to her plight.

"Is this Judge good or bad news for us?" she whispered to Benedict.

She knew from listening to Anthony that the right Judge for the right case could make all the difference. Would a man not always be tempted to help out a fellow male? There should of course be complete impartiality in a court of law but could it nonetheless slightly tip the balance? Benedict's reply was a subtle wavering hand, signalling 'fifty-fifty'.

The Judge motioned that they should all sit down and after approximately twenty seconds of shuffling and throat clearing the court was silent.

"Case 20454," introduced the usher. "The Applicant is Claire Ruth Sarah Jackson, formerly known as Mrs Anthony Aidan de Klerk. The Respondent is Mr Anthony Aidan de Klerk. Could counsel please approach the bench?"

Claire kept her gaze ahead as the two bewigged barristers approached the Judge's desk and the three of them started conversing in low, measured voices. *What on earth are they talking about?* A couple of minutes later the black gowns of the two barristers swished as they turned around. David Sherwood QC took a seat next to Anthony whilst Benedict stayed on his feet, calmly shaping the papers in front of him into a neat pile before squaring his shoulders and addressing the Judge.

"Your Honour," he began. "This hearing is to seek permission for the Applicant to remove hers and the Respondent's child from the United Kingdom to go to reside in the United States of America. The case has been brought to the court as a matter of urgency, namely because the Applicant and her fiancé Jonah Kennedy, a resident of the US, have recently learned that they are expecting twins……

At the word 'twins', Claire zoned out. A few chairs and a faux corridor safely separated Anthony from Claire but, as Benedict mentioned the t word, Claire could clearly see her ex-husband's body tense and a silent sigh pass his lips. The number of babies she was expecting had clearly taken him by surprise. She would never have done it because it would have looked odd, but her instinct was to reach out and take his hand in hers. She wanted to apologise for any discomfort he might be feeling, to empathise with him. She knew how it felt to learn that your ex was having a child with another person and it was strange as hell. It shouldn't matter whether it was one baby, two, triplets or quads, but Benedict had mentioned that the fact it was twins did serve to strengthen their case. Perhaps that's why Anthony had physically reacted, when normally his professional demeanour would have given nothing away.

Claire forced her attention back onto Benedict. He was now offering up the character witnesses, holding out documents for

409

the court usher to pass to the Judge. It wasn't permitted for them to be written by family members, so both Georgia and Orlando had kindly accepted the task. A wave of nostalgia washed over Claire. Would Orlando's testimony still be valid now that he was no more?

The Judge put on his spectacles and perused the documents whilst a heavy, respectful silence descended on the room. Tissues were taken out of pockets. Noses were blown. The journalists were making notes in pads, or perhaps they were just doodling. Jonah looked at her and gave her a slight but encouraging smile, squeezing her hand once again for the briefest of moments, the tiniest of gestures which somehow made the air easier to breathe. Once the Judge had finished, he laid down his glasses and nodded towards Benedict.

"You may continue, thank you."

Benedict readjusted his wig as he took to his feet again.

"Thank you, Your Honour," he began. "It is also pertinent to point out at this stage that not only does the Applicant have a job lined up in the United States which commences in three week's time, but so, too, does the Applicant's fiancé, who has recently signed a full-time contract with the television network

NBC which will tie him to San Diego, California, which is where they propose to reside......

Once again, Claire could sense Anthony's frame tense and this time he released a more audible sigh. She never liked confrontation at the best of times and right here, right now, felt like the most hideous confrontation imaginable. What's more, she knew there was worse on the agenda. The way Benedict was building the picture made it clear to her what was coming next.

"Indeed," said Benedict, "there are other compelling reasons why it might be preferable for the Applicant to take hers and the Respondent's daughter out of the country............"

Benedict had told her to dig up some dirt on Anthony, to remember something which could help throw his character into disrepute. Most of the time he was a competent father, but it hadn't taken long for her to recall a couple of incidents which Benedict reassured her were perfect.

"Your Honour, it's been brought to my attention by the Applicant that the Respondent has a tendency to be forgetful. Two years ago, there was an incident where he went grocery shopping with his daughter. When he returned home he had a

411

car full of groceries but he'd left one key thing behind in the supermarket."

Benedict paused for dramatic effect and then added very loudly and clearly: "His daughter."

There was a snigger from the press box. This time, Anthony didn't flinch. If anything, Claire felt she could detect a slight smirk, as if he were laughing along with the journalists and saw the funny side.

"Six months later," Benedict continued, "he showed a more violent side to his character, one I'm sure he would prefer not to recall. The Applicant was so traumatised by this incident that it still makes her shudder to think of it. Both the Applicant and Respondent were at home with their daughter at the time. The Respondent had many piles of work papers laid out on the dining room table. His daughter was walking around brandishing a plastic mug of orange juice. Her father repeatedly warned her to not get too close and that the papers were important, but you know how it is with children. His daughter was only seven years old and wasn't taking him seriously, to her peril as it turned out. When the inevitable happened and the contents of the cup upended over the Respondent's papers, his reaction was violent and totally out of proportion to the misdeed. He grabbed his daughter by the arm

412

and flung her across the room with such force that she was thrown, stomach down, onto the hard wooden floor."

Claire half-expected another audible sigh to come from Anthony's direction. *She* certainly felt like sighing. She felt regretful and dirty at having to portray a perfectly decent father in such an imperfect light. Anthony's expression, however, remained impassive. If anything Claire felt that his slight smirk was getting broader. There was something sinister about his expression which made the air feel as if it was laced with arsenic that stung her throat with every breath she took. Her palms were becoming stickier by the minute. Beads of sweat were breaking out on her brow. Glasses of water were set on the table in front of them. She leaned forward to take one and took gentle, calming sips as Benedict started to sum up.

After a short recess for an early lunch, it was David Sherwood QC's turn in the limelight. Claire wondered if it was hard for her ex-husband to sit back and let someone else do the job he was normally paid to do. It didn't look as if he was finding it awkward. If anything, he now looked more at ease than before, as if he'd been invigorated by the break. If Jonah was in the commentary box, she imagined he'd liken Anthony's demeanour to that of a tennis player who'd been losing before rain stalled play but who returns to court once the sun's come out, sharper than before, ready to turn things around. Claire turned towards Jonah. She wished she could ask him if that really *was* what he was thinking but his expression was unreadable.

"Your Honour," David Sherwood commenced, "the Respondent appreciates the Applicant's change in circumstances but has instructed me to state for the record that he thoroughly rejects the application and doesn't believe it's in his daughter's best interests. At the moment the Respondent has contact with his daughter every other weekend and one night during the week, which already doesn't feel adequate to him and he would like to push for more. I'm sure you will appreciate that San Diego, California, is six thousand miles away and, with return air fares costing an average of £900.00, it would be unrealistic to expect him to be able to maintain that same level of contact. Furthermore, he would like to challenge the fitness of the Applicant and her fiancé to co-parent his daughter. It has come to his attention that recently in the UK the Applicant suffered from a moth infestation in the house in which she resides with their daughter. The fact the infestation was so bad…..

Claire was heating up from the inside out. Christ! Miriam must have told Anthony about the moths. She didn't blame her. One couldn't expect an eight year old to be a reliable keeper of secrets. She wished that she had a fan to cool herself down. She was starting to feel nauseous. There was a flutter in her stomach and a slight lurching sensation. Was that the babies or nerves? David Sherwood wouldn't leave the damn moths alone. He was claiming that she'd been too distracted with her new television career to notice that there was a problem and by the time she had realised, harmful chemicals which could have been damaging to their daughter's health needed to be used to clear the pestilence.

Claire longed to stand up and defend herself. *It wasn't like that. The moths were before I even had my first screen test and it's bloody hard to work out there's a problem until it's already out of control. The pest removal man said as much himself.* Instead she was forced to remain impassive and just listen. She feared there was worse to come and she was right. David Sherwood was clearly only at the beginning of carrying out the most extraordinarily unfair character annihilation of her.

"Recently the Respondent learned from his daughter that, little over a month ago when she was staying with the Applicant and her fiancé in San Diego, they visited the San Diego Zoo Safari Park. The Applicant's fiancé has an eight year old daughter and all four of them went to the safari park where the two little girls, age nine and eight respectively, were allowed to go zip-lining. May I state for the record, Your Honour, that the rules and regulations of the park clearly stipulate that children must

415

be a minimum of ten years old to go zip-lining. The fact that their children were underage and the two adults still allowed them to take part in this activity shows both reckless disregard for rules as well as reckless disregard for safety and surely points to the fact that the Applicant and her fiancé are irresponsible parents.........

Claire's stomach started churning. She tried to take deep, long, calming breaths, but the deeper she breathed, the sicker she felt. Her eyes began to dart manically, wondering if there was a bowl nearby or whether she might dare make a dash for the bathroom. The more David Sherwood spoke, the worse she felt. Thankfully he'd stopped speaking and was instead quietly addressing the court usher, who duly nodded and then walked to the nearest wall to dim the lights. Her ex-husband's barrister went to a table next to the press box and turned on a machine which looked a bit like a photocopier. He stood tall, flamboyantly swishing his black gown before recommencing:

"Furthermore Your Honour, the Respondent had the good fortune to witness firsthand the type of absent parenting we can expect from the Applicant and her fiancé. If you look at this picture here....

David Sherwood pressed a button and a magnified image of Miriam and Martha swimming in the pool outside Lily Beach came up on a projector screen to the right. The girls' faces had been blurred to protect their anonymity and the picture was a wide shot which included the entire poolside area, complete with the surrounding sun beds.

"You can see clearly that the two girls age nine and eight, were left swimming in the pool unsupervised. As the photo shows, there is not an adult in sight. In fact, there is nobody else at all in sight."

Claire's vision was deteriorating. She held her tongue, but she wanted to explain, to stand up and point with a rod to the gym in the photo. *Jonah was in that gym, watching the girls with an eagle eye. We are not foolish parents. He was as close to them as if he'd been on one of those sun beds. Plus I was watching the girls through the kitchen window.* Stars were forming to the side of her sightline, right and left, and everything in front of her was turning into a fuggy blur. She was gulping frantically for air, like a fish caught in a net. She leaned forward to fetch her glass of water, spilling a little as she wobbled it towards her lips. She was feeling ever so slightly better when David Sherwood clicked a button and replaced the picture of the girls swimming with another image. It was of Jonah swinging back a tennis racket. Claire looked towards Jonah worriedly. It was one thing for Anthony to attack *her.* It was another to attack her fiancé. Jonah didn't deserve any of this. He'd been nothing

417

short of wonderful to Miriam. Jonah was raising an eyebrow, a spark in his eye as he slightly nodded, as if understanding something more clearly. What was it that now made more sense to him?

"I'm going to show you a series of photos," David Sherwood QC clarified, "which will show you the most shocking of incidents where the Applicant's fiancé is deliberately harming the Applicant's daughter."

He clicked through the photos fast, showing a story rather like a flip book, where pages are turned so rapidly that the pictures appear animated. Jonah holding back his racket; Jonah swinging it forward; the strings on the racket meeting a tennis ball; the ball whacking Miriam in the arm; Miriam's blurred face crying out in pain, her cheeks pinched in a wince, her mouth so wide you could practically see her tonsils. Damn Anthony, damn him, damn him, damn him. Poor Jonah, this just wasn't fair. He was turning to her, taking her hand in his, a look of concern on his face. She really couldn't breathe now. The more she tried, the more starved of oxygen she became. Her eyes felt like two round pebbles popping out of their sockets. She was going to throw up. No, not here, not in front of everybody, please. *Can someone get me a bowl and quick?* More and more stars began to dance psychedelically in front of her and then they started to spin and spin and spin. "Duchess,

418

are you ok?" she thought she heard Jonah ask. And then her world turned black.

CHAPTER TWENTY-EIGHT

CLAIRE

What's this tube in my nose? Claire's fingers toyed with the stringy-like plastic glued to the inside of her nostril, lightly at first and then more urgently when it wouldn't come out. She tried to take in her surrounds, eyelashes flickering feebly, but a fog of fatigue made it impossible to lift her lids. Instead she allowed her fingers to trail south. There was something tightly wrapped round her stomach, too tight, it was suffocating. It was a thick rough belt with ridges in the material. It felt almost like canvas. *Where am I?* She tried to speak, but her lips wouldn't cooperate and the words remained lodged at the back of her throat.

"She's exhausted. Why don't you go and grab yourself a cup of tea and perhaps she'll come round in an hour or so."

The voice was female. Who the hell was she? *Where* the hell was she?

"I think I'll stay here if that's alright with you."

The voice was male, accent American. It was Jonah. She tried to say his name. She mouthed the word, aching for her diaphragm to do the job it was designed to do. No sound came out. What is *wrong* with me? A hand took hers. For a strong grip the touch was surprisingly gentle. A thumb lightly caressed her knuckles.

"Shall I hold her other hand?"

It was a little girl's voice. Miriam. Oh darling, yes, please hold my hand.

"I'm sure your Mom would love that."

A chair scraped along the floor and then something heavy landed next to where Claire was lying, brushing her leg. Afterwards a delicate little palm found its mother's counterpart, fingers wriggling to interlock with hers.

"Will she be ok?" asked Miriam, worry tingeing her voice.

"Of course she will, honey. Your Mom's just very tired."

"Are the babies ok?"

The babies – is that thing round my waist hurting my babies? Someone's got to save my babies. Her body felt weak, nothing was working as it should, but a mother's job is to be strong. She *had* to be strong. Instead of trying to open her eyes she screwed them even tighter shut, summoning every ounce of strength in her body towards her vocal chords. *Come on, you can do this.*

"Are the babies ok?"

The voice she heard didn't sound like hers at all. It was thin and raspy, a waft of nothingness in the air. A lump landed heavily on the other side of her body and then she felt somebody lean over her and kiss her forehead, stroking her hair.

"Shush baby," said Jonah. "You're fine. Everything's fine. You're in hospital and the babies are doing great."

Phew, thank goodness for that. Tears of relief started to build behind her closed eyes, the moisture acting as a catalyst for the lids to blink and open. Jonah and Miriam blurred into vision, sitting on the bed, one on each side of her. Why was she here? She didn't understand.

"What happened?"

Her voice was diminutive and frail. Had there been an accident? Was she involved in a car crash? Jonah grinned. Good, if he was smiling things couldn't be that bad.

"You passed out in court. It was very dramatic. An ambulance brought you here."

The court case, oh God, now she remembered.

"How long have I been here for?"

"Twenty-four hours."

Twenty-four hours? How could a whole day pass by with her not knowing about it? And if that much could happen with her being unawares, what else could have happened?

"Did we win?"

Perhaps the case had been adjourned. Perhaps when she was fit to leave hospital the whole horror of it would recommence.

Jonah's smile disappeared.

"No honey, we didn't win."

Claire turned her attention to Miriam, who was looking at her with such love and concern that she decided to let the subject of the court case go. She didn't want Miriam to become worried about any of this when what really mattered was that all her children were well.

"What's this?" she asked, tugging at the tube in her nose.

"The doctors put you on oxygen for a while just to play it safe."

"And this?" she asked, pointing at the belt around her waist.

"That is to monitor the babies' heartbeats, just to check that all is well."

"But all *is* well?" there was panic in her voice.

"All is well," he reassured, stroking her hair. "Don't let anything get to you. It's not worth it."

How could she not let this get to her? They didn't win, which now meant that she would have to go to the States to start her new job without Miriam. Goddamn it, she wasn't going to leave Miriam with Anthony when she went. No sir. Miriam could stay with her grandma instead. Or maybe she'd just have to give up on that job altogether. Perhaps it wasn't meant to be.

"I'm going to the toilet," Miriam announced.

Miriam hopped onto her feet and swished through the blue curtains pulled around her mother's bed. She was clearly familiar with the surrounds, as if she'd been to the restroom several times here in the last twenty-four hours and now knew exactly where to go.

"I knew it," said Jonah quietly, once Miriam had gone. "I knew something was up. I never told you at the time because I didn't want to scare you, but I swear, the day that that lovely ex-husband of yours took all those photos of me playing tennis with Miriam and the girls swimming in the pool, I'd *known* that someone was spying on us. I'd felt it. I just hadn't realised who it was. I should have put two and two together."

Claire gasped, clapping a hand over her mouth, remembering those photos in court and how Anthony had tried to make it look like Jonah was some kind of hideous child- abuser.

"I'm so sorry," she apologised, shaking her head. "I feel so bad."

425

"Shush," said Jonah. "Don't worry about it. I'm made of sterner stuff than that."

He dug into his trouser pocket and pulled out an envelope. It looked very official, with the name of a law firm on the front: **Slaughter & Jay**.

"This came for you this morning," he said. "It looks important. I had to sign for it."

Claire had had enough of lawyers for a lifetime. She didn't really want to open the letter. She wanted to dispose of it as quickly as possible, to toss it in the bin. Lawyers, courts, they all spelled bad news.

"It's probably more rubbish from Anthony," she pushed the letter away. "I don't want to know."

Jonah put the letter into her hand.

"I showed this to Benedict Pendleton this morning, just in case it was relevant. He said it had nothing to do with our hearing or Anthony whatsoever. So I think you should open it."

Claire tried to open the letter, but there was a cannula inserted into a vein on the top of her hand and it was uncomfortable.

"Why have they put this in me?"

"Apparently you were dehydrated as well as exhausted so they've been pumping you full of minerals and liquids via a drip."

Claire turned and saw a bag of clear fluid hanging from a hook behind her.

"You open the letter," she instructed, handing it back.

Jonah tore roughly at the envelope and pulled out a cream sheet of paper. He started reading it to himself, his eyes widening as his eyes scanned along the lines.

"Stop that," Claire barked, smiling warmly. "Either give it to me or read it out loud."

Jonah cleared his throat.

Dear Ms Jackson

I do hope this letter finds you well.

I am the Executor of the final will and testament of the recently deceased Orlando Goodman. I am pleased to inform that you have been named as the beneficiary of the recently deceased's maisonette in Kings Cross. I met with my client just a few days before his passing and he was keen that you, over all the other beneficiaries, should learn this news swiftly. He also wanted you to know not to feel compelled to live in the property. You are at liberty to rent it or sell it so that proceeds can best be utilised to enhance life with your soon-to-expand family.

My client expressed his immense gratitude for all you have done for him – he was most fond of you. Please do get in touch as soon as possible to let me know how to proceed.

Yours sincerely

Jonathan Finger

Claire held out her hand and Jonah placed the letter in it. She read it once again, to herself and a couple of rogue tears tumbled down her cheeks.

"Wow," she said quietly.

"Don't upset yourself," said Jonah.

Claire shook her head.

"I won't," she promised.

This was so unexpected. She always had such a soft spot for Orlando and it moved her that he felt the same way. The blue curtains swished open and Miriam poked her head through.

"What's that?" her daughter asked.

Claire folded up the letter.

"This is a gift from Willy Wonka," she said, opening up her arms for Miriam to fall into.

"What, a golden ticket?" she asked, wide-eyed.

"Yes," Claire replied, "kind of."

CHAPTER TWENTY-NINE

ANTHONY

Why doesn't this victory feel so sweet? That was the question which had plagued Anthony most of the weekend. True, there'd been one major hiccup en route which somewhat dampened proceedings. Watching his ex-wife collapse to the floor stirred mixed emotions within him. His first instinct was to run over to check that she was alright, but of course that would have looked a tad bizarre. Plus that dimwit Jonah was fawning all over her, preventing anyone else from coming too close, claiming that she needed 'air'. Was he a doctor now or something? And then it had dawned on him, perhaps this was all an *act* to win over the Judge's sympathy. Perhaps this had all been staged by their idiot barrister who he'd heard through the grapevine was famed for his maverick tactics. Stranger things have happened in court. Lord knows, he'd tried some of them himself.

When the ambulance arrived and Jonah left with it, Anthony half expected the case to be adjourned, but due to the urgency of the hearing, it continued. Strictly speaking none of the parties involved actually needed to attend anyway. And so the rest of Anthony's fabulous photos had been played out like a slide show to a few select members of the press who appeared less interested now that the Applicant and her famous fiancé had departed. Part of the fun of the photos was to see the reaction they made on Claire and "dimwit". Without them, their impact was greatly diminished.

At the end of the day the Judge scheduled judgement for the following morning at 10.30 a.m., same time, same place. When Jonah turned up alone Anthony freaked out, although he'd done his best not to let it show. He wanted to ask how she was and *where* she was, slightly concerned that perhaps he'd pushed things too far with his photos. But as a lawyer himself, he knew well enough to keep his distance. They were on opposing sides: 'never the twain shall meet'. However, after the judgement was made and permission was *not* granted for Claire to remove Miriam from the jurisdiction indefinitely, Anthony tried to brush aside those barriers. He kept his expression impassive, not wanting it to appear that he was gloating. At least, if any expression *were* on show, he hoped he'd managed to display a soupcon of sympathetic commiseration. He sauntered over to Jonah, hand outstretched, hoping that they could let bygones be bygones and brush any misunderstandings under the carpet. They were grown-ups after all. Moreover, his training had taught him to shake hands

431

with the opponent, win or lose. And damn it, Jonah's training was exactly the bloody same. Tennis players shake hands over the net after a match, win or lose. Not dimwit Kennedy though. No. Dimwit Kennedy turned his back on him, ignoring his outstretched hand and giving him nothing but the cold shoulder. Maybe something awful had happened? Maybe Claire had lost the babies?

The next morning was perhaps the most awkward of his life. Actually, there was no 'perhaps' about it. It just plain *was* the most awkward moment of his life. It was his weekend with Miriam and he'd gone to pick her up as planned from Gladstone Road. Gone was the nice relationship with his ex-wife which he prided himself on. Before Gwyneth and Chris Martin had consciously uncoupled, Anthony felt that he and Claire were great examples of how couples could amicably separate and co-parent. But now, relations were clearly strained. Claire didn't even do the hand-over. It was Jonah, who was courteous but monosyllabic. And then, to make matters worse, Miriam hadn't even wanted to come with him. She cowered away from his advances, scurrying to cling to Jonah's legs. "I don't want to go," she said. "Tell me I don't have to." Jonah wasn't even her father! How could she favour the Dimwit over her own dad? Being attacked by a swarm of bees couldn't sting any more.

The weekend with Miriam had gone from bad to worse. She seemed to have taken a dose of Jonah's medicine, managing to last from morning till dusk being perfectly courteous whilst remaining irritatingly monosyllabic.

"What do you want to do today?"

"Don't care."

Well, ok, that was two syllables.

"Do you fancy going to Madame Tussauds?"

"Fine."

Miriam had been pleading with him to take her to the waxworks for ages, so this should have elicited great excitement. There was even a brand new model of Katy Perry. Miriam adored Katy Perry. She was word-perfect on the lyrics to *Roar, California Gurls* and *Firework*. Anthony presumed that once they got to the museum she would perk up, and yet she walked around the place as if it was a funfair without any rides. Even the offer of lunch at McDonalds couldn't cheer her up. She'd longed to go there because her nutrition-obsessed mother would never take her. But when he walked her through

433

the golden arches and told her she could finally have a Big Mac and fries, she looked him in the eye and said "yuck".

It wasn't until much later in the evening that she strung more than one word together in a sentence and her first attempt wasn't pretty.

"I hate you," she said.

His skin prickled but he kept calm.

"You are the most selfish man I've ever met," she added.

Still he didn't react.

"All you ever think about is yourself. You don't want Mummy to be happy. She'll never be happy if she stays here. You know that. You're keeping her a prisoner in this country, just so that she can stay with me. And you nearly killed mummy's babies. You're horrid."

Ah, so the babies were still fine. Nonetheless, her words slapped him in the face. Her mature grasp of the situation surprised him but he wouldn't let on.

"Sweetheart," he sidled up to her, stroking her back. "This is all very complicated and I wouldn't have done any of it if it weren't in your best interest."

"My best interest is having a mother who is happy."

And your best interest is having your father still in your life and not on the other side of the world. That's what Anthony wanted to say but he didn't. Instead, he stuck to condescending platitudes.

"Sweetheart, I don't expect you to be able to understand all this yet. You will when you're older."

Miriam crossed her arms defiantly.

"I'm tired. I want to go to bed."

It was only 7.30pm. She normally delighted in staying up late on the weekend, to watch a reality show or a family movie.

"If that's what you'd like," he said.

At 8.00pm Anthony had checked up on her. She'd fallen asleep on top of her duvet, an open book still gripped between her fingers. He gently prised the book from her grip, turned the bottom corner of the page and placed it on the bedside table. Then he scooped her into his arms, pulled back the covers and slipped her underneath, kissing her gently on the forehead. He stood watching her sleep for nearly half an hour whilst an internal dialogue played in his head. How had it come to this? It felt like only yesterday that this mature little girl was a tiny baby, barely bigger than the palm of his hand. If he could, would he rewind the clock back to when things weren't so complicated, when all that mattered was changing a nappy and feeding her a bottle? You bet he would, even though, when she was a baby, he longed for her to be older, to be able to communicate with him, to tell him what she was crying about. Was he selfish? No, he was just doing what any right-minded father would do. Had he done the wrong thing? It wasn't possible that wanting to play a proper role in your daughter's life could be wrong. Would Miriam hate him forever? She needed time to get over it. She would get over it. They would all move on from this.

He went downstairs to join Ali who was watching TV whilst cradling Jasper in her arms. For once their son was fast asleep at a sensible hour.

"Everything ok?" she asked.

He sighed as he sat next to her on the sofa.

"Do you think I've done the right thing with Claire?"

He'd not dared to ask her this before because he didn't want to be dissuaded from the path which he absolutely knew he had to follow. But now he needed an opinion and he prayed she could be objective. He didn't want any of this to tarnish his relationship with his daughter or even Claire for that matter.

"What makes you think you haven't?" she asked.

"Miriam hates me. Claire hates me. Jonah hates me. What if all this hate never goes away?"

Ali was silent for an age. For a while he thought that perhaps she was more absorbed by the programme on the television in front of her than in his dilemma but she'd clearly just been cogitating. She turned to him and placed a hand on his arm.

"Darling, I know this is hard and I know you don't want to hear it. There's no right or wrong. I can absolutely understand where you're coming from and perhaps if I was in your shoes I would have done exactly the same. But seeing as you're asking for my opinion, I'll give it to you. I was really impressed with how you and Claire had moved on following the divorce and now, all this bitterness, I'm not sure that it's worth it. There must be another way. It's not like you will never see Miriam. And it could be worse. It could be New Zealand or Australia. America's not around the corner, admittedly, but it's easy to get to. There's holidays and lots of them. There must be some arrangement you can come to that will be better than storing up a lifetime of bad feeling which will be unhealthy for everyone's relationships?"

Now he remembered why he hadn't sought Ali's opinion. She was staying stuff he didn't want to hear. How could there possibly be another arrangement that could work for them? Clearly Ali was incapable of being impartial. Miriam was becoming a problem and it would be convenient if she could be got out of the way. Isn't that why Ali was saying what she was saying?

With a heavy heart he called Claire early Sunday morning. What he needed to do had come to him in an uncomfortable dream which made him toss and turn and dampen the sheets. He wasn't due to return Miriam till the end of the day but this needed to be sorted out now. Procrastination would only be his enemy. He was surprised when she picked up the phone to him. She hadn't bothered the day before.

"We need to talk," he told her simply. "Is it alright if I bring Miriam back now and we go somewhere neutral?"

Claire hesitated on the other end of the phone.

"If we must," she said.

That was better than a 'no'. Her generosity was already putting him to shame. He deserved to be blanked. Miriam didn't ask any questions when they rolled up at 77, Gladstone Road. Far from it, she seemed delighted by the early return and when Jonah opened the front door she ran into his arms. Jonah chose that precise moment to finally look Anthony in the eye, delivering a glassy, stony glare, as if to say: "Look what I've got buster. I've got something that's yours and I'm not giving it back." In the absence of not being invited into the house, Anthony hovered on the doorstep uncomfortably. Claire rescued him, coming to the door jangling keys in one hand as she fought to slip into her jacket with her other. She bent down to kiss her daughter and whispered something in her ear which Anthony couldn't quite work out. Whatever it was seemed to satisfy Miriam, who nodded sagely and whispered "bye".

"I thought we could go to World Cafe?" Anthony suggested.

It was a café round the corner which served superior cappuccinos and brunches.

"How about we go to the park instead? There's a kiosk there for drinks."

Whatever she wanted was fine by him, and perhaps staying in the open would be preferable to being cooped up in an artificial environment.

"Do you want me to drive?"

He thought he should offer, seeing as she was pregnant. She cast him a weird look.

"It's a two minute walk away. I think I can manage it on foot."

He wondered if it was best to start vocalising his ideas en route to the park. Why wait after all? But then Claire asked him what he'd done with Miriam over the weekend and he allowed banal chit-chat to continue until they reached the kiosk, where they ordered two polystyrene cups of tea and settled down on a bench. They were side by side, but a cavernous space divided them, as did awkward silence. She was waiting for him to speak.

"I'm really sorry about everything," he began.

Claire nodded, not turning to look at him, preferring instead to concentrate on a dog chasing a squirrel. She would not speak though. And she certainly wasn't about to forgive him. Why should she? He was trying to ruin her life.

"And I really hope we can work through this and move on from this. I don't want you or Miriam or even Jonah for that matter to hate me for the rest of your lives," he continued.

Claire remained impassive, transfixed now by a toddler who was chasing the dog who was chasing the squirrel. He knew what he had to say next but was he really sure? It was going to change the landscape of his life forever. He took a deep breath and swallowed sharply, downing a gulp of tea for courage.

"I've been doing some thinking."

His body was turned to Claire's. He wanted to tell her to look at him and not the damn dog, so that she could see he was serious, but he wasn't in a position to issue commands. He took a deep breath.

"I'm going to let you go to America," he said.

441

Now she turned to him.

"Sorry?" she asked, as if she'd misheard.

"I want you to go to America and take Miriam with you, if that's what you want. That's not to say that I *want* you to go but I've come to the decision that it's wrong of me to prevent you from leading your life, especially with your two little babies on the way."

Claire leaned forward, fussing with her right arm, raising it a little. For a moment he thought she was going to hug him but in the end her hand found her ringlets instead, fingering them agitatedly. Her eyes glistened.

"If you really mean that," she whispered, "then thank you. Thank you."

For a second Anthony remembered why he'd wanted to marry Claire in the first place. She had such sensitivity and an allure which cut to his heart. He'd never met anyone like her before and probably wouldn't again. Goddamn it, he never cried, but he felt on the edge.

"And I wanted to congratulate you on the twins," he said.

There, was it really so hard to be nice? No, it felt good.

"Thank you again," she said.

"I'll get my lawyers to speak to your lawyers to decide how best to proceed."

Claire held up a hand.

"No, no lawyers. Can't we just arrange this between ourselves?"

Anthony smiled. Yes, that would be infinitely preferable. This was what he wanted, no animosity, just the two of them working it out between them, wanting the best for their daughter.

"Of course we can."

Claire returned her fingers to her tea, strumming the cup nervously as she cradled it, as if it were a piano keyboard.

"Also," she said. "I appreciate that the flights to America are expensive. I've come into some money recently and I'd like to use that to help you come out to the States as much as possible and to send Miriam back to the UK. I don't know. We can work out the details. It's just that I'd like to help. It's not your fault that I'm choosing to live so far away. I'm sure, and hope, that we can find a way to make this work which will make everybody happy, even my mother who hates flying. The QE2 transatlantic voyage from Southampton to New York costs a bloody fortune."

Claire smiled, her joke lightening what was a heavy conversation.

"Thank you," he said, extending a hand. "I appreciate it."

She took his hand in hers and they shook on it, firmly, decisively and gratefully.

EPILOGUE

ONE YEAR LATER

"Come back here you two," called Claire as the girls scampered off. She'd successfully tied sashes round their waists but they each had a round floral headpiece which still needed to be attached. Miriam and Martha returned, rolling their eyes like prima donnas, hands on hips. "Aren't we done yet?" asked Miriam. She was only feigning haughtiness. In truth, she couldn't remember feeling so excited and was as uppity as a jumping jack. This was a big day. Lily Beach resembled a magnum of champagne about to be uncorked. Rooms were filled with people buzzing about in a hurry, constantly checking their watches. A dozen cooks had taken over the kitchen and – apart from entering or exiting via the front door – downstairs was now officially out of bounds.

"Right, you little monster," Claire pulled a giggling Miriam into her arms and clipped the headpiece onto her hair. Martha was the next victim and thankfully was slightly less wriggly. Job done, Claire surveyed her two special girls. Martha referred to their identikit white outfits as 'posh sundresses', an apt description. They were thin and floating with spaghetti

445

straps over the shoulders, waists accentuated with burgundy silk sashes. The most perfect pair of bridesmaids. Clearly they weren't the only ones being admired.

"You look beautiful, Mummy," Miriam cocked her head appreciatively.

"Not as gorgeous as you two," Claire bent down, taking the girls in her arms and kissing them each delicately on their heads, anxious not to damage the positioning of their halos. As she stood, she checked her reflection one last time. What she was wearing could hardly be called a bridal gown, but then again, they hadn't wanted a conventional wedding. She'd spotted an ivory, three-quarter length figure-hugging dress in a local shop window. When she tried it on, it was as if the simple but elegant robe had been waiting for this moment since its creation. Its plunging neckline complemented her décolletage and the V-neck back showed off her shoulders, drawing the eye away from her slight post-partum bulge. She'd have paid good money for it but it had been in the sale, reduced to $55. $55 for a wedding dress, she still couldn't quite believe it! She'd left her fiery ringlets loose, just how Jonah liked them, with just one comb in the side to match the bridesmaids' headdresses.

There was a sharp knock at the door.

"Come in," said Claire.

Her voice was tight. She was getting jittery now, too. The door opened and it was her mother.

"It's time," said Dolores. "Everyone's ready."

Claire was so grateful that her mother was here and proud that she'd braved the journey. The fear-of-flying course appeared to have done the trick. It hadn't quite taken away the fear but it *had* got her on the plane, minus the narcotics. She'd been in town for a while now, helping out with the babies. Claire would miss her when she was gone.

"Ok," Claire took a deep breath and the girls' hands. "Let's go."

Dolores followed them out of the bedroom and down the corridor towards the stairs.

"You've forgotten your shoes," she cried.

"Mum," Claire turned round smiling, observing her mother's completely unsuitable high-heels, "the wedding's on the beach. We're going barefoot."

Claire and the girls had enjoyed a pedicure the previous day, selecting a shade of varnish to match the bridesmaid's sashes as well as other décor details. Claire hadn't been to the beach since first thing this morning when Rosa, a Mexican caterer who was friendly with the complex's caretaker, had been dressing the hundred or so chairs for guests in white linen covers with burgundy bows on the back. She then decorated a small gazebo where they would make their vows, twisting trails of white and red flowers along the poles holding the canopy. Rosa and half her extended family, so it felt, were now in the kitchen, preparing a feast of enchiladas, tacos, moles and sangria. So no, it wouldn't be a conventional wedding but what Jonah and Claire wanted most was a great party. There was so much to celebrate.

Claire began to walk down the aisle, with Miriam and Martha a couple of steps behind. Watching from under the gazebo was Jonah. Claire had known exactly what he was going to wear because he'd sought her advice but, seeing him standing there with his toes in the sand, dressed in smart black long shorts with a matching waistcoat and white shirt, made her heart melt. She smiled at him and, in return, the entire congregation smiled back. Their beams broadened when Snow Patrol's *Just Say Yes* started booming through the speakers. Jonah had wanted this ceremony to take place a year earlier but Claire was pleased they'd waited. Now felt like just the right time.

Please take my hand
Please take my hand
Just say yes

People swivelled to admire the little procession as it went past. Richard from *Morning Cuppa* had made the trip and was sitting next to Will Ryan from ABC. Gordon Ramsey was here with his wife and in front of him was Gwyneth Paltrow. After she'd made a guest appearance on *Taste of the Place* ten months ago, whisking up a Brussels sprouts recipe featured in one of her cookery books, she and Claire had become firm friends. Jonah's two brothers had been given the task of 'looking after her' and they were revelling in the honour, one sitting on either side of her. Jonah's parents were adjacent to her parents and her sister had made the trip from Hong Kong. Anthony and Ali had even come. Yes, who would have thought it possible? A lot of progress had been made in the last year. In the front row was Georgia's husband with their baby Jack on his lap. Georgia herself had been given two other very important babies to look after, Jonah and Claire's six-month old twins, dressed to match their father, looking cute as can be. Georgia was balancing a waist-coated baby on each of her legs, bouncing her thighs up and down, pulling funny faces at them as a distraction. Orlando Goodman had been spot on. It was two boys. Two beautiful sons with white blond hair and eyes

449

the shade of today's unblemished sky. Doctors claimed they weren't identical but most people struggled to tell Toby and Eli apart. Framed and in pride of place on their bedroom wall was the post-it on which Orlando Goodman had scrawled his prediction. Claire felt sure that her favourite client was here in spirit, watching over them.

Claire joined Jonah under the canopy. He took her hand and she stood on her tip-toes, leaning her lips towards his ear, laughing. Nobody but him could hear. Snow patrol was still playing: *You're the only way to me. The path is clear.*

"We should have invited Kate Middleton," she whispered.

"Sweetheart," Jonah whispered back conspiratorially, "there's only room for one Duchess at our wedding."

Just say yes, coz I'm aching and I know you are too.

Friends, family and loved ones……..This wasn't to be a religious ceremony or a long ceremony. The vows that they'd written for each other weren't for anybody's ears but their own. They both felt incredibly blessed to have found each other again and promised to treasure what they shared with every ounce of their being for the rest of their lives. *We are here*

450

today to join two souls that have already been united as one.
As the Officiator began, Toby and Eli started to protest,
holding their arms out in vain towards their mother and father
who were standing side-on in front of them. Out of the corner
of her eye Claire caught Georgia struggling to hold the twins
steady, performing a variety of facial acrobatics to keep them
entertained. Miriam and Martha were starting to giggle. *This
new journey will be at times both richly rewarding and
extremely difficult, but, most importantly, it will be a journey
you take together.*

Having twins had been a real learning curve. It didn't feel like
double trouble - triple or quadruple trouble more like,
compared to having a single baby. The most fascinating
observation had been that if one twin was fussing, the other
would usually keep quiet. It was rare for them both to complain
simultaneously. Whether this was out of mutual respect or had
some deeper significance related to survival, she didn't know.
All she *did* know was that today of all days, for whatever
reason, Toby and Eli decided to fuss together. Toby was the
first to begin exercising his vocal chords with Eli starting up a
split second later. Claire turned to them and couldn't help but
smile at their outstretched arms, begging for her to pick them
up. *Today Bride and Groom proclaim their love and
commitment to the world-*

Claire did what came naturally, wedding or not. The twins were clearly intent on being part of the action. She stepped towards them, scooping one into the crook of each arm, before heading back under the canopy, where Jonah took Eli off her.

"Shall we cut to the main event?" suggested the Officiator, with a twinkle in his eye.

Claire and Jonah nodded, smiling, and whilst the congregation laughed at what was turning into a particularly unique service, one of Jonah's brothers delivered the rings. A wedding planner might have baulked at how the next five minutes panned out, at how choreography that had been planned for the ceremony was dismissed in a flash, but Claire thought the naturalness of what happened was absolutely perfect. Babies were balanced on knees as rings were slid awkwardly onto fingers. Jonah and Claire's respective "I do's" were drowned out by Toby and Eli gurgling enthusiastically. The only thing that went vaguely according to plan was the "you may now kiss the bride" instruction. That was carried out with such passion and tenderness that the two bridesmaids and twin page boys insisted on joining in. As waves gently chased each other to the shore, the newly formed Kennedy family became lost in a tight embrace and a shower of confetti.

THE END

ABOUT THE AUTHOR

When Jo was ten years old she wrote a short story about losing a loved one. Her mother and big sister were so moved by the tale that it made them cry. Having reduced them to tears she vowed that the next time she wrote a story it would make them smile instead. Happily she succeeded and with this success grew an addiction for wanting to reach out and touch people with words. Jo lives in London with her husband and three children where she works as a TV and print journalist. Since becoming a mother anything remotely sad makes her cry. She's a sucker for a good romance and tear-jerker movies are the worst. She's that woman in the cinema, struggling to muffle audible wails as everyone else turns round to star. Jo's pretty certain one of her daughters has inherited this gene.

Other books by Jo Kessel

Lover in Law
Weak at the Knees

Made in the USA
Charleston, SC
15 August 2014